Printed in the United Kingdom under licence.
London Rogue Press 2021

ISBN Number: 9798704886280

FOR DB
FOREVER

THE SPARKS
IN MY SKULL

I D ATKINSON

CHAPTERS

1: BITCH

We're fakers, all of us.

We fake it to ourselves and to each other – we make out like we're totally bossing it, owning it, on point, #livingmybestlife…

…but it's mostly bogus.

Especially me. I am not nearly as together and confident as I make out.

My confidence is painted on with the Urban Decay lipstick that matches my berry-coloured skater dress. It wilts in the flower tucked behind my ear. And it wobbles in the skyscraper heels my parents don't know I own.

I'm trying to style it out while on the inside, I'm a total disaster.

Where r u gorg? (Thinking-face emoji)

I look at my phone: it's Jazz.

I've literally just arrived (Face-throwing-a-kiss emoji)

…I reply. I look around to see where she's at and a boy stares back, smiling. Not a warm smile – his eyes are all over my dress and they're glassy, like he's thinking about something else.

And then I see Jazz! My BFF. She squeezes her way through the tightly-packed bodies and we hug like long-lost twins – even though we literally saw each other four hours ago.

'How do I look?' she asks. I look her up and down, nodding.

'Like a hot Disney princess,' I say.

'Exactly the look I was going for,' she grins. 'And you look amaze too – switched up your hair with the flower, nice. And that dress! Very boho beautiful.'

'These heels are torturing me already,' I reply, looking down.

'Oh, but they are totally worth it!' says Jazz enthusiastically, always with the compliments.

Me and Jazz – Jasmine – everyone says we're like sisters. Except sisters bicker, and Jazz and I *never* do.

We're almost the exact same height, we've the same body shape – which means we basically share our wardrobe, which is great for me as she's always sooo on trend. But Jazz has amazingly-straight, shoulder-length blonde hair, while I've got long, dark brown hair with a fringe and a kink.

Oh, and we think the same about almost everything – everything important, anyway. We're both vegan, for instance. Well, sort of. I'm vegan, Jazz is 'a vegan who has dairy'. Which is a vegetarian, but try telling her that. I absolutely love all animals. With Jazz it's maybe a bit more about watching her weight. We went through this phase of trying every diet going – the 5:2, the Paleo, GI, Keto – basically everything the magazines we read said.

Wow, this party has actually got a really nice vibe. Usually you get super-excited about a party and they end up being pretty lame, but tonight it feels like everyone's really getting into it. It's Noolie's, a girl from school. It's been all over Whatsapp, the 'No Class / No Principles' party, probably the last one before college starts.

Noolie's done a great job, she's cleared a load of space, she's put up a trillion fairy lights to make it nice and she's snagged some *major* speakers from somewhere, you can really feel the bass shaking your insides.

I can't see her though – it would be good to see how she's doing after the demo yesterday. Noolie is… she's the only person I know with the same condition I have. Aether. And after the anti-aether protest, well, it would be good to hang with someone going through the same thing, you know? Not that Noolie and I are tight or anything – I've always kept my stuff low key whereas she's all 'my aether game is strong' kinda brazen.

Ugh, I can't see Noolie, but I have just spotted the biggest fakers of all: Ronny and her glossy posse. Pretty girls with ugly make-up, all drinking Apple Sourz and dancing vaguely to the pounding, bass-heavy music because oh, so much sexiness.

'The chic clique are here,' says Jazz, noticing me noticing them.

Jazz and I were sort-of friends with Ronny a few years ago, 'til Ronny turned into this pretentious mean girl who did everything for the 'Gram. Totally self-obsessed and all about building herself up by putting the rest of us down. While we were still friendly I told her about my aether – a moment of weakness – and she's held it over me ever since. Whenever I see her she'll throw shade and make out like she's about to tell everyone my secret.

'What's up hun?' says Jazz. I'm obviously looking anxious.

'Just.. you know,' I say. 'The demo in town yesterday? I can't get it out of my head. All those angry people, marching and shouting. Like aether was some evil thing. Just seems to be getting worse, you know? And apart from you and my fam, Noolie and Ronny are the only people in the world who know about me. Noolie's got aether too so that's ok, but Ronny…'

'Hey, don't stress about it,' says Jazz. 'Those dumbasses protesting – it's just some temporary drama, babes, got to be. Soon, everyone will realise that actually, aether is cool as. I'm sure of it. Then you won't need to hide it babes – you'll be worshipped as a triple threat! Brains, beauty and aether. No wait, should be… Brains, beauty and broomsticks?' She tries to keep a straight face.

'Oh, great!' I say in mock indignation. 'Now my BFF is hating on aether.'

'No way babes,' replies Jazz. 'You know I am totally woke when it comes to aether. Hey, why don't I grab us a couple of Cosmos from the kitchen, then you and me, we slay it on the dancefloor, k? I've just seen Jay and he is looking hot.'

I grin and roll my eyes at her. 'Sure, I'll be here 'til you get back,' I say, sinking into the sofa.

As Jazz disappears into the crowd, someone immediately squishes in next to me on the sofa. Oh, it's the boy from earlier – the one with the glassy stare. He smiles and offers me a pill.

'I'm good, thanks,' I shout over the music.

'Sure?' he says loudly, practically holding it under my nose. 'You're Echo, aren't you?'

'No, thanks anyway,' I say, shaking my head. As if I'd take drugs from some random boy! I guess it's Ecstasy, but really, who knows.

'This is a tune,' says the boy approvingly as the beat changes. 'Hey, remember Nate's Rubik's Cube party?'

Oh yes, last term. I remember. You ever been to a Rubik's Cube party? They're a total drag because you have to wear clothes in six different colours which means a) you have to wear a lot of stuff if you're a girl and b) your chances of looking good are zero. Then at the party it's just a writhing sweat-fest of horny boys trying to swap clothes with you so you're all in one colour.

'I remember,' I say. 'I wore purple. Turns out that's not a Rubik's Cube colour, so I didn't have to swap a thing. Shame.'

'Yeah, cool,' he says, not really listening. 'I was hoping we'd link up you know. Seth reckons you're high maintenance, but I think you're cool.'

Oh, thanks. High standards is not the same as high maintenance, douchebag. He's really staring and nodding slowly, like he's trying to be all deep or something, I dunno. If he can sense vibes between us then truly, they're just the vibrations of my skin crawling.

'Scuse me, I need the bathroom,' I tell him, trying to pull myself out of the sofa. He starts to protest, actually groping at my arm, but I wriggle free.

OMG, the stairs are impossible, it's like a queue for the toilets at Glastonbury. I do my best to tip-toe between all the St Tropez legs, abandoned jackets, paper cups and fingers that are either updating their Snapchat streak or sliding inside the pants of the hot guy / girl they're with.

The bathroom door is locked. Course it is. There's a glum-looking girl rattling the handle.

'Hey you guys, come on,' she yells. 'I actually need the actual bathroom.'

Ugh. I'll just wait in this bedroom for a minute – it's empty, probably because there's no lock. I go in and sit down on the bed to rest my feet – these killer heels really are killing me.

But a few seconds later in comes the boy from the sofa. Dead-eyed pill boy.

'Yo Echo!' he says faux-enthusiastically. 'Thought I'd lost you!' he adds, like that would be the worst thing ever. Now he's standing I see he is tall, over six foot, with hair that makes him seem taller.

'I was just going back down,' I say. 'My friend Jazz...' I trail off.

'Oh yeah, I know her, "all that Jazz",' he replies. 'I just saw her dancing with a guy... Jay, is it? She won't bother us,' he says, closing the bedroom door behind him.

Oh... shit.

'So it's cool, we can just chill here for a bit. You know, just talk.'

Oh right there: alarm bells. When a guy says they just want to talk you know that's bullshit. That's their brain drowning in a fug of testosterone, saying the first stupid lie it can think of to –

– OMFG he is suddenly kissing me, out of nowhere! He's pushing at me with his mouth all hard and angry, his tongue is jabbing at me, it's so gross, my head tips back to get away at the same time that he's pushing me and I'm now I'm back on the bed and he's on top of me...

WTF? I should cry out. I do cry out, I think. But on the other side of the door is a wall of distorted bass that drowns out everything.

No no no

this is not happening

Jazz, Jazz, god she's so close, so close

she's literally just here

if I could just cry   out

— but he's pawing at me, wriggling his body to smother me. Christ, he knows I'm struggling, trying to get him to stop but he doesn't care, he's got one hand on my throat while his other pulls at my dress, scrabbling and stretching... he's pulling at his jeans button, I'm having a panic attack I need an inhaler even though I don't have asthma, my limbs are filling with heavy, icy water. It's like they say: fight, flight or freeze, and flight isn't possible so I'm freezing up...

...wait, no. Hell no. Not freeze. Fight. I'm going to fight, course I am.

I mean, I made a mistake, daring to sit on a bed in an empty bedroom? That was something I did wrong? No. This guy. He's the one who's made the mistake.

There's a shelf above the bed. I'm staring at it right now. I can see the thick handle of a heavy glass jug sticking out. If only I could reach it, I could use that.

And... I can. Reach the jug, I mean. Not with my arms. With my aether.

I block out what's happening and I focus on the jug handle. It has bubbles in the glass. Solid handle, I can imagine holding it, feel its weight. I can picture it in my head. I can feel it in my head. And…

The jug shivers. I can move it. Come on.

His hand is stroking my throat, pressing on it, his face is bruising mine, his other hand… oh Jesus, move, MOVE!

The handle of the jug swings wildly right with a judder.

– he's got my dress up, he's got his hands in my pants as I yank on the jug with everything my aether-infected brain can summon, the jug is spinning like a fire juggler –

and …

…it topples, turning three sixty in the air as I try to guide it with my mind, direct it to fall just so, and…

SMACK

…it hits the boy, the sharp, bottom corner of the jug hits him right on the back of his head. With what you might call a sickening thud. But I'm thinking satisfying thud.

He screams out and instantly rolls off me sideways, grabbing the back of his head like he's trying to hold his brains in. He's doubled up like he's going to vomit there and then.

I roll away, my knees coming up to my chest as I take in a great wracking gasp of air. I think I might hurl too. OMG.

I literally fall off the bed, my knees thud onto the thin carpet and I push myself up with shaking hands. The boy looks scared / angry / I don't know what.

I scrabble for the door handle, trying to twist it, shaking at it like I've forgotten how to open a frickin' door, in a panic like in some horror movie when someone's being chased.

'Hey, no, ugh, you little bitch, where do you think –' he slurs, starting to rise, stumbling as he clutches the back of his head…

…and the door opens and I tumble out, back into the throbbing party. I falter and fall down the stairs, out the front door, staggering into the bleak, black night – out, away from the boy.

OMFG.

I'll message Jazz in a sec, tell her I feel sick, that I've had to go. In a sec.

Just as soon as I can stop these hot, hateful tears.

2: CYCLOPS

"Just... give me a moment. Let's put it in context. At school, children learn the 'ages' of human civilisation. Stone Age, Bronze Age, Iron Age, yes? The Roman Age, Medieval Age, Industrial Age, The Atomic Age, and then we get to The Digital Age. Most recently, The Information Age.

"And then... it was going to be The Artificial Intelligence Age. Drones, blockchain, The Internet Of Things, machine learning. Cyber warfare, driverless cars. Artificial intelligence. The machines take over.

"But just as our obsession with technology was overwhelming everything... along came aether. And suddenly humans were relevant again. Interesting.

"Corporations, governments, organized crime, religions – everyone got interested in what humans could now do. And what they might yet be capable of. Because of aether. We've entered The Aether Age."

– From the TS (Top Secret) Interviews
with Doctor Magellan-Jones

There were a couple of reasons Flynn's life sucked so hard. And right now he didn't want to think about either of them.

So instead, he looked down... and dropped over the side.

Flynn had been a skateboarder forever. His mum told people he could skate before he could walk. He didn't know how many hours he'd spent here at the skate park, but plenty. Learning to ollie, kickflip. And the first time he dropped in on this vert ramp – well, the first time he'd wiped out, but still. It was a release. Made him feel alive. Which was the best kind of distraction from the truth, the first reason his life sucked: he was dying.

It was past seven and the sun crouched low, watching him. It glinted off the grind rails and bathed the concrete hips and hubbas in a deep orange glow. Flynn pushed off hard in his beat-up Converse.

Yeah, it was a good distraction from dying.

Except… he was being distracted from his distraction. A group of kids in the half pipe to his right were baiting each other, their voices too loud.

'Come on, pussy, gis a go,' he heard one say. 'Don't be a prick, it's fine, don't be such a little baby. Just gis a go, k?'

He looked over. Five kids – two youngers, maybe ten or eleven with a birthday skateboard, and three guys about his age crowding round them. Oh yeah, definitely his age, he recognised two of them; they'd gone to his school. Dicks.

He ignored them and skated where he was, squinting in the fading sun. He would have to go soon, his mum was on earlies this week and would be off to bed in a couple of hours.

Gliding and rolling round, he pulled a high kickflip for old time's sake… but there was a cry to his left just at the wrong moment and it broke his concentration, his board squirmed under him, his foot turned over. He felt the sprain instantly, the sharp twist shooting from his ankle across his foot, up his leg. Shit.

He looked over. The three he'd known from school, they'd got hold of the boxfresh board and were messing about on it, skating badly and probably scuffing that shiny new design. Flynn sighed. Bollocks. What could he do? It wasn't his fight. He needed to get home. His ankle hurt. Bollocks.

'Hey, trying to skate here, k?' he called out, hoping that might diffuse things. Though it probably wouldn't. Because they were dicks.

The one on the skateboard stopped. 'What you saying bruv?' he called back. Then he smirked.

'Oh my days, look who it is fam! Cyclops!'

Bollocks.

They came up the ramp. Hyenas with new prey to snap at.

The one who'd called him Cyclops was first. Maxen, that was his name.

From the same estate as him, different block. A tall, nasty waster who'd been done for nicking on the estate and who they said had robbed and pushed an old lady down the concrete steps. She'd been in hospital for three months.

'Yo yo Cyclops, how you doing bruv?' he asked. He waited for his two mates to join him before facing up to Flynn. 'Long time no see,' he grinned, checking his mates had got his hilarious joke. The one Flynn had heard a million times before. Cyclops, because he was blind in one eye. And people could always tell there was something wrong with his eyes because they were different colours. The left – the blind one – was green, the right was blue.

'Bit old to be skateboarding ain't it though?' said Maxen. 'You feel me? Or maybe you like hanging round kids, is that it? You a batty boy, Cyclops, you here to score a date with one of these little pussies?' He was right up in Flynn's grille now as the other two lads moved either side of him. Shit.

Flynn was maybe two inches shorter than Maxen, but several inches wider. He'd done gymnastics since he was ten, and while he was never going to make the Olympics, he'd benefited from all the training. He could take this dickhead, he was sure of it.

But all three of them... not so much. And they were crowding him, there wasn't much space, just a sharp drop onto hard concrete.

'You're right, it's for kids,' he replied. 'So why don't you give the kid his board back.' He looked down into the dip below where the two boys were standing huddled together, desperate to go but not daring to leave without getting the new skateboard back.

Maxen pulled a face. 'You telling me what to do, fam?' he said.

'No, said Flynn quietly, I'm just – '

'What you sayin' then?' said Maxen. 'You calling me a thief, Cyclops? I'm just playin'. We're just playin' right?' he called down to the scared kids below. 'You wanna call me a thief, you front up and say it to my face, batty boy, you feel me?'

'Remember this here is Keel's boy!' said one of the others. 'My old man says he gets out soon. Don't wanna upset daddy's littl' un,' he laughed.

'Oh yeah, Keel Dallas,' said Maxen, bouncing on his feet a little. 'Yeah, daddy's a badass, that right, fam? You gonna go runnin' to daddy when he gets out? Or maybe you the badass? Apple don't fall far from the tree, is it though? You a tough guy like pops, Cyclops?'

'I'm nothing like him,' said Flynn quietly. He took a calming breath. 'Look, I'm not calling you a thief. All I'm saying is…' he paused, searching for the words. 'I'm saying, you're not a thief…

'… you're just a… you know, a shit-for-brains bedwetting fuckwit who pushes small kids and old ladies arou –

– And just before Maxen lashed out, Flynn's mind went flicker flicker flash.

That's what it was like: a stuttering camera flash.

It left an after-image of Maxen's right arm smashing out at him.

It would send him toppling over the side.

It would dislocate his shoulder as he hit the ramp.

It would split his head open.

It would.

But it hadn't happened yet.

Because it was a flash-forward, from his *aether*.

And just in time, Flynn twisted sideways and slapped his board out at Maxen and the plywood edge caught Maxen's swinging forearm with a dull, painful clatter.

'Aargh, fuck!' yelled Maxen in reflex, clutching his stunned arm.

Flynn let go of his board and dropped off the side and just caught onto it with his feet.

'You're fucking dead bruv, you hear me? Dead!' yelled Maxen after him.

No, not dead, Maxen. Dying.

They ran at him like wild dogs, yapping and snapping. Flynn heard them drop the board with a clatter. So the little kids would get it back at least.

Ugh, his ankle was hurting hard. He got to the edge of the skate park and kicked his board up into his hand. Come on.

Grimacing, he ran across a grass verge – yellow from the recent heatwave – but they were closing, smelling blood. His ankle felt like it was going to give way.

'Cyclops! You're dead!' screamed the voice again.

He survived the next five seconds. Then the next five.

He turned sharply into an underpass, a short tunnel covered in tags, under a path to the train station. They were behind him, their baying calls bouncing off the curved graffiti walls. 'I know where you live, you blind pussy!'

And then he was through. Down a short embankment. Along a narrow cut-back, almost hopping, gritting his teeth through the pain. Give up, give up he willed them. Just let it go.

But they still came. It was like they could sense he was injured. Hyenas zoning in on the sickly animal in the herd. He stumbled, starting to panic.

He turned a corner then limped up some steps and doubled back in the direction of the skate park, before – there – he collapsed behind a buzzing electricity / phone cable box.

And then… he waited, trying to not to pant loudly. His heart was pounding. He had to rest his ankle.

Bollocks. Some kids with a new skateboard, nothing to do with him. Why had he got involved? And they'd mentioned him. The other reason Flynn's life sucked so bad. Keel Dallas. His dad.

Flynn could imagine his old man hearing them calling him a 'badass' and a 'tough guy'. He'd lap that up, wouldn't imagine any irony. He'd be standing there with a shit-eating grin, sucking on a fag, his yellow rodent teeth, tattooed, scaffolder arms like bridge cables and his cold, glittering eyes. Keel Dallas was the other reason Flynn's life sucked so bad… and he was getting out of prison in a month.

The minutes passed. If they found him now, he'd be fresher. Maybe his ankle was better. And maybe they were unnerved by his ninja skills, blocking Maxen just as he was going to smack him over the side.

Not that Flynn did have ninja skills. It was the flash-forward: pre-cog. Occasional, random flashes when he'd see something just before it actually happened. Something he could do because he had aether.

The irony. Aether was killing him, but it had – maybe – just saved his life.

Flynn got up gingerly. No sign. It was getting darker, the sun had dipped behind the horizon. He got back on his board and made his way home.

Twenty minutes, skating in silence and finally his block of flats appeared, looking down at him black against the blood orange sky. He popped his board up and limped slowly up the hill, still wary. Maxen knew, more or less, where he lived.

He hobbled up the four flights of steps – even with a bad ankle it was better than taking the piss-stinking lift – and along the concrete walkway. He could see their door, and the lounge window; the light was on. His mum would be settling down – on earlies for her cleaning job, she'd be off to her room soon, leaving him the lounge and sofabed. He already had his keys in his hand and –

– Wait. Voices. He could hear voices from the other side of the door. A male voice – shit, had Maxen talked his way in? Panicking, he put his yale in the lock, turned and –

No. No! Bloody hell, no.

Staring at him from across the lounge, tapping a cigarette over an ashtray, a nasty leer on his lips. Not Maxen. Worse, much worse. Flynn's knees gave way a little, his injured ankle buckling.

It couldn't be. A month, they still had a month 'til he was out. This apparition, this monster, he couldn't be here, it wasn't possible. Shit – they hadn't let him out early, not for good behaviour? That was a sick joke.

Flynn felt his face go cold.

'As I live and breave,' said the man with a sneer. ''Ere 'e is, and still wiv the skateboard like a little kiddywinks.

'ello son!'

3: TERRORIST

There's a line I saw once, on Pinterest I think. Be yourself because everyone else is taken.

But I don't think *anyone* wants to be themselves. I only have to look on Instagram and it's like wow, everyone else's life looks sooo much better.

We all want to be that girl, that guy, that person we've seen with the perfect boyfriend, perfect skin, perfect job – the perfect life.

Except… no-one's life is perfect. It might look that way from where you're standing, but the truth is: everyone has their own shit to deal with.

I mean, they haven't got your shit to deal with, you might look at them and go, 'Oh they're so lucky, they weren't just almost raped at a party by some disgusting sleaze-bag.' But they've still got their own drama.

Like the people we're watching on the news.

They're all about to die.

I'm at home on the sofa, Piper (my gorgeous Westie) is on my lap and my parents are watching too, transfixed by the horror on screen. The footage is taken on a phone inside a passenger jet. The picture is jerky and the sound all muffled, panicking voices as anxious faces go in and out of shot.

Suddenly there's a piercing scream as everything lurches violently to the right.

The yellow masks drop down with their plastic bags and tubes pulled out behind them.

There's a garbled yell and – bam – everything flips over, bodies go flying and the phone is dropped. It hits the ceiling (which is now the floor) and the screen goes black.

Then the news report cuts to professional footage of a vast, choppy ocean and my heart lunges at my throat.

The camera pans in on a scatter of white objects floating on the surface. The biggest is a huge mid-section of passenger jet. The circular windows are more like portholes now. But there's no inflatable slide attached to the door. No life-rafts filled with waving passengers in life jackets. Just their belongings, bobbing on the ocean.

And the camera goes in close, really close, on something colourful, kinda horseshoe shaped. It's… I think it's one of those neck pillows. Oh, frick. It's a stripy orange neck pillow with a smiling cat's face on. OMG. It's a kid's neck pillow.

And the news reporter gives us the deets in a flat, calm voice. British Airways flight BA09984 has crashed into the North Sea just eleven minutes after take-off. It's the worst UK air disaster since World War Two. All one hundred and fifty-two passengers on board are missing or dead.

Then the voiceover says this awful tragedy is being treated as a 'terrorist incident'. Caused by someone like me. Someone with aether, who tried to hijack the plane.

'Oh my god, Echo!' says my mother in horror.

'This is unfortunate,' says my father.

'Unfortunate?' screeches my mother, turning to him wild-eyed. 'A hundred and fifty people are dead! Echo… they're blaming people like her. They'll be out for blood!'

Oh, jeez. Those poor, poor people. All dead. And their families, oh god, they must be just distraught, I can't even… this is something else.

And they're calling it a terrorist attack by someone with aether. I take a shaky breath.

'I'm taking Piper out,' I say to my parents. Piper leaps up.

'What? Have you not seen the news?' says my mother. 'They're calling people like you terrorists, Echo! And after that stupid anti-aether demo in town last week? Tell her, Virgil!'

'I… I really need to clear my head,' I say, getting up. Oh, my legs have gone all wobbly.

'I'm not sure that's wise,' says my father. 'Have you thought this through?'

Classic dad. I tell him I'm taking Piper out and he asks if I've thought it through, like I should have spent the last hour carefully planning a dog walk.

'Look, no-one knows I have aether,' I say. 'Well, hardly anyone. They might suspect, but… either I can take her for her walk or she can pee in the garden, up to you,' I finish.

'I'm going to my study,' he replies sternly, standing.

That's typical of my father. He's a neuroscientist, which is a lot less interesting than it sounds. It basically means he spends a lot of time away at conferences and a lot of 'do not disturb' time in his study. Since aether he's been in big demand, so I've seen even less of him. He's never been one of those 'Hey, let's go catch a movie' or 'Who fancies pizza?' kinda dads. But he has helped me with my aether, I guess.

'Look, take Piper,' he says, glancing at my mother. 'But make sure you take your phone too, have you got it?'

I waggle it at him.

'Ok,' he says. 'But twenty minutes, no more. Any longer, I call the police.'

My mother glares daggers at him. 'Virgil!' she hisses.

'The situation is getting worse,' he says, looking distracted. 'And soon, well maybe Echo won't be able to go outside freely. But for now… I don't think there'll be vigilantes with pitchforks at the door just yet.'

'Thank you. I think,' I say.

I flash my mum a reassuring smile, but really all I can think of are those poor passengers as I go into the hall, Piper scrabbling after me. I'm wearing denim cut-offs and a vest top, so I slip on a pair of flip-flops, grab my linen blazer and some poo bags then pocket my keys and slip out into the warm evening air.

It's not quite dark as Piper and I make our way down the street. I've had Piper, my pure white Westie – West Highland Terrier – since she was a puppy (she's seven now) and she and Jazz are the loves of my life. Piper is awesome, just totally lit. She's a better person than most people for one thing. And whenever I'm at home we're inseparable, she sleeps on the end of my bed, she follows me from room to room and even going to the bathroom alone is a struggle.

Talking of Jazz, I did tell her about the party, BTW. The next day. And she did go abso-frickin-lutely mental, as expected.

She wanted to find out who he was and cut off his dick and make him eat it. But I calmed her down eventually, and I said no to the police too, not with the whole aether thing. In a few weeks it's college, a fresh start, a whole new chapter – we'll probably never hear or see that guy again. I just want to forget about it, for it to just fade into the background. A scar you can barely see anymore.

And Jazz understood, she really is my rock, and after we talked on the phone she came over with a tub of Ben and Jerry's Chunky Monkey non-dairy and we watched Netflix and ate the entire tub.

The street is totally deserted, BTW. Every house and flat has its curtains pulled, slivers of light peeking through when the curtains don't meet properly. Everyone glued to the TV, watching the news about the 'terror attack' I guess.

Piper and I get to the end of my road and turn down; the next road slopes as we go past the back of the church and then the graveyard. It's a lovely cemetery, really well maintained and always lots of flowers. But it's a totally different vibe in the dark obvs, and I hurry past just a little bit quicker. Despite acting all cool with my parents, inside I am butterflies. The party left me pretty shaken, I haven't got over that yet. And now this story about a plane crash caused by aether, just a week after the anti-aether demo.

When aether first became 'a thing', it was just some weird trick kids with migraines could do.

Migraines have been the bane of my life. *Chronic* migraine I mean, since I was a child. It means I missed loads of school, I have to be careful what I eat… and every so often I'm struck down by this just horrendous pain, like there's a crazy snake writhing around in my head, trying to eat its way out.

And then around two years ago something super-weird happened. If you were young (like, under twenty) and you got chronic migraine, you also started being able to do stuff. Not normal stuff. 'Abilities'. And they call it aether.

No-one knows why it started (not even people like my dad), just that it had some link with migraines. Like all this time, maybe migraines were just a symptom of the human brain evolving. But not evolving fast enough, because they say that actually, our brains aren't really able to cope with aether. So having it is fatal.

The scientists, doctors whatever, they can't really say what your life expectancy is. You could have a year, you could have ten. *Maybe* even twenty. What they are sure about is that there's no way round it. One day your aether will cause a sudden, lethal brain aneurism and that's it. Game over.

I still remember the day my dad explained it to me, how I cried and cried. I can still remember my pillow, how I had to turn it over in the night because it was so wet from my tears.

But anyway, the thing is, until it kills you, aether, means... well, I can do a couple of different things, like move the glass jug at the party, but also I have a special bond with animals. So for instance, I haven't got Piper on a lead. She doesn't need one – she always knows exactly what I'm feeling and she always knows the exact right thing to do.

In fact right on cue, we turn and there are the large, green, wrought-iron park gates and Piper – just ahead – stops and turns to look at me expectantly.

yes

...I tell her with my aether. And that's it, she's off like a firework, shooting down the lane. I follow her, glad to be away from it all for a few moments.

Then my phone buzzes. Oh, it's a message from Alekzandr, a boy who was in the same maths and science classes as me at school. I think he may have had the hots for me actually, but the feeling was *not* mutual.

Hey Echo Noolie missing for 3 days. Did u know? Call me kk

What? Noolie's missing? Since a couple of days after her party?

I go through the gate and see Piper just ahead, rooting around in some ferns. She sees me and dashes off, keen to extend her trip. I follow her between the neat, even grass, still holding my phone.

God, Noolie. The only other person at school with aether, as far as I know. She was better at it than me and she showed it off.

Right, that's it. We've gone far enough.

to me piper to me

Piper appears immediately, barking good-naturedly and sprinting towards me, just totally one hundred percent reliable. 'Good girl, good girl,' I breathe. I pet her a little and turn back home.

Christ, Noolie's missing. This is getting dark. You know? There have been all these negative aether stories in my feed for months now. And trolls attacking anyone who admitted to having aether. Plus some pretty nasty stories in the news. The demo in town last week, that was just one of loads that have been happening all over the country. Today the plane crash story… and now Noolie's vanished? I'm starting to feel a bit overwhelmed, TBH.

Then my phone buzzes again and I nearly jump out of my skin with the sudden vibration. I look at the message, a news alert I have turned on, the screen making me glow like a firefly.

And *boom*. That's when I see the news that totally slays me.

4: NAPALM

"All I'm saying is... humans were old news. Anyone who was around in 1997 will remember it as a turning point: the year a computer beat the world champion at chess. Back then it was considered incredible, the idea that a machine could beat the world's best player at this most complex and subtle of games.

"As the years went by, chess engines continued to improve – and today no chess grandmaster can beat the best computer at chess. So in a way, 1997 marked the beginning of the end. The year when artificial intelligence began to overtake human intelligence. Then aether appeared. And at a stroke, humanity got its edge back."

– From the TS Interviews with Doctor Magellan-Jones

Flynn felt a knot of pain in his stomach. His old man was back. Keel Dallas was back.

Last night he'd been forced to sleep on an airbed in his mum's room so this hateful man could have the sofabed. And today Flynn had stayed in, stuck in their small flat all day so he could guard his mum against this menace. And all the while his ankle throbbed from the incident with Maxen. Bloody hell.

The day hadn't been completely wasted: he'd read some theories on his iPad about where aether came from, then a kickstarter project for someone claiming to have invented an 'aethereal rig' to augment your ability (which sounded like bollocks) and some stuff about an 'aether sanctuary' called The Farm. He'd also seen the news report, how someone with aether – an aethereal – was being blamed for the BA plane crash, and then written the phone number for The Farm down, just in case.

The man pulled a fag packet and yellow disposable lighter from his trouser pocket and took out a cigarette, lifting it to his eager lips.

'No!' said Flynn's mum. 'I mean…Keel, please. It's just… Flynn is very healthy.'

'Well he should be fine with a bit of fag smoke then, shouldn't he?' said the man, his cigarette bouncing up and down as he spoke.

His mum's face was strained, her voice pleading. 'Please Keel, please… maybe you could smoke it outside?'

'Christ,' said the man, pushing the cigarette back in the pack. 'Pardon me for breathing.'

They sat in awkward silence for what seemed like an age, the man on the green sofa, Flynn in the sagging armchair, his mum perched on its arm. Inbetween them was the fold-down table, picked up years ago from a charity shop. It was normally up against the tiled fireplace, but his mum had opened it out, put a tablecloth on and set it with plates, cutlery, salt and pepper and a big wooden spoon. Like some make-believe family dinner she'd seen on TV. The oven started beeping.

'Oh, it's ready!' his mum said, leaping up. She went into the kitchenette and pulled on the red spotty oven gloves.

'Ok, who's hungry?' she called through brightly. 'Sit up, I've got a real treat.'

The man got off the sofa to slouch in a chair at the table. Flynn sat at the other end, as far away as possible.

His mum came thorough holding the casserole dish high like a trophy.

'Hey, budge round love,' she said to him. 'I can't squeeze past you with this.'

Flynn froze. He took a breath. He stood… and moved round. Next to him. He could smell him, that sharp, stale smell of him.

'Shepherd's pie,' said his mum, putting the dish down on the table with a hint of pride. 'Your favourite,' she nodded to the man.

'Don't know where you got that idea, Sylv,' said the man with a melodramatic frown. 'Lasagne's my favourite.'

Flynn saw his mum's face fall, a wrinkle of worry on her forehead.

'Oh. Oh. I was sure –'

'No no, Sylv, lasagne every time. But don't worry, I'm sure this will be fine.'

His mum nodded. 'I'll remember,' she said quietly, picking up the wooden spoon to dish up.

Flynn said nothing.

'It's good lamb mince,' his mum added, perhaps to break the silence. 'You don't mind, do you Flynn?'

Flynn shook his head.

'Flynn often cooks with Quorn,' said his mum as she spooned out a large portion of the steaming mashed potato and mince.

'What's that?' said the man, taking his heaped plate of shepherd's pie from her.

'It's vegetarian,' she said, spooning out Flynn's plate. 'Vegetarian mince.'

'Oh Christ!' said the man, slamming his fork down on the table. 'This is goddamn veggy mince?'

'No, no, not today, this is real lamb,' said Flynn's mum quickly. 'Tesco's Finest this is.'

'Thank eff for that,' said the man. 'I can't be doing with all that nancy rubbish. Christ, I ate better in the nick than that. Tell you what,' he said, shovelling a huge forkful of food into his mouth, 'they do a good lasagne in the nick, do the lads. Very decent.'

'It's lovely, mum,' said Flynn, taking his first mouthful. 'Really tasty.'

She smiled at him gratefully.

The man took the salt and shook it liberally over his food. 'Tell you what shepherd's pie reminds me of,' he said. 'Robbie, this fraggle from inside.'

'What's a fraggle?' said Flynn's mum, sitting down finally with her own portion of shepherd's pie.

'Someone what is a bit soft in the head. Easy meat.'

'Oh,' said Flynn's mum.

'Yeah, 'e was a fraggle and also a grass. Always on privileges, always got the cushy jobs – like working in the canteen. And always off having words with this senior kanga in his office.' He looked at Flynn's mum. 'Kanga – you know, kangaroo, screw.'

'Right,' said Flynn's mum quietly.

'Grasses and nonces, they're the lowest of the low,' said the man, warming to his theme. 'And what made it worse was a lot of the drugs were comin' in with the food deliveries. So havin' a grass in the kitchens was a big no no.'

The man paused to scratch the stubble on his throat and jawline with his fingernails, making a loud, rasping sound. He picked up his fork again and jabbed it towards Flynn and his mum for emphasis.

'You know? Can't be avin' a grass. So one day the firm bringing in the meow meow, they decides as to make a show of Robbie. Give him a wet up.

'Prison napalm, they call it. What you do is, you get some boiling water and you start dissolvin' sugar in it. Much as you can. More and more, keep stirrin', keep addin' – the more sugar you puts in, the hotter the water boils at, see? Plus it makes it all sticky. So it sticks to you while it burns – prison napalm.

'Now normally it might be a mugful. But in the kitchens, well you got all the water and all the sugar too.'

The man took a theatrical forkful of food, making them wait for his story.

'So poor old Robbie is peelin' spuds in the back room, for our shepherd's pie that evenin'. He hears a noise, turns to see who is it and – blam – they tip this huge steel bowl, wider than I am and full of the sweetest prison napalm, all over him.

'Poor blighter was fried like a doughnut, blisters bubblin' up all over. Burns all over his face, throat, chest, arms – a right screaming mess I can tell you. We didn't see him for nearly two weeks while they were treatin' him.

'Then one day he's back, all pink and raw, blind in one eye. First night he was back in his cell, he hung hisself. From his bunk, with a TV cable. He had a TV on account of his privileges, see.

'Course the meow meow firm are delighted. The grass is gone, now they've got open season on bringin' the gear in through the kitchens. But about a week later, they get busted. Turned out Robbie weren't the grass all along.

'Everyone thought his privileges and office visits was cos he was a grass – but in fact it was cos the senior kanga liked fraggles and was bummin' poor Robbie. Probly why he took his own life, actually.'

The man looked around at Flynn and his mum like he'd delivered some great piece of wisdom. There was a heavy, tense silence while he attacked his dinner.

'Anyway, that's what shepherd's pie makes me think of.'

Flynn shook his head. 'What a lovely dinner time story,' he said sarcastically.

The man frowned at Flynn, a fork of food just inches from his mouth. 'What you sayin', son? You tryin' to mug me off?'

Flynn said nothing.

'Well?' said the man, eyes blazing cold.

'He meant nothing by it Keel,' said Flynn's mum, 'You know, it's just that… well, this is a nice family meal. It's not a very happy story.'

'Yeah well, sorry I ain't spent the last three and an 'alf years in Disneyland,' said the man.

'I know, I'm sorry –' began his mum.

'And just let the boy answer for hisself, eh Sylv? Big boy now, don't need to hide behind mummy's skirts. Not that you're wearin' a skirt Sylv, but you know what I's sayin.

'So, let me say it again son: are you proper tryin' to mug me off?'

Flynn turned and stared back at the man now. He met his gaze and focused hard on not swallowing. The seconds of stalemate ticked by, until suddenly the man broke the tension.

'Nah, I'm only messin' with ya!' he exclaimed in a fake, jokey way. 'I'm only messin! Did you see that Sylv, did you?'

Flynn's mum smiled, not knowing what to say.

'What's that smell?' continued the man. 'It's either your cooking or I think little Flynn's had an accident! No I'm only joshin' with you son. You should see your face!'

Even though he was more than halfway through his meal, the man reached forward for the salt again, shaking it animatedly, his elbow practically in Flynn's face.

'Oh, watch out. Careful, Flynn son,' he said. 'Bit tight in 'ere, ain't it? No room to swing a rat. I was a bit surprised to find you still 'ere when I got back, tell truth. Thought you'd be in your own little shag pad by now. Place ain't big enough for the three of us, is it?'

'Flynn's not going anywhere,' said his mum quickly. Bravely.

'No, no, course not, that's not what I'm sayin', don't misunderstand me,' said the man in mock indignation. 'It's fine, course it is. For now. Besides, I got this new business venture, gonna net me plenty of readies, gonna be a blinder. We can all move to a bigger place soon.'

'Oh, that sounds nice!' said his mum.

'Too right,' said the man. 'Just need a little start-up capital, you know, a few quid to play with, then it's all gravy.'

'Oh, well, ah – I've just paid this month's rent so I haven't got much…' his mother began quietly.

'You're not lending him anything,' said Flynn quietly.

The man stared intently at Flynn.

'No no Sylv love, you're misunderstanding me again,' he said, still looking at Flynn. 'I'm not asking you for any cash, course not. What kind of man do you think I am, begging for scraps from a woman? No, just sayin' it'll take a few days, that's all.'

He pushed his empty plate away, ruffling the tablecloth.

'Right, where's the beers?' The man stared at Flynn's mum like a challenge.

'Beer… oh no, yes I didn't think, I forgot, I mean I'm not sure –'

'Hey hey, come on, I just mean a coupla light beers, nothing heavy. You know I ain't into gettin' wasted, I am a reformed character. Didn't even touch the pruno inside. Just a couple of beers but, to wet me whistle. This being my homecoming dinner.'

'Yes, of course, yes you're right – I was just planning the meal, I didn't think – I'll go now,' said Flynn's mum, putting down her knife and fork from her half-eaten dinner and standing up quickly, banging her thighs against the table with a rattle of cutlery. 'I'll be quick, it's only close.'

'No mum,' said Flynn. 'It's fifteen minutes away, it's too late.'

'He's right love, you've done enough. Let the boy go.'

'I'm not going,' said Flynn sharply. 'No-one's going.'

'Well, fine family reunion this is,' the man spat dismissively. 'Not even a drop of beer to wet me lips,' he went on, folding his arms. 'Treated better inside than I am 'ere.'

'No no, it's no problem, it's my fault. We need milk anyway, I'll go –' continued his mum, shuffling and edgy as she dithered as to whether to get her purse or her coat or clear the dishes first.

Flynn felt his insides grow heavy, seeing her like this. Seeing her sense of self ebbing out of her, her confidence faltering. This man – this shit – should not drink at all, but at least Flynn could do the rationing.

'I'll go,' he said, standing.

'What? No you can't,' said his mum, as Flynn reached for his top hanging over the armchair.

'It's ok mum. I'll run. I can do it in half the time. It's good exercise.'

The man nodded. 'Let the boy go,' he asserted. 'You've done enough. 'Bout time he started helping you round the house a bit. You put your feet up. The washing up can wait.'

He took his cigarette pack back out of his pocket and took one out. Flynn's mum's eyes widened.

'It's ok Sylv, boy's going out, ain't he?' said the man. 'No harm done, me smokin' while he's out. In't that right son? Christ, you'll be havin' me on them e-cigarettes next, talking 'bout passive smoking like some effin' doctor's leaflet. I tell you what Sylv love, ever since his childhood accident you've smothered him. Boy needs to grow up. Needs a man to show him what's what. I'm back just in time.'

Flynn stared back. And said nothing. He just went out the door, pulling it to behind him, and ran down the first flight of concrete steps, stumbling once and then tripping badly the second time, smacking his hip into the wall.

He stopped and sat on the bottom step, his arms folded tightly around his body, trying to squeeze his heart to calm it down.

His childhood accident. That monster had no right to call it that.

Flynn had been a child, that was true. He'd just turned seven. Wearing new pyjamas, a birthday present from his mum. But he'd woken up in the night with a jolt. He heard shouting. And screaming. It made him scared, hearing the raging temper through the thin wall, the anger of his daddy, the frightened, begging voice of his mummy. He'd started crying right there in his little bed, pulling the shabby patterned blankets around him.

The noise had got worse, there'd been a crash; things breaking. He'd scrambled out of bed, the blankets twisting around his legs, knotting him up. But he'd managed to get free and into the room.

And there had been his daddy, snarling like a mad dog, holding his poor mummy up against the wall by her throat, smacking the side of her head with the heel of his hand again and again, smudging her hair across her face where it stuck to her tears and snot and blood.

And Flynn had hurled himself at the man. Stop hurting mummy, stop hurting her he'd yelled, beating his small hands against the man's tree trunk legs.

And the man had looked at him with cruel, dead eyes and casually kicked out like he was shaking off a fly.

His size ten boot had caught Flynn full in the face. Shattering his cheekbone and splitting his left eye.

He'd had four days of surgery. Nurses gave him soothing words and strong painkillers as he fell in and out of consciousness. It was over a week before that little seven year-old boy had opened his left eye again, and the nurses noticed that his pupil had changed colour. So now he had one blue eye and one green.

He remembered it so vividly, lying in the hospital bed, staring up at the ceiling with his right eye… as he tried to open his left through the crust of gunk gluing his eyelashes together.

The bewilderment of his eye opening… and his field of view not changing.

Not getting any bigger.

Blinking, panicking, wondering where his mummy was as everything beyond a certain point remained completely dark…

…and he learned what it was like to be blind in one eye.

5: WITCH

The bus hits an overhanging branch with a smack that makes me jump. I'm basically jumping at everything at the moment.

The aeroplane tragedy – Flight BA09984 crashing into the North Sea – was four days ago. Everyone on board is now officially confirmed either dead or missing.

It's also four days since I heard that Noolie has gone missing – which means she's actually been missing for a week.

And four days since I got the *horrendous* news alert on my phone: that because of the plane crash, the government is introducing a 'state of emergency'. They're putting anyone who might be able to do aether on a watchlist… and they're making plans for everyone who has aether to wear an electronic tag.

I'm going to be tagged?!? It's just so … scary. Sitting upstairs on the bus, my head is spinning. Aether terrorists, disappearances, demos, tags, a state of emergency… it's just horrendous.

And all over social media – even some of the newspapers – people are calling the government's new plans for aether The Witchcraft Act.

I mean: FML.

I take a deep breath. I wish I had Piper with me, but she's not allowed at work. She always knows when I need cheering up, and how to too. Probably because of our connection, because of my aether. It's an ability called animus.

There are, apparently, six aether abilities. They get called the six 'aspects', I don't know why. There's:

1. *Psychokinesis.* Only my dad calls it that, everyone else just says PK. Being able to move things just using your mind. I'm not great at it, but I can do it a bit – the glass jug at the party, that was about my limit. But I've seen clips of people in masks lifting motorbikes off the ground or hurling TVs against the wall with their PK.

2. *Pre-cognition.* Shortened to Pre-cog. Amazingly, it means you can see into the future. Which is just weird. But you can't make it happen, it's just random (that's what they say, it's never happened to me). And it's only a second or two into the future. So it doesn't sound like anyone with pre-cog is going to be predicting the lottery numbers any time soon.

3. *Thiriokinesis*, also called Animus. My best one. It's not animal control (which some people think), it's just you can connect with an animal's mind, bond with them, kinda make emotional suggestions. A bit like hypnosis, maybe. Well maybe, it's hard to explain. There are no instruction manuals for this stuff. But basically it's why Piper and I have such an incredible connection.

4. *Psynaptic shock.* Normally called Snapshot. I can do it, according to the EEG monitor my father uses to measure my brainwaves. It's like a stun gun to the brain. Fries your synapses. If you did it on someone it could make them dizzy, or concussed or even knock them out so it's a bit gross. I've never tried it on anyone, obvs – that would be like GBH or something.

5.   *Telesthesia.* Most people call it Scry. It's not telepathy, which some people think, it's just the ability to sense someone's state of mind. If they're tired, if they're angry, if they're faking or hiding something. You can't actually read their thoughts. And I can't scry anyway.

6.   *Wispr.* I've never done this either. But according to Wikipedia, two people who can Wispr can talk to each other with their minds, like a mobile phone. It sounds quite cool, I've just never had chance to try it with someone.

I've read stuff by bloggers who reckon there are more than six aspects, like pyrokinesis (being able to conjure up fire), stuff like that. Probably all fake, but... well, six aspects is the official story. I also think that – oh, this is my stop.

I leap out of my seat, thank the driver and walk the ten minutes to The Cat's Pyjamas. It's a cat café run by my boss Melinda (who is just lovely).

And how awesome is it having a job where you're surrounded by beautiful, super-friendly cats the whole time? I absolutely love it. People often say 'are you a cat person or a dog person?' but I don't buy that you can only be one or the other, I totally love both.

'Hey, Echo my gorgeous,' calls out Melinda, looking up as I walk in. She's Australian and she calls everyone gorgeous or babe or poppet. Even if she doesn't really like someone I think she still calls them sweetie.

Mr Tibbles rubs himself against my legs. Mr Tibbles is a cat, obvs. A ginger and white moggy, very confident and very sociable.

'How are you then babe?' asks Melinda, restocking a couple of the cake stands as I hang up my coat and take my pinny out of my bag.

I nod more enthusiastically than I feel. 'Good thanks, really good.'

'Did you see the news? State of emergency mind, is it?!'

I nod again, my heart sinking.

'Yeah, it's a shocker though isn't it? You can't feel safe anywhere nowadays.'

I nod again, biting my lip and looking around. 'Table four?' I ask.

'That's right babe, just sat down. We've a newbie on the menu today, orange and pistachio cake and totally delicious if they're interested. If not I'm going to eat it all myself, really I am!'

I smile and go over, but I am butterflies inside. Even Melinda's talking about the news and aether. FML.

It's pretty boho in The Cats Pyjamas. Lots of mismatched pattern, upcycled items and vintage pieces.

The three people on table four (all women, all in their mid thirties I'd guess) have never been before so I explain how it all works and take their order. I also use my aether to usher over Maleficent, a black Persian with gleaming long hair. She pads over at my gesturing (a cover for actually using aether) and I stroke her between the ears and get her to jump up onto a nearby pouf covered in Cath Kidston fabric. The women coo appreciatively.

When I applied for the job Melinda asked me if we had any pets at home and I said yes Piper my Westie. Melinda screwed up her face – ah, the cats won't like you because you'll smell of dog, she said. Then I went in to meet the cats and they were all over me like I'd showered in catnip. Fair dinkum, Melinda said, pretty amazed. So I got the job!

The next hour goes by pretty fast. I dart from group to group, carrying trays of orders while cats weave in and out of my legs. I can hear snatched moments of conversation about the news, about 'aether terrorism'. Everyone's putting the world to rights and saying something must be done. I keep nervously biting my lip.

Then the café door opens, I turn to see who's going to take the last table… and OMG: it's Ronny and Gigi. The leading ladies of the glossy posse. I've worked here nearly five months and never seen them in here before. But now, after the week I've had, to top it all I have to go over and take their order. Yay.

'Hello ladies,' I say, walking over and trying to be coolly professional. 'What can I get you?'

At first they act like they haven't heard me. So I stand there for a few seconds, just being ignored.

'Excuse me ladies,' I say more loudly after an awkward pause, 'Can I help?' Ronny glances up.

''sup waitress,' she says in a such a fake urban accent. 'What is this place?

'All these cats everywhere? It's so lame.' She looks me straight in the eye, challenging me to react. And she acts like she doesn't recognize me.

'Ehm… it's a cat café,' I say, stumbling a little over my words and cursing myself inside for doing so.

'A café for cats? Run by dogs?' says Gigi. They think that's hilarious.

I breathe as slowly and calmly as I can.

'No,' I say, 'it's a café for people. It's just got cats because some customers like it.' I can't believe I'm explaining it to them.

'Well I don't want a saucer of milk,' says Gigi. They laugh their fake laughs again.

'Would you like a few more minutes?' I say.

Ronny's brow furrows. 'Wait a minute,' she says in mock realization. 'Aren't you that girl from school?'

She looks at me questioningly. What am I supposed to say? Seriously? Am I 'that girl'? What does that even mean? Like I'm so famous or something.

'I – how do you mean?' I say.

'Oh, yessssss!' says Ronny, smacking her head with her hand. 'The school witches! There was Noolie, she was actually ok, and this one, what was her name... Echo!'

'You can say that again!' says Gigi. Oh, that joke. Sooo hilarious.

'Are you allowed to be here?' Ronny says. 'Does your electronic tag let you this far from home?'

'She must be here for the black cats,' adds Gigi. 'That's what witches have isn't it?'

'Now, now Gigi,' says Ronny, 'We must mind ourselves. Echo might not want everyone to know she's a witch. They'd probably choke on their tea if they knew it was made in a cauldron!'

'Yeah,' says Gigi, looking dismissively at our (generally older) customers. 'It's all very Fifty Shades of Earl Grey.'

'Oh Gigi, you are too much!' says Ronny. 'Look witchtress, just bring us the least awful thing on the menu – do you think you could manage that?'

God, this is so crap.

I steer clear of them for the next twenty minutes, as much as I can. But every time I go close, they laugh at some mean joke, or lean over to each other to whisper about me.

Then I take an order from two large ladies in vivid dresses sitting at the table next to them and Gigi snaps her fingers at me. 'Waitress. Oh waitress,' she trills in her most patronising voice. They want the bill, apparently this place is just too lame. I go and fetch it, then I give one of our regulars, Mrs Daniels, a free refill. She's 'nearly seventy-six' as she told me once and she loves cats but she isn't allowed them in the sheltered accommodation where she lives.

I turn back, but there's no Ronny and Gigi. I go over to the table… and yeah, they've definitely gone. Without paying. There's just the abandoned bill, with something written on it in black eyeliner pencil.

'Everything ok gorgeous?' I feel a concerned hand on my shoulder and I turn too fast, my face flushing, having just read the note. It's Melinda.

'Huh?' I say, hopelessly.

'Those girls – I saw them dash off suddenly. Have they paid?'

My throat tightens. 'They – uh – well, I'll pay,' I say.

'What? No, if they've done a runner I'll call the cops,' says Melinda.

I shake my head quickly. 'No! No, they haven't done a runner. They – they're friends from school. I said I'd treat them,' I finish weakly.

'Ok love,' she says gently after a moment, taking pity on me. 'That's no problem. Hey, things are a bit quieter now. Why don't you take your break, poppet.'

I nod limply and quickly run out for my break, those butterflies bouncing around inside me again.

As I go, my fist squeezes around Ronny and Gigi's bill, tattooing a mirror image of their message – of their hate – onto my palm in greasy black eyeliner:

Burn the Witch

6: RUNT

"I was the first person to realise the link between aether and migraine. Look back and you see migraines and remarkable brains have had a long association – some of history's most influential people suffered from migraines.

"Military leaders including Julius Caesar and Napoleon. Political leaders like Thomas Jefferson. Writers – Lewis Carroll and Virginia Woolf. Scientists such as Darwin and Freud, and philosophers including Nietzsche.

"Inventors too – Alexander Graham Bell got them, for instance. A number of artists: Monet, Van Gogh – you can see the pain poured into his art. Tchaikovsky. People with incredible minds… that were prone to migraine.

"The signs were there. Migraines meant something. They were a symptom, a growing pain… of the brain developing in a quite extraordinary way."

– From the TS Interviews with Doctor Magellan-Jones

Flynn needed to see the news but the man – this stinking, drinking, simmering bastard – was sprawled out on the sofa watching some shit about bounty hunters.

The lounge felt smaller and darker since he'd come back, filling the space with his grim, menacing mass. Even his heavy breathing was oppressive, like he was trying to take as much oxygen as possible, leaving none for Flynn.

But he really needed to see the news. A week ago there'd been a plane crash which was being blamed on an 'aether incident', now they were talking about tagging anyone twenty-five or under who got migraines, to monitor them as a potential 'aether terrorist'. And online there was nonstop aether trolling and death threats and all kinds of stuff. There were even rumours of aethereals going missing. A girl from his town, Noolie Dunn, had gone apparently vanished off the face of the Earth. It was a big story on the local news.

Oh, this prick. Flynn would read the news online instead, in the bedroom. He got up off the sagging chair to reach for his iPad…

…and saw that his rucksack was unzipped. Weird. He didn't leave things open. It wasn't the kind of person he was. He was the kind who, if he was drinking a bottle of water, would put the lid back on between sips. Yet here was his Berghaus rucksack unzipped, gaping open with a wide, black scream.

He thrust his arm inside its mouth, feeling around anxiously. His fingers probed the corners. Nothing. Its stomach was empty. He spoke as calmly as he could.

'Where is it?' he said. His voice came out more raspy than he wanted. And the man ignored him.

Flynn stood up and turned slowly, his back straightening and his fingers curling inwards with tension.

'Hey – I said, where is it?'

The man, sprawled on the green dralon sofa, turned his gaze lazily away from the TV for a moment.

'Where's what, sprat?'

'My iPad,' said Flynn, his voice wavering a little. 'Where's my iPad?'

'I don't know what yer squawkin' about,' said the man dismissively, turning back to the TV and taking another swig from his lager can.

'I think you do,' said Flynn angrily, his face beginning to flush. Through the wall next door he could hear Bollywood music playing.

'All right everyone?' said his mum, coming through from the kitchenette.

'My iPad is missing,' said Flynn.

'Your – oh, I'm sure it must be around here somewhere.'

'No mum, you know I don't leave it lying around. It was in my bag and now it's gone.'

'Keel,' said Flynn's mum nervously, 'Have you seen Flynn's iPad?'

'Eye what?' said the man. 'I don't even know what one is. Sounds like summat for women, time of the month.'

Flynn's mum took a breath. 'It's Flynn's computer, isn't it,' she said, her voice wobbling a little. 'Just like a square screen. Silver. Thin.'

'Oh that, now someone's startin' to make some sense, talking some English. Yeah, I borrowed it.'

Flynn's mum's face transformed from worried to relieved in a heartbeat. 'Oh, there you go Flynn, your dad just borrowed it.'

Flynn wasn't so easily convinced. Not by this bastard. 'Well where is it then?'

The man muted the TV, an angry wrinkle across his forehead. 'Told you boy, I has borrowed it. For my business. Gonna get us out of this dump. Tell you what, I'll get you a new one next month, how about that, will that stop yer gripin'?'

'I don't need a new one, I want mine. With all my stuff on it.'

'Fine,' said the man, 'That one then. Just wait 'til next month, like I said, and I'll get it back then. Now enough, ok?' he said, his temper starting to show through. He took another swig, his fingers making the aluminium of the can click and wrinkle.

Flynn's mum looked at the man, confused. 'Get it back? What do you mean Keel? Where's Flynn's iPad?'

'Now I'm sayin' it nicely Sylv, you need to stop badgerin' me, you and the boy 'ere. All these questions when I's just tryin' to have a relax, watch a bit of TV, hopin' that mebbe for once you got a good tea goin', a decent spread.

'I got this great business opp, I keep tellin' you. Gonna make a bundle. And if 'e don't want a new iPad computer thing, fine. Old one it is. Message 'eard loud and clear.

'As it happens, now that I know what you're blabbin' on about, it's tucked up nice and safe in that Quids Inn down the high street. They gave me a couple a hundred notes for it, but it's not sold, they're just holdin' it. On a buy back. I get it back in a month or so – payin' over the odds mind – and in the meantime, it helps towards me startup cash, for the business venture.'

Flynn's head started to throb and his eyebrows snarled towards each other, like stags about to lock horns. This man. This bastard. His mum was ashen, shock all over her tired face. 'You… you've hawked Flynn's iPad?'

The man put the lager can down on the carpet and swung his legs off the sofa, sitting forward now and looking almost as angry as Flynn felt. The Bollywood music through the wall seemed louder than ever, joined by the noisy pulse beating in his eardrums as the pressure in his head built.

'I don't know why you're gettin' your knickers in a twist!' said the man. 'I told you: I ain't sold it, no-one's usin' it, no harm done. Look at the pair of you, all riled up. And look at this shitty dive too. Shameful. Me sleepin' on this pile of broken old springs,' he added, nodding down at the sofabed, 'I had a better mattress in the nick, though.

'It takes money to make money, you know that? Workin' capital,' he said, saying the words slowly, like he was teaching economics to children. 'I just got out, yeah? They don't wave you off with no golden handshake. I got no ready cash, and no-one's gonna give an ex-lag a job. So I'm goin' self-employed, gonna be my own entra-prun-ooer. But I need funds. Christ, I told you whingers this the other day.

'Now, I suggest you both settle down before tempers get aggro. Nice phone, by the way, son,' he added, gesturing at the pocket Flynn had put his phone in. 'Pricey, was it?' He stared at Flynn with a sly half-smile, baring his nicotine-stained teeth like a rabid dog.

Flynn swallowed. He could taste acid in his mouth. 'Go get it,' was all he said.

The man sat back on the sofa, indicating going anywhere was the last thing he was planning. He looked down at his big, veiny hands and began massaging a knuckle. 'Simmer down lad,' he said. 'I'm not some schoolgirl to be ordered about. Be a good boy and everything's gravy. You just have to wait for your toy, a few weeks, that's all. Money's invested now.'

Flynn began to pace a tiny space of worn carpet. Was he getting a migraine? His head felt heavy, full of blood and anger. His mum looked distraught, reaching her arms out to touch Flynn, to hold him still, but not quite doing it.

'What… can I…' she stuttered, '…how did you invest your money, Keel? she asked hesitantly. Your money.

'Oh, you don't need to know 'bout that, Sylv,' said the man. 'All legit, nothin' for you to worry about.' He picked the remote up and waved it at them both. 'Now, can we all just shut up with this silly nonsense and watch a bit of telly?'

Flynn stopped pacing like an animal in a Chinese zoo.

'No,' he said clearly. 'Get the money back, and buy back my iPad. First thing. I need it.'

'Watch yourself, son,' said the man, throwing him a dark glance. 'I don't take kindly to bein' given orders. Didn't take it when I was inside, not from the kangas, not from the nutjobs, not from the gang bangers – and I'm certainly not takin' it in my own home from some sad little geek.'

Flynn's body twitched involuntarily. His mum lurched forward, her hands on his shoulders to keep him still, to hold him back.

'This is not your home!' yelled Flynn down at the sofa. It was the first time he could remember raising his voice in years. 'You don't belong here! This is not your home, you're not welcome, you're not wanted! I hate you, mum fears you, you're a disgusting bloody parasite!'

The man stood quickly. Flynn had grown considerably over the years, but the man still looked down on him, a full three inches taller and a couple of stone of prison-gym muscle heavier.

'You gobby sprat,' the man seethed in his face, bubbles of beery spit forming on the yellowed teeth. 'Who do you think you are, runt? I've made an effort with you since I got back, tried givin' you a man's influence, and this is the respect you show me?'

'Please,' said Flynn's mum, 'Please, Flynn, Keel.'

'Why are you like this?' shouted Flynn. 'You're disgusting, you —'

Flynn stopped talking as fingers strong as pliers clamped around his throat. He felt his Adam's apple being squeezed by the hard, rough pads at the base of Keel's thumb and forefinger.

''Bout time you started listening to what I said,' the man asserted with his stale lager breath. 'What's the matter with your ears? As useless as that left eye of yours is they?'

Flynn's mum grabbed the man's arm, the arm that was crushing Flynn's windpipe. 'Keel, stop it, please, stop it!' she cried. 'You're going to kill him!'

'No, no,' said the man. 'Boy's been pushin' me since I got back. Pushin' and proddin' and bleatin' and bitchin'. 'Bout time we sorted this thing out. I blame you as much as him, mind,' he added, throwing her a mean look. 'You've indulged 'im Sylv. Mollycoddled 'im since his accident, and he ain't never gonna get on in life if he continues badmouthin' 'is betters.'

He swung Flynn round with one arm, up against the wall where the music was coming from, knocking a swimming trophy off the tiled mantelpiece.

'Stop hurting my boy, stop hurting him!' his mum screamed.

It was like ten years ago all over again. Except this time it was her trying to protect Flynn, rather than the other way around.

With his right hand locked around Flynn's throat, the man grabbed Flynn's mum by the wrist with his left, wrenching her off him with a loud crack. She screamed out in instant, down on her knees, then scrambled back, holding her shattered right wrist by her left arm as she fell onto the sofabed.

And something snapped in Flynn.

He and the man were just centimetres apart. Flynn concentrated as much as his oxygen-starved faculties would allow. Everything felt blurry. He let the hate blossom in his mind, lighting up the neurons in his brain, connecting, glowing, growing. Then, focus. Focus the hate. Focus the rage. He might pass out any second, and the desperation concentrated his mind. He could feel it.

Hold in the rage, the adrenaline and focus it all. Focus. Hate. Focus…

'Dear oh dear,' said the man, ignoring Flynn's mum sobbing on the sofa, 'the two of you gangin' up on me. Who'da thought it. But let me tell you the way it's –'

...*Strike.*

There was a flare in Flynn's mind, a blinding white light as he let go a snapshot at the man, right at his head. A burning, coruscating flare of aether.

The man's eyes glazed over like a stunned animal. His jaw slackened. And the choke hold around Flynn's windpipe went loose. All for a fraction of a second.

And in that instant, Flynn threw his head forward with all the force he could manage, aiming the top of his forehead at the bridge of the man's nose. There was a sharp, brutal crunch.

The man staggered back, clutching his nose as blood streamed through his fingers. Flynn's head throbbed harder than ever and he sucked oxygen from the air in wheezing, rasping breaths. It felt like the man's fingers were still around his throat, they had dug in so hard. And he could see his mum cowering, collapsed into the sofabed, clutching her injured arm and whimpering in pain.

'You dirty little shit,' growled the man, still looking groggy from the stun.

He reached into his pocket, smearing it in blood, and pulled out a thin black plastic handle. He pushed a metal stud on the side; a blade swung out and Flynn's mum shrieked in horror.

Flynn stared at the blade and twitched his head sideways, and the knife – slippery in the man's bloodied hands – flew across the room and hit the window with a crack, then dropped down onto the sofa next to his mum.

'What the –' the man said, confused and angry, staring at the curtain where the knife had hit. 'You – you did that! You freak!' he snarled at Flynn. A light went on behind the dull, unblinking stare. 'Yeah – you did it. You're one of them… headcases, on the news!' he said, gesturing at Flynn like he wasn't human. 'Well shit the bed, ain't this a pretty mess,' he added, spots of blood dripping from his nose onto his white polo top.

'Do you know what I think?' he said, stepping forward, his bravado back. 'I think little boys shouldn't play with knives. And maybe you're all outta tricks!' And on the last word he swung a huge roundhouse punch at Flynn's head with a fist like a circus mallet. He was a big man, broad-shouldered and prison-ripped. And he was right, Flynn was all out of aether tricks.

But he was still ready. He'd had years to be ready. To think it over and over a million times, what it would be like to face this man in anger. And not as a seven year old in his pyjamas, but as an adult looking for justice.

And as the fist swung in – the predictable, clumsy hook – Flynn stepped in with his right foot, blocking the man's in-swinging blow with his forearms. Then Flynn twisted his hips with his own punch with his left hand, bringing his right arm in tight to his body as the left shot forward, perfectly straight: unblockable and unstoppable into the man's snarling jaw followed by another with his right, straight onto the man's broken nose.

Crunch.

'Uhh,' groaned the man, staggering sideways, catching his foot on the hearth…

…and stumbling onto the edge of the mantelpiece, the side of his head smashing into the tiled corner with a juddering pop, falling in slow motion, crumpling to the floor.

Motionless.

Silent.

His body lay twisted awkwardly, his left arm bent up between the fireplace and their small, folded dining table.

And for the first time all evening there was a moment of perfect quiet in the flat. Then Flynn's mum let out a weak, frightened moan.

Flynn went over to her on the sofabed, stepping over the man's body. She was holding her arm against her body. He put his arm around her, being careful to not touch her damaged wrist. The man's knife was wedged at the back of the sofa, and Flynn discreetly folded it closed and put it in a pocket out of sight of his mum.

'Are you ok?' he said to her. 'We should get you to a hospital.' His mum just stared at the heaped body on the floor.

'He's smashed his head on the fireplace,' she said. 'I saw it.'

Flynn nodded gently. She was in shock.

'Is he… have you… is he… alive?'

Flynn turned to look at the man.

'I don't know,' he said. 'Probably,' he added. 'Probably just unconscious.'

'Maybe…' she said, trailing off.

'Look mum,' said Flynn, 'we need to get you to a hospital, have someone look at your wrist.'

She turned to him as if seeing him for the first time. Her jaw wobbled and her sad eyes went glossy with tears.

'Oh Flynn, I'm sorry,' she said. 'I'm so sorry, my wonderful boy. I should never have let him back in. I should have stood up to him.'

'Hey, it's ok, it's ok,' said Flynn, 'it's not your fault. He's a bully.'

'I just thought, maybe this time…' she said haltingly. 'Perhaps this time maybe we could be a proper family.'

'We are a proper family,' replied Flynn. 'You and me. We don't need him. We never did. We don't need anyone. We're a proper family, mum, we are. And no-one is going to hurt you ever again.'

The man's arm fell behind the folded table and Flynn's mum jumped back, a small shriek coming from her lips. Flynn got off the sofa and went over. He could see a dark, sticky patch in his hair where he'd struck the mantelpiece. He wasn't sure – and he wasn't going to touch to find out – but it looked like maybe a piece of skull was sticking out, from which a treacle-like trail of dark red was oozing. Slowly, he put his hand down in front of the man's mouth… yes, he felt slight movement of air.

'He's breathing,' he told his mum. 'Now please, we need to get you to the hospital.'

As he stood, his mum twitched at a sound behind her: a distant siren. 'The police!' she exclaimed.

Flynn realised: it had been perfectly silent because the Bollywood music had stopped. Charminda next door must have called the cops. He wouldn't come round himself, he wouldn't want to get involved, but he'd have called the police when he'd heard the yelling and banging through the thin walls.

'We'll just tell them what happened,' said Flynn. 'Apart from…' He was thinking about the bloodied knife in his pocket.

'Oh!' said his mum. 'Your powers? The things you can do. Oh Flynn, he saw it – Keel saw.' She grabbed Flynn on the shoulder with her good arm. 'When he comes round he'll tell the police – he'll twist it all on to you, you know what he's like!'

Flynn bit his lip. He didn't want anyone to know about aether. Especially not the authorities. Especially not in connection to a grievous injury. Especially not with all the stuff that was in the news about plane disasters and electronic tags and witchcraft.

He sat back down on the sofa. The knife handle dug into his side, prodding him like an accusing finger.

'No, no – that would make him a grass,' he said. 'He wouldn't do that. Remember his story from the other night, Robbie from prison? The "prison napalm"? He won't say anything.'

'Oh Flynn,' wailed him mum, 'we can't trust him. When – if – he wakes up, he'll be mad you got the better of him. He'll tell, I know he will!'

She was right. The man was a thug and a bully but he was also snide. Silent tears were sliding down his mum's face. 'I can't lose you,' she said. 'They can't take you away from me. They nearly took you back then… you know. Into care. I can't go through that again. I can't lose you.'

The siren was getting closer.

Flynn leapt to his feet. 'I should go.' His mum looked up, horrified. 'Just for a few days, 'til things settle down,' he said as reassuringly as he could. 'When he's in hospital – when he comes round, I'll go see him. Tell him there's more to come if he says anything to the police or ever comes back. I'll tell him I could fry his brain. And if he doesn't come round… well, either way we'll be free.' Flynn was thinking fast. 'But I need to get away for a bit – if they arrest me now, I won't be calm enough, I won't be convincing. And if I'm in custody I won't be able to visit him in hospital.'

His mum looked at the motionless body again, slightly dazed. 'You stood up to him,' she said, looking back at Flynn with pride in her wet eyes. 'You showed him you weren't scared. And you showed me I don't need to be either.'

The siren sound outside became very loud, then stopped.

'I can't lose you Flynn, I can't. Go on, get out of here before they find you. I'll make sure they don't come after you. I love you.'

Flynn had more emotions fighting for room inside him than his body could contain. His throat felt crushed and bruised and his head hurt. He stared into his mum's eyes for a moment then bent forward, hugged her briefly and kissed her on the forehead. Her arm might be broken, and she was weeping and distraught, but inside, something seemed to have healed. Perhaps, like with him, healed back stronger.

'I'll see you soon. Bye mum.'

He went to the door and grabbed his jacket off the hook, not even glancing back at the sack of wet meat on the floor. His head was really starting to throb.

'Take care, my beautiful boy,' his mum called out after him. 'I love you so much.'

7: ABDUCTED

Where is Noolie?!?

I'm sat on the bus (again) looking at my phone. She's still not been found. She's literally vanished off the face of the Earth.

I'm swiping through page after page of pictures, comments and likes. It's like… wow. Her parents, brother, friends, distant cousins, local media, someone from Hollyoaks, complete strangers who never met her – they're all posting sweet messages and photos. Some of it's really lovely and moving. But mixed in there are all these other posts too. Complete strangers throwing shade at Noolie just because she's aethereal. Some of it is so… extra.

The worst are some of the sick replies to her parents, who made an appeal asking for her safe return (which means they think someone's taken her?). There's a video of them making this emotional appeal, breaking down as they do, it's really heartbreaking.

I'm not sure my father would ever break down like that. Like when he told me about aether being fatal, mum was in absolute bits and I was too, but he was just the same as always. Never loses control, never has a greying hair out of place, his designer specs are always perfectly straight and his expensive shoes are always gleaming and on point. And he's always totally sure of what to do, like he *never* doubts himself. The total opposite of me, in other words. Probably why I drive him so mad when he's giving me aether coaching in his study.

Oh, phone. It's Jazz.

'Hey beautiful,' I say. 'What's new?'

'I'm standing around nekkid,' she replies. 'I've just showered, scrubbed and shaved my legs and I'm letting the body butter soak in.'

'Oh so I'm just a distraction while you stand around bored?' I say.

'Yup,' replies Jazz with a grin in her voice. 'So watcha up to shorty?'

'I'm on the bus home,' I say. 'Looking at all the stuff about Noolie.'

'Oh good grief, I know,' says Jazz. 'It's totally cray. The irony is Noolie would love all this attention, but she's had to go missing to get it!'

'Ha,' I say softly.

'Hey, don't worry babes,' Jazz says. 'You've always kept your aether on the down-low. But she always had her aether swag on, you know? Truth is, I bet she's realised that shouting about being an aethereal was a dumb move at the moment, so she's gone off somewhere to lay low. And I bet she is reading all the posts about her and loving every minute of it.'

D'you know, that does kinda make sense. More than the theory that Noolie's been abducted. Trust Jazz, she's so good at making me feel better.

'It's like funerals,' I say. 'You have to die to hear all the good things people think about you.'

'I'd love to go to my own funeral!' says Jazz.

'Err… everyone goes to their own funeral?' I say.

'No, while I'm still alive, I mean!' says Jazz. 'Hey we should write a speech for each other's funeral, then read it to each other,' says Jazz.

'Morbid!' I reply.

'Here lies Echo, my BFF,' intones Jazz down the phone in a sombre voice. 'Brains, beauty and broomsticks, she had it all. Now she's gone, all I have to remember her by is a phone full of memories that really need better filters. Plus of course, in her Will she did leave me everything she ever owned, including her super-cute Westie, her ridiculous collection of sunglasses and the vintage Kate Spade bag that by rights should have been mine in the first place.'

'Still on about the bag,' I say (we both spotted it at the same time in this posh charity shop last year, I ended up getting it). She laughs.

'Talking of broomsticks,' I say, lowering my voice, 'Ronny and Gigi came to the café. I've never seen them in there before but Ronny was really being blatant about my aether.' I've now gone down to a whisper so no-one on the bus overhears. 'And she called me a witch.'

'Oh that stuck-up cow,' says Jazz. 'All that stuff about "The Witchcraft Act" online, it's so cringe. Ronny is totally out of order. Better witch than bitch.'

That makes me laugh. 'What I don't get is how come if you're an aethereal and a girl you get called a witch, but you don't see guys being called "wizards" or "warlocks",' I say.

'You are right babes, there is no equality,' agrees Jazz in mock-indignation. 'To be honest it was much cooler when they were calling you all vampires!'

Oh yeah, vampires. Sometimes aethereals get called vampires – I didn't get it at first, but it's because of the migraine thing. Basically, if you get migraines, you can be more sensitive to light. Bright light can trigger an attack or make it much worse, so you might wear sunglasses more often (I have eight pairs) or you might just want to keep out of the sun. Like a vampire.

'Vampires are always thin, aren't they?' I say. 'I think I put on about three pounds after that Ben and Jerry's splurge the other day,' I say.

'Hey, a rhinoceros is just a unicorn with curves,' says Jazz.

'Sure,' I say, 'but who wants to be a rhinoceros?' Talking of bodies, something has just occurred to me.

'Wait – why are you shaving your legs?' I ask.

'Well I said I'd catch a movie with Jay later, so…'

'OMG!' I gasp. See, I've been so caught up with my own drama I've completely forgotten that other people have lives too. Jay is the guy Jazz spent most of the time at the party with, after I suddenly bailed. She's liked him for a while.

'So it's Jay and Jazz now, how cute. Except your names are too similar, you can't even turn it into one joint name – wait, of course… Jay Z!' I exclaim, delighted.

'Well now I *have* to marry him,' says Jazz, 'that is just too perfect. No, I guess – I'm not sooo into him…' she says unconvincingly. 'But he's quite cool, don'tcha think?'

'Yes,' I say back immediately, 'Jay's one of the good guys.'

And I do think that, one hundred percent. Jazz and I have had it before where a guy has cracked onto us both, or one of us might have had a thing with a guy, but then he slyly starts messaging the other one of us. Just sleazeballs, basically. And don't they realise best friends tell each other everything? Jay's never been like that though, he's a straight-up guy, and pretty cute I have to admit.

'And he is totally hot…' adds Jazz, as if reading my mind.

'Oh god,' I say. 'Jay this, Jay that, I'm sick of this new relationship already. Like, "Jay's so hot, Jay's so cute, Jay really understands me, Jay's strong but sensitive",' I tease. 'I'm never gonna hear from you now, not until the day you break up with him am I?'

'No way babes!' says Jazz. 'He's still just some guy. He will never come between us. You know we could go on a double date, we just need to find a guy for you. What about Alekzandr, he's always had a major crush on you!'

She's joking of course. Alekzandr is the boy who messaged me first about Noolie going missing, but I wouldn't touch him with a barge pole. And after the boy at the party, I am staying away from all guys for a while.

'I'd rather stick with a dog,' I say. 'Piper is more loyal and reliable than any guy. She loves my friends, never sulks or ditches me for her dog mates … and I don't have to shave my legs for her!'

'Ha, fair enough babes!' cackles Jazz.

'Right I'm almost home,' I say. 'I'll call you back when I'm walking Piper, k? And thank you.'

'What, for calling my BFF? It's nothing, babes!'

I shake my head down the phone, totes emosh.

'It's everything,' I reply.

I hang up and send her a yellow heart best friends emoji and she sends the same one back a fraction of a millionth of a second later.

This is my stop. I get off and my phone buzzes again. Oh, it's not Jazz this time (or Alekzander, thankfully). It's... Christ, according to my phone, it's Noolie.

Hey Echo its me Noolie

And I literally stumble in the street. What? Is it? Really?

Hey there? Is that really you?

....I reply. There's a pause, then:

Yes its me remember that time when we talked that time about aether and you said it just blew your mind ha ha

Oh yes, I think I do remember. Me and Noolie weren't friends or anything but we did talk about aether a few times, before my dad told me to keep quiet about it. And I did say that to her, I was making a stupid joke about how it ends up killing you – it literally 'blows your mind'. Not a great joke I know.

Where are you Nools? Are you safe?

...I message.

Yes I am in a place called THE FARM a refuge for aethereals. Great place to hang out with other people like us and lie low while these troubles are going on!!! In the countryside not far. Call 07542 21503 if you need a safe place to stay for a few days would be good to catch up. Just call and youll speak to Jane a lovely lady whose son has aether she owns the farm very safe and quiet and vegan food too!!! Come say hi its safer here

…she replies, ending with a (smiley face) emoji.

Right ok Noolie, maybe I will, glad you're ok. Lots of people worried about you you know.

…I send her. I even include a (thinking of you) style emoji.

Don't tell anyone about this keep it our secret please please not safe to be aethereal in public at the moment must not show anyone just come to THE FARM 07542 21503

And then as I'm replying my phone actually rings. It's my mother, wow, quite the drama tonight.

'Hi mum,' I say, 'I'm literally just five minutes –' but she cuts me off mid-sentence.

'Echo quick, come home!' she yells down the phone at me. 'Haven't you seen the news?'

'What today? Err no mum,' I reply. 'Why, what's happened now? I've just been –' but she cuts me off again.

'Hurry Echo!' she yells. 'Hang up and get home – you're in terrible, terrible danger!'

8: BLIND

"Aethereals will become more prized than the world's best scientists, engineers, coders or business leaders.

"Just look at the UK: around 15 million aged 19 or under, the age at which aether first began to manifest. Fewer than 1% are affected by chronic migraine, which brings the number down to 150,000. But children under 10 have no control over their latent ability, so the viable aethereal population becomes 10-19 year olds who get chronic migraines – that's just 75,000 people in the whole of the UK. And we know that not all of them will have significant aether.

"So it's smaller than the UK's prison population or the number of people who die from smoking each year. The nation's entire aethereal population could comfortably fit in Wembley Stadium. That makes them a rare and extremely valuable resource."

– From the TS Interviews with Doctor Magellan-Jones

A car alarm woke him, its repeated cry wailing: this is a shitty part of town, get me out of here.

Flynn glanced at his G-Shock: 5:32. Might as well get up. He didn't know what time the first joggers or dog walkers would appear, but he wanted to avoid being seen.

He sat up on the park bench slowly, every ounce of him aching and complaining. Some was from last night. From the man, crushing his windpipe. Some was his throbbing skull, the mournful warning of a migraine trying to force its way into his brain. And some of it was from spending the night sleeping on a park bench.

What a cliché. Did homeless people really do that? He'd seen people in sleeping bags and on cardboard in shop doorways and underpasses, but he didn't want to risk being picked up by the police that way. And he could have checked into a B&B – he had almost three hundred pounds in the bank, but he didn't want to throw money away just on a bed for the night.

He sat up. Big mistake, his head told him, exploding with sickening colours. His back protested too, all bent out of shape.

Gingerly, he rested his head back and rotated his shoulders. His phone had buzzed several times last night, but his head was too sore and his eyesight too blurry to read them or reply.

The car alarm stopped. Flynn stood, then sat down again quickly, a wave of nausea running through him. His head was getting worse; it could turn into a full-blown migraine any moment. He didn't have his migraine medication, hadn't even thought about grabbing it as he fled. There was a Tesco Express near the park, he could get some tablets once it opened. But if he wanted prescription-strength… maybe he could swipe some from Boots, using PK. Maybe?

He tried to stand again, this time more slowly, lifting his head as gently as possible – as if he was ninety years old with chronic arthritis. The pain was horrible, but bearable.

Sunglasses. He'd need some of those too. He began to shuffle out, past the silent, turned-off fountain, towards the children's playground area and the lane that led him out.

The next few hours were grim. He managed to get some Migraleve from Tesco, taking two pink and two yellow tablets almost immediately, but the harsh tube lighting in the store was blinding and he was sick as soon as he got outside, throwing the tablets up. The next four stayed down, and he sluiced his mouth with a bottle of water and cleaned his teeth with a toothbrush he'd picked up. They didn't have sunglasses, but he managed to stagger down towards town and picked some up from a pound store. It wasn't a sunny day, so no-one else was in shades; like a celebrity trying to go unrecognised, wearing sunglasses probably made him more conspicuous, but he really needed them. The world was a spinning, nightmarish blur of sky and buildings and people.

He stumbled sideways and bounced off a shop window. He was going to draw attention to himself. There was one of those big, bland bars just up ahead, one of those chains. All blond wood and fake blackboards. He made himself get there, left foot, right foot, eyes down to avoid the sun, willing his feet into moving.

As he collapsed onto the bar stool, sunglasses still on, the tight black t-shirt with a long beard looked at him suspiciously.

'Heavy night, dude?'

'No. Headache.' His voice was rasping and strained; it was the first time he'd spoken today and he could still feel the man's hydraulic, claw-like fingers on his throat.

The guy behind the bar looked back at him, unsure.

Flynn concentrated on speaking normally. 'I just want an orange juice and lemonade.'

The guy seemed reassured. 'Pint or half?'

Normally he'd only drink diet, but the sugar in the orange and lemonade revived him a little. He washed down another couple of the yellow Migraleve pills.

There was a muted TV screen hanging from the ceiling. News channel, footage of a police security van on its side, the back busted open, all cordoned off, police everywhere. He could just make out the text on screen:

Gangland kingpin escapes with help of aether crew

Bloody hell. He wanted to know more but the screen was too bright and he looked away, grimacing. He was starting to burn up, so he unzipped his jacket, wiping away a mist of sweat on his forehead with the paper napkin the pint glass had sat on.

The man had been his usual hateful self about Flynn's migraines, of course. Saw it as either weakness or an act. 'Jus tryin' to get attention,' Flynn could remember him saying dismissively once, as Flynn lay in bed writhing in pain.

A wave of tiredness washed over him. He had barely slept. He could do with a strong coffee. Except caffeine was bloody rocket fuel for a migraine.

He willed himself to check the texts from his mum, ignoring his stinging, blurry eye.

12:22am

I told police he was drunk and fell when we had a row and said you were away with girlfriend I didnt no name or address xx

1:35am

Hope you ok safe and warm x

7:21

Good morning my amazing son hope your back soon i miss u x

8:04

Pls call me when you can?? xxxx

He texted her back:

Hi mum don't worry all ok will call you later

He finished his drink and stood as slowly as he could. Oh Christ, the pain was still there, that feeling of seasickness or concussion. The pills were a couple of riot police, just about keeping the angry mob at bay. But they needed reinforcements – and quickly.

Back outside, the sun had strengthened and the cheap sunglasses weren't up to shielding him from it.

Migraine sufferers were the world's vampires. They had superhuman abilities, but when the pain came, they needed to hide from the sun. Within minutes he felt woozy again. His head was spinning and he was starting to get bright spots of light at the edge of his vision.

He sped up.

The Boots was round the corner. He went past a pop-up falafel shop, ignored someone in an Oxfam tabard trying to get him to donate and bounced – again – off a large shop window. If he was a vampire, he was one whose drink had been spiked with holy water.

Somehow, he reached Boots, squeezing between the hoards of people coming out with their lunch meal deals. There – the pharmacy counter. Diclofenac, or if possible Sumatriptan. Whatever was closest and easiest to get. He shuffled up to the counter, but away from the queue and the tills. He didn't want someone to try and help him. Surely indifferent British service would save him here.

Ah: he saw some Voltarol. That was twenty-five milligrammes of diclofenac. It used to be available over the counter, 'til the government made it prescription only. A blog he'd read on the dark web said it was part of a conspiracy to tag everyone who got migraines, by making them go to the doctors for a prescription – and the doctor then passed their details onto the government, which lo and behold, was now introducing an aethereal register and electronic bloody tagging.

He closed his eyes a moment, to rest and focus.

'Can I help you?'

He opened his eyes, fearing the worst. Sure enough, a pharmacist was looking at him. She was black and pretty, her white coat matched by her even, sparkling teeth.

'Do you have a prescription?' she ventured.

He felt his pale, waxy complexion flushing. 'No, I – I'm just looking.' That was a stupid thing to say – who browsed at a pharmacy?

'Ok... well if there is anything you're looking for, you can ask me or anyone else here in complete confidence, ok?'

Oh, Christ. She thought he was embarrassed about what he'd come for – condoms or pile cream or something. He smiled thinly and nodded. She seemed to take the hint, and went to help someone else.

Right. He could do this. He had to.

Staring at the white box with the orange stripe, he told himself to reach out and take it. He willed it. He had the ability. PK. His mind could just pluck the Voltarol from the shelf before anyone noticed...

...nothing. The box didn't move. And he couldn't block the throbbing, stinging boom boom boom out of his mind.

Come on. Think about that man in hospital; the demon he had to protect his mum from. He stared at the small oblong box on the shelf; it was made of iron and he was a magnet. It was dust and he was a vacuum. It was a bouncing ball he had thrown against the wall and now it was going to hurtle back towards him.

Come on! He screamed at the box inside his head, pushing the pain away. And then it did move. No, shit, the box next to it did – his aim was off. It plopped uselessly face down onto the shelf.

There was a firm tap on his shoulder. Flynn turned: security. He hadn't even realised Boots had security – where had he come from?

'Excuse me sir,' said the security guard, 'could we have a quiet word please?'

What did the guard think? That he was trying to steal drugs? Well, come to think of it, that was true. And Flynn was looking suspicious, pale and sweating like an addict. He even had his hands in his pockets, like maybe he was concealing something. A weapon, perhaps.

'Err no, it's ok, I just want to buy some… painkillers,' he said. The security guard's expression didn't change at all. 'If you just step away from the counter, I'm sure we can sort this all out.'

He couldn't go anywhere, he'd collapse if he didn't get something now – he couldn't go and talk and explain himself and give his details. He turned back to the display. 'I just need some, err – ibuprofen,' he said. He stared back at the Voltarol. If he could just quickly pluck it, make it look like it just fell off the shelf but then pull it over… quick quick quick quick

'Just come with me sir,' said the security guard, putting his hand on Flynn's shoulder. It was a big, heavy hand like the one the man had tried to hit him with last night. He whirled drunkenly to face the guard…

…and the shelf of drugs flew sideways. Boxes and bottles shot out in a sudden, noisy splurge making people jump and someone scream and the security guard's eyes go wide.

'PK!' a woman yelled a second later, pointing at Flynn. 'Terrorist!'

Flynn turned and ran in panic-fuelled desperation.

The pain of his sore ankle was numbed by all the tablets he'd taken, but he was three-quarters blind and he half fell down the steps as the security guard yelled out and came after him. Nobody else tried to stop him, but he careered into an aisle of lipsticks and jars, knocking dozens to the ground.

He just managed to get out and around the corner, onto a side street away from the pedestrianised area.

Then a wave of nausea overwhelmed him and his diaphragm spasmed. He doubled over in pain and was sick again. It was watery; just the orange juice and lemonade from the bar and he realised he hadn't eaten all day.

Forcing himself to his feet, he staggered around a corner into a dead end alley and collapsed behind two huge shop bins.

The spots of light around his vision were closing in.

And the ice cold pain behind his eyes was becoming unbearable.

9: BURN

BURN THE WITCH

BURN THE WITCH

That's my phone.

BURN THE WITCH

BURN THE WITCH

BURN THE WITCH

Again and again it comes. I've blocked the number a couple of times, but after a few minutes, more come through. I'm guessing it's Ronny and Gigi since that's what they wrote on their bill at the café, but who knows for sure.

And the latest news, the story my mum has seen that's freaked her out, is that aethereals are being targeted for acid attacks. They are literally being burned alive – by acid.

And now she's seen the Burn the witch message coming up on my phone on repeat she's gone nuclear.

BURN THE WITCH

My relationship with my mum has never been super-close. We've never had that 'We're more like sisters!' thing that's for sure, even though I'm an only child. People say that maybe we're too similar, but I don't know. She's way more highly strung than me, that is for certain.

Not that I have this 'daddy's girl' relationship with my father either – it's just that he's a neuroscientist so he understands more about aether than most people. He reckons that if you learn to control your aspects – the aether abilities you have – it makes you less likely to have a migraine, and might even delay the day you have a fatal brain aneurysm. So over the last eighteen months I've spent a lot of time with him in his study, working on aether. Which is why I'm better at it than I should be.

I still remember the first time he sat me in his study to try PK. He got me to try and lift a sachet of sugar he found in a drawer, taken from a café. Just a tiny, featherweight sachet of sugar. My uncontrolled PK tore it apart. Exploded everywhere. He's still finding grains of it. Hiding in pages of his scientific journals or resting in the mesh grille of his vintage valve radio. I thought mum would go spare as she's pretty OCD, but she took one look at the sugar and my dad's annoyed expression and just burst out laughing. Which made me laugh too. Which made my father even more stern, which just made us laugh even more. 'You always were a messy child,' my mum said.

Which I just have to take her word for as my parents don't have any pictures of me from when I was a baby or toddler. Zero. All their photos were on a computer – not in the cloud – and there was a house fire which destroyed the computer and everything on it was lost forever. So there aren't any photos of me til age seven, and even then not many. Thanks, mum and dad!

BURN THE WITCH

Anyway. I look at myself in the full-length bedroom mirror propped against the wall next to my bed. Piper is sat at my feet, her head cocked to one side like she's trying to figure out why this strange girl is always looking at her own reflection.

I am, I think I said before, about five seven, size six, with dark, slightly-wavy hair pulled back in a pony tail with a fringe.

I have a bit of a tan from the awesome summer we've had and the sun has brought out the freckles across my nose and cheekbones. I have a wide smile, people tell me, and I like to dress a bit boho but not too much. As Jazz says, 'Fashion never goes out of fashion'. Today I am wearing a floral shift dress with tan suedette sock boots. No jewellery apart from a single silver bangle and no make-up other than a little primer. This is my going-away-for-a-few-days outfit.

BURN THE WITCH

And *that* is why I'm leaving. The whole deal with aether right now, it's too much. I'm not freaking out the way mum is, but it is pretty sketchy – there's a national state of emergency and the government reckons they'll be rolling out electronic tagging in the next six weeks.

The anti-aether demos are getting worse, in the news aethereals are getting blamed for every major crime going, there are reports of aethereals being abducted and now these acid attacks… basically it's non-stop doom scrolling bad news for aethereals.

And my mum is saying someone must know I'm an aethereal because of the burn the witch messages so I'm in danger so I should just get the hell out of dodge and lie low (like Noolie I guess / hope, who I haven't told mum about).

BURN THE WITCH

BURN THE WITCH

I mean, I'm not sure if I really have to actually leave home, maybe that seems a bit OTT but my mum is here in my room right now, packing. Panicking.

Oh god, not that – I pull a mullet dress back out of my rucksack. Jeez mum. It's kinda dusky pink and the top half is covered in pink sequins, like a fairytale princess. My mum bought it – the last time I ever let her buy me clothes, I think. 'I don't think there's room for this,' I say, quickly putting a black polka dot tea dress in instead.

BURN THE WITCH

'Oh Echo, Aunt Marianne would love to see you in that,' says my mother. 'It's so lovely, I don't know why you don't wear it more often.'

No. Just no. I mean, I know it's the end of the world, but that's no reason to dress badly. I should try and go out with some style. The doorbell goes, Piper starts barking and thank god, it's Jazz. Good, now she's here I can turn my phone off.

She throws her arms around me in the hallway and I do the same. While Piper watches, we stand there like that for several seconds in total silence. Sometimes a hug is the only thing to say.

'Oh god Eks,' she says when we finally pull away. 'The world has gone insane!' I look into her clear green eyes with my own speckled hazel ones.

'I don't really know what to do,' I say. 'My mum thinks I should leave. Go stay with her sister, Aunt Marianne and her husband – they live by the coast – until it all dies down.'

'Well that makes no sense,' says Jazz. 'You need your friends around you at a time like this!'

'Well you tell her,' I say, grabbing her hand and pulling her upstairs, Piper scrabbling on the stairs to follow.

'Oh Christ,' mutters Jazz. Oh Christ is right.

Back in my room, my mother is doing a terrible job of packing – normally it's OCD perfect, but the contents of my rucksack look like they just lost a pillow fight. Plus she's putting all the wrong stuff in *again* – it's like she doesn't know me at all. Which, to be fair, she probably doesn't.

While she gathers up the vegan supplements I take (calcium, iron, vitamin D and vitamin B12) I grab my rucksack off the bed away from her and sort through it.

'Hi there,' Jazz says breezily.

My mum looks up. She has a dazed expression like she's got PTSD or something. 'Oh, hello Jasmine,' she replies. 'Echo is going away for a few weeks.'

'Echo could come stay with me,' says Jazz helpfully. 'No problem at all. We won't tell anyone.'

'What? No, no thank you,' says my mum firmly. 'She needs to be out of town to be safe. My sister lives in a very small village by the sea, very secluded. Echo will be safe there, out of harm's way.'

'Sure, I get that,' Jazz says, 'but are things really that bad?' she asks, trying to sound casual.

'Yes Jasmine, things are really that bad,' my mum replies loudly. 'Aether people are being abducted or melted with acid!'

That's my mother for you: blunt words from a sharp tongue.

'Well actually, only two people have been attacked with acid,' I reply. 'So maybe, since not many people know about me..?'

My mum turns to me, her eyes blazing.

'You don't understand the danger you're in!' she seethes.

'What about dad?' I add, 'what time will he be back? I can't just disappear while he's out – have you called him?'

'Don't worry about your father!' she snaps. 'He's not worried about your wellbeing!'

Brilliant, my mum is in one of her rages: mad at everyone and impossible to reason with. Jazz looks at me with 'I tried,' eyes. Piper nuzzles the back of my leg sympathetically. So. It really looks like I'm going.

The thing is, deep down I know she's right. The world has gone to absolute shit and I just don't want to admit how scared I really am.

Jazz helps me pack while my mum flaps around. I take a wistful look around my bedroom: butterfly fairy lights woven between the cream metal headboard of my bed; an IKEA wardrobe with clothes all over its open doors; bookshelves crammed with young adult fiction; a wall of photos arranged into a heart shape; the vintage gilt-framed full-length mirror I picked up from a flea market; a polished iroko wood memory box full of silly keepsakes, and piles of shoe boxes poking out from under the bed. Memories on every shelf, in every drawer.

'Aunt Marianne will love seeing you, you know that,' my mum is saying. 'And Uncle Bo too, he's always had a soft spot for you.'

Yeah mum, that's cos he's a perv.

Jazz and I tramp down the stairs with my rucksack, and mum hands me her credit card. 'It's eight one four four,' she says. I take it from her.

'But really, what about dad?' I say as I take my linen blazer off a coat hook. 'Are you sure we shouldn't wait for him?'

'No!' says my mum emphatically. 'It's too dangerous for you to stay here any longer. You get off now – if you get the bus to the train station you could be at your Aunt's before eleven,' she adds. 'She's expecting you. I'll speak to your father. He's all for this, you know.'

Hmm.

'Ok then,' I say. I take Piper's lead off the coat hook by the door; you have to put dogs on leads some places, and she is definitely one hundred percent coming with me. She barks once when she sees me take the lead.

dont worry not to use not to use

…I tell her with animus.

adventure adventure!

She jumps up happily, showing her bright white teeth and little pink tongue. She's more excited about this than me, that's for sure.

My mum hugs me stiffly. 'Take care Echo,' she says. 'This really is for your own good. One day you'll realise this was for the best.'

Hmm. 'Ok thanks mum,' I say, 'love you.'

'Call me when you get there,' she replies.

'I'll walk to the bus station with her, Mrs J,' says Jazz.

I open the front door and pick up my rucksack. Suddenly I feel very emotional and tears break the dam of my eyelashes and run down my face. This is so crap. I'm being driven out of my own home by politicians and placards and poisonous lies. Burn the witch. FML.

Outside, the evening is cool and clear and Jazz helps me pull on my rucksack. We start to walk slowly down the street, my beautiful Piper happy to be outside, running ahead then turning to look until we catch up, then running a few steps ahead again. Bless her.

'Don't go,' Jazz says suddenly. 'Come and crash at mine. You know my parents adore you and no-one would know you were there so you'd be safe as. We can spend the days sat in the not-at-all-overlooked garden, evenings we just load up on Netflix and skinny popcorn, and then at night we stay up planning where we're going travelling after we finish college. It'll be awesome!'

I smile, wiping the tears away. Having a bestie like Jazz is just amazing, it's a privilege really. And what she's saying does sound wonderful. I really want to say yes. But I say no.

'I can't,' I say. 'I would love to, it's a great idea but my mum's probably right, I should be out of town while it's all so crazy and, I dunno… I just feel like if I was at yours, instead of making me safe, it would be putting you in danger,' I say. 'And I just couldn't bear that, I wouldn't be able to sleep.'

'Ah, babes,' says Jazz, touching my wet cheek, 'but what's the alternative? Go to some dull-as seaside town to stay with "Aunt Marianne"?'

'Oh god,' I say. 'I dunno. I mean… Uncle Bo weirds me out, he's a bit of a lech.'

'Oh Christ, no way then babes, you are not going there!' Jazz says, stopping in the street and putting her arm around me.

Question is, what am I going to do? Maybe a b&b? Then something occurs to me.

'Wait,' I say. 'Look at this.' I get out my phone and show Jazz the messages and she checks the number against the one she has on her phone.

'Yep,' she confirms. 'That's Noolie alright. And she literally is "alright"!'

'Yeah, looks that way,' I reply. 'And she's talking about this place, The Farm… run by some woman called Jane? Maybe I should check it out. Noolie seems to think it's legit.'

'Jeez, I don't know,' says Jazz, looking at Noolie's message. 'I mean, maybe. Let me speak to her.'

Jazz calls her, but it goes straight to answerphone, like Noolie's phone is switched off. The same it's been for everyone who's called her I guess.

'Well why don't I call the number, speak to this Jane?' I say. 'Can't hurt to talk to her.'

'Yeah, but Noolie always was a bit odd. She sounds even odder in the message. What if it's dodge?'

'Hey, I can look after myself you know,' I reply, giving her a nudge. 'Have you not seen the news recently? I'm one of them aethereals, I'm dangerous!'

Jazz grins.

'Any trouble and I'll just snapshot their ass,' I say. 'Besides, I've got Piper.'

'Well, totally,' agrees Jazz, bending down to stroke her. 'Piper is just increds, aren't you?' Piper wraps herself around Jazz's legs appreciatively as Jazz stands back up and looks at me. 'She's not exactly the biggest though, Eks.'

'Yeah but you know what they say,' I reply, 'it's not the size of the dog in the fight, it's the size of the fight in the dog. Isn't that right, Piper?'

Piper yips excitedly, she is practically bouncing up and down like she's on a trampoline.

Jazz grins again. 'Jeez, ok then you pair of ninjas, give your new bestie "Jane" a call then. But if you do go – and we're not saying you will, right? – but if you do, it's just a week or two tops, k?'

'Absolutely,' I say to Jazz. And then we stop walking and hug again in the street, filling the evening with our embrace. I'm an absolute melt. Jazz's clothes all fit me – but it's her hugs that fit me best of all.

'If I go, I'll miss you like crazy,' I say to her.

'I'll miss you like the deserts miss the rain,' Jazz replies.

'I'm missing you already,' I whisper.

Someone once told me that in French, the phrase is *Tu me manques*. It doesn't quite translate as "I miss you", it's more like, "You are missing from me." Which is so much better, don't you think? Because that's what it feels like, just the thought of being apart from Jazz.

'It's so unfair Eks,' she says. 'Why are people so dumb? Why aren't they working on saving your life, instead of ruining it?'

It's a good question. But I have abso-frickin-lutely no good answer.

'Two weeks tops,' I repeat as we finally pull apart. I am a total melt.

I can see Jazz's face is as wet with tears as my own. 'Come on then,' I say. 'Let's find out where this place is.'

And I tap the number in Noolie's message.

And I call.

10: MONSTER

"There are many theories as to what was the catalyst for 'The Aether Age'. Environmental. Experimental. Evolutionary. Extraterrestrial. Groundless garbage, all of them.

"The brain is a notoriously difficult organ to study. It's also extremely complex and adaptable. What caused young people with chronic migraine to suddenly become aethereal... we may never really know.

"For example: take sunflower oil. It's popular to cook with and it's high in omega six. The problem is, too much omega six in someone's diet can effectively 'force out' the omega three. This can result in significant changes to brain chemistry. Perhaps that was the trigger for aether? Or perhaps it was magnesium. Magnesium has an established link with migraines and levels of environmental magnesium are at an all time high – perhaps it reached a critical level that triggered aether? Who can say: to isolate all the possible causes is quite impossible.

"As for the ludicrous conspiracy theories that aether was caused by a secret government research programme... well, I refute those claims utterly."

– From the TS Interviews with Doctor Magellan-Jones

Flynn got out his phone. His bleary, migraine-blind eyes struggled to read his mum's Whatsapp messages.

11:33am

Hi you i just had a call to say Keel is in a comer could be weeks may be even months b4 he comes out of it x

11:46am

Every thing will b ok please call me when u can xx

He called her; she answered in the first ring. It was emotional, her tears triggering his. He admitted to having a migraine, he had to, to explain his shaking, slurred speech. Then he asked about her wrist: it was fractured but not broken, and in a sling.

He told her he couldn't come home yet, not while the man was in a coma – not until he came out of it and Flynn had the chance to talk to him before the police did.

But he said he'd be back as soon as he could and agreed that yes, of course everything would be ok – though he wasn't sure if she believed him, or if he even believed himself.

He told her he loved her. She was still crying when reluctantly, eventually, he hung up. He could barely speak, barely see. His phone popped up a message:

Low battery 10% remaining

He took another Migraleve, exceeding the daily recommended dose.

He was almost out of battery. And options.

He was exhausted and hungry and suffering. The migraine was consuming him and without proper medication he was going to collapse. Maybe worse – maybe this was the ruptured brain aneurysm that everyone with aether got one day, and he was as good as dead already.

Or maybe… it was possible someone could help. Someone who wouldn't ask questions. Maybe.

He reached inside his Nebraska jacket and took out his wallet. Inside was a scrap of paper he'd kept. It was from the first day he'd been at home with Keel in the flat, missing work so he could make sure his mum was safe. He'd been browsing, just looking at stuff about aether, and he'd written down the phone number of a place that claimed to be a sanctuary for aethereals.

The Farm.

Holding the piece of paper flat on the palm of one hand he used the last of his strength to bring the number into focus.

And he called.

11: ANTHRAX

I can taste diesel.

My lungs are filling with black globs of the stuff, I can feel it. My skin feels like it's had an actual misting of spray glue. I'm worried for Piper's tiny lungs. She's sat on my lap and I'm stroking her, soothing the both of us as I pet her white fur. We've been in the back of the van for over two hours now, this can't be good for her. And I can tell she doesn't like it. I don't like it either.

'Are we nearly there?' I ask.

'Oh yes, not too far at all, don't you worry,' says Jane. You know how some people look like their names? Well, Jane Brown does not look like a Jane Brown.

So: I called 'the farm' and Jane answered. She sounded pretty friendly, Noolie was apparently out horse riding (which I must admit, got me interested) and Jane said I could come and have a look around and if I didn't like it they could drop me back wherever.

And now I'm in the back of her farm van with her. Fleeing 'The Witchcraft Act'.

Upfront a man drives us to Jane's farm, which is… I don't know where. Jane won't tell me, she says sorry, it has to be kept secret to protect the aethereals already there – especially as they don't really know me, I could be anyone and texting someone the location.

Except I couldn't do that, because my phone's got no reception.

It's weird. My phone had been turned off, because of all the burn the witch messages. But as I left, Jazz said to turn Find My Friends on so she could follow me on the map, see where I was at. So turning my phone back on was the first thing I did as we got into the back of the van. But I've got no signal, not a single bar. Weird. So I haven't been able to message Jazz, see where we are on a map, nothing. All I can see is the time: over two hours since we left. In her message, Noolie said it was closer than that.

Anyway, Jane Brown does not look like a Jane Brown, not to me. It's like a nice, homely name, and this lady does not look homely. She's pretty old, I'm gonna guess late forties, with scraped back, greying yellow hair. But her mouth is twenty years older than that – her lips are like *super* dry and lined, her teeth are ratty and dark, and – I'm just throwing it out there – she has a moustache. I guess farmers don't go in for personal grooming much. Or for chat, actually. She was pretty friendly on the phone, but since we started driving she's barely said a word.

'Do you have other animals on the farm then, as well as horses?' I ask.

'Some,' she replies.

I'm starting to think maybe this was not such a hot move on my part.

It's just that, well, I didn't want to put Jazz at risk, staying with her. And I definitely didn't want to stay with Aunt Marianne, not with her second husband. I still remember the way "Uncle Bo" was at a family barbecue last year. The way he would look at me and make inappropriate jokes or "accidentally" brush past me. No, I could definitely not stay there. So instead Piper and me are stuck in the back of an old van and I'm starting to feel anxious.

I've always suffered from anxiety, BTW. I can get anxious about anything – my freckles, putting on weight, my hairy legs. Not getting the right grades, missing the bus, not getting into the right uni. Plastic pollution. Climate change. All the species of animal and plant that are being wiped out. We lose eighty thousand acres of rainforest every day. Eighty thousand. That makes me *really* anxious.

And dying, I worry about that. Well, maybe not dying exactly, being dead. With aether… I'll be lucky if I make it to thirty. Alive for thirty years, then dead for a billion, billion, billion (etc) years. That freaks me out – it literally keeps me awake at night. Then I lie in bed worrying I'm not getting enough sleep… which keeps me awake. Which makes *no* sense.

Jeez, really, what is up with my phone?

'Err, Jane, do you know why my phone isn't getting any signal?' I ask. 'There's nothing about the van or anything is there?' I say timidly.

Jane looks at me like I'm speaking a foreign language and shrugs. She's like a different person in real life, it's like I've been catfished.

Then suddenly the van lurches to the side, rocking as if it's on two wheels.

There's a pained crunch from the gears and it lunges forward and accelerates and I grab hold of Piper to keep her from flying into the wall of the van. Jane (she's wearing a thin boyfriend shirt and tough tan trousers, like cargo pants) gives me her most reassuring smile / show of rat teeth.

'Nothing to worry about,' she says. 'Just avoiding traffic.'

Yeah sure, whatever. Not even my mum in one of her black moods drives that crazily. I shouldn't be here, really I shouldn't. I don't have scry, but still, this doesn't feel right. What have I done?

We drive on... it's another tense hour and my nerves are shreds. I try to comfort Piper and she tries to comfort me. It's eleven thirty pm. Then there's a squeal of brakes and I'm flung to the floor, Piper is thrown out of my arms and my rucksack skids along the length of the inside of the van, just missing squashing her. The van comes to a stop. Frick!

The door handles abruptly squeal and the back of the van opens, sucking in a blast of cold night air. It is perfectly dark – the kind of pure, uncut '100% dark' you only get when you're a million miles from anywhere and there are no streetlights and even the moon doesn't want to venture this far out.

Piper barks, she's keen to jump out and escape this diesel-stinking tin box but she wants me to come too and I'm thinking yeah I should run for it though I don't know where I am and I'd have to leave my rucksack and it's pitch black but yeah, I should definitely bail *right now*.

Then there's a bodiless voice, cooler than the night.

'Hello Echo.'

A shape moves forward – a faint silhouette in the oppressive darkness. Oh frick.

'You have made the right decision,' says a man's voice. Then why is this feeling shadier by the second?

Jane gets out, and the driver comes round to the open doors, I recognise him from when we got in. Clean-shaven, buzz cut hair, black t-shirt and jeans. And combat boots. He doesn't seem to feel the cold, and before I can grab it, he reaches in and picks up my rucksack like I only packed it with tissue paper.

'So, you have met Jane,' says the man's voice again, the shadow. 'And this is Rasputin, he will take your bag. My name is Hagen. Come out.'

Well of course I was always going to get out, but now he's told me to, it's like I'm doing it to obey him. I feel like the real me is slipping away.

My legs are stiff and shaky. Piper is glad to be out, but she's not sending out happy vibes. And we might have had a great summer but it's a cold night and my linen blazer can't keep it out. Christ, where are we? This is not even a road, it's like some tiny country lane, lined by giant trees and wild hedges. I'm not sure where I could run even if my legs were up to it. Oh god. What have I done?

'A tiny dog,' says Hagen, looking at Piper. That's all he says about her. Then: 'The Farm is less than a kilometre up the track.' He points into blackness, past a silent Land Rover. 'Let us not waste any more time.'

He is tall, with slicked, longish hair and a side parting. He has a humourless manner, like he's never found anything funny, a bit like my father. He's wearing all black as far as I can tell, but there is the tiny red light of a cigarette in his right hand.

He gestures with it now at Rasputin, who slams shut the van doors and takes my rucksack and throws it in the back of the Land Rover. The van starts up – I realise Jane's no longer standing here, she must be taking the van.

'Yes,' says Hagen, gesturing for me to follow my rucksack into the back of the Land Rover. Jeez. What can I do? I need to bide my time. Think about my aether. Could I really do a snapshot, if I needed to? My brain is fuzzy. I am getting those butterflies again and my mouth is dry. Oh god. I get in with Piper – she is really not psyched to be getting in a vehicle again so soon, and I try to calm her as best I can, try not to pass on my own rising dread.

Hagen follows me, flicks his cigarette into the air and pulls the door closed as he gets in, and we start off up an unlit country lane lined by trees, with literally nothing beyond them. Oh frick frick frick, what have I done?

I try to fake that I'm ok with all this.

'The Farm,' I say, trying to keep my voice from wobbling. 'It's Jane's farm is it?'

Hagen's nostrils flare for a second.

'Jane Brown, it is her farm,' he confirms. 'Her son has aether. Over time, they have made it a refuge for other people with aether. This is necessary. Out there,' he says, gesturing dismissively, 'things are worse every day. For you. Aethereals are in a serious risk. The Farm is safety.'

'Like Noolie?' I say. 'Will I see her tonight?' The Land Rover is bumping up and down as the track becomes stonier and more uneven, I can see why we got out of the van.

'No,' says Hagen. 'There has been an outbreak of anthrax. People already there are quarantined.'

'What?' I say.

'It was some weeks ago,' he says without expression. 'Three horses. We have fixed this problem, but until the quarantine period passes, you will be separate from the others and there are areas of The Farm that are cordoned off. Do not under any circumstances cross the quarantine tape, do you understand me?'

I mean... what? Anthrax? My brain is *so* fuzzy with tiredness and my body is weak from pumping adrenalin around because of the anxiety, but this just feels sooo sketchy. And – wait, Jane said Noolie was riding a horse earlier, how does that work if there's anthrax? My anxiety levels are through the roof, I can literally feel my heart bouncing between my throat and my stomach, it's almost painful. My phone says it's just after midnight... and I've still got no signal.

'I should call my family,' I say. 'My phone, it doesn't seem to be getting reception, I don't know... could I borrow yours please, just for a minute please?' I ask.

Hagen shakes his head.

'There is no signal,' he says. 'It is remote. No cellphone signal, no internet. The Farm is cut off.'

'A landline at least,' I say weakly.

'No,' he says firmly. Oh frick. What have I done? Then he reaches into one of his shirt flap pockets... but only to get out a pen and a blank red card, like a postcard.

'Take the card and write a message,' he says. 'Put your address on and it can be with your family tomorrow.'

'Well… I might go back tomorrow anyway,' I say haltingly. 'Jane said just to take a look, you know. It was just my mum really, she'll have calmed down by tomorrow.'

Hagen's nostrils flare again, and he runs his hand along his jawline – it looks like there's something weird about his right hand, but I can't really tell for sure in this light.

'Take the fucking card,' he says quietly, with a tone like he's used to people doing what he says first time. 'You will not leave soon. To do so, it would not be safe. It would not be a smart thing to do. And you, I think you are a smart girl, Echo. A smart aethereal.'

OMFG.

I feel sick, like back at the party. I feel like I'm going to hurl, my stomach is twisting inside. And what about Jazz, she'll have sent me loads of messages and be wondering why I haven't replied.

This is all a terrible mistake.

And this man, Hagen, he has a coiled-up menace that terrifies me.

What have I done?

12: KNIFE

"In the twentieth century a man called James Hydrick claimed to have psychokinetic powers. He was a complex character and also a criminal. In fact, he escaped from prison three times, once karate kicking his way through a concrete wall.

"His demonstration of PK was rather more modest: he would crouch down, eyeballing an open old phone directory on a table in front of him. He'd hold his hand out, show a great deal of concentration... and then, as he moved his hand, a few yellow pages would turn over without him touching them. It was later shown he did it by blowing a quiet, controlled jet of air through his mouth.

"Nowadays it seems incredible that people were fooled by him, and that such a feeble demonstration captured public attention. But it gives you an insight into just how overwhelming the birth of aether – with acts far more impressive than turning a few sheets of paper – was for most people."

– From the TS Interviews with Doctor Magellan-Jones

The knife hit hard, punching through the target mid-way between bulls-eye and the edge.

'Poor,' said Hagen.

Flynn had been at The Farm for just over a week. He'd spent most of it in a makeshift hospital, half-paralysed, three-quarters blind and completely exhausted. They'd given him two hundred milligrammes of diclofenac a day, soup and water. After two days the paralysis had begun to fade and his vision had started to clear. He was weak as a new born foal, but they gave him a battered, seized-up wheelchair. After five days he'd felt his strength returning. His sore ankle had had chance to properly rest. His throat, crushed by Keel's fingers, felt less tender too, though with faint bluish-green bruises striping it. A reminder of that night every time he looked in the mirror.

Then they had moved him from the makeshift hospital into what they called a 'shepherd's hut'. It was a small wooden shed with a domed roof and steps up to the door, because it was raised up on wheels. There were a dozen or more of them dotted around The Farm.

And Flynn had answered Hagen's questions: which of the six aether aspects do you have? Precognition? Psychokinesis? Psynaptic shock? Telesthesia? Thiriokinesis? Wispr? Which are you best at?

Flynn hadn't wanted to admit to anything, but as he'd so obviously been having a migraine attack when they found him, he couldn't deny being aethereal. Still, it had taken his fragile brain a moment to translate the aspects into their more common names:

Precognition – pre-cog – yes, he'd had half a dozen 'flashes' over the last two years.

Psychokinesis – PK – yes he could do that too, perhaps that one best.

Psynaptic shock – snapshot – yes, he was pretty sure he could do that too, but he didn't say how he knew. Hagen had stared at him, but hadn't asked any more.

Telesthesia – scry – he didn't think so.

Thiriokinesis – animus – no, he'd never had any gift with animals.

Wispr – he wasn't sure, he'd never met another aethereal to try it with.

And now, a week on and able to get around without the wheelchair, he was out in a field – one of the anthrax-free ones he assumed – demonstrating his 'best' aspect, PK: trying to grip throwing knives with his mind and direct them to the painted straw target. So far: four in the target, nine lying scattered around it.

'Again,' said Hagen. Again.

Flynn bit his lip and picked up another of the knives – a thin sliver of black metal with paracord wrapped around the handle and a ring at the end.

He felt the balance as he gripped it between his red, blistered thumb and forefinger. He looked at the circular target thirty feet away and focused.

He brought the knife up to his shoulder and stood a little sideways, peering at the target, trying to amplify it in his mind. He took a breath, exhaled slowly… and threw.

It span through the air, first arcing up in order to make the distance. As it flew he tried to guide it with his PK, directing it as it span in its violent ballet, homing down to the centre of the target with deadly intent, unswerving, unstoppable…

– and then he had a momentary flashback to that night, when he had used PK to pull a knife from Keel's bloodied hand –

...and the knife wobbled in the air and missed its target by two feet and embedded itself into the soft moorland mud with the other nine.

Hagen ran his tongue over his teeth behind his lips.

'Very poor,' he said. 'Again.'

Flynn sighed. 'I have no depth perception,' he said. 'From being blind in one eye. I think it's that as much as my PK.'

Hagen didn't answer for a moment. 'Perhaps,' he said. He looked at the expensive chronograph watch he always wore. 'But excuses are easy,' he added. 'Being good at something is hard. Try again.'

Hagen was an unnerving, intimidating character and Flynn was in no mood for a fight, so he picked up yet another knife. He closed his eyes and just felt it in his hand. He let everything else fall away – the gentle breeze, the trees, the moor, the farm buildings behind them, Hagen, even the target. It was just him and the knife. No, in fact he was the knife. And suddenly he was soaring up and away, turning and spinning; he looked out and saw the target, saw it below him, in front of him, he flew towards it and...

...bang, the knife hit only about three inches from dead centre.

'Better,' Hagen acknowledged. 'Again.'

Flynn looked at Hagen and raised his hand. 'My fingers are starting to bleed,' he said. 'This is great and everything, but

I'm not actually planning on a career in the circus,' he trailed off with a shrug.

Hagen took a step towards him. He was tall, suntanned, dressed in the kind of dark, rip-stop clothes someone in the military might wear off-duty, and utterly lacking in any sense of humour. Flynn had grown up around a dangerous man, and Hagen reminded him of Keel a little. Not just that they both smoked; their manner. Men who acted calm, but who you could tell held a terrible rage inside. It made you nervous, because you never knew what might set them off.

'Bleeding fingers. I see,' said Hagen. 'But having acid thrown in your face would be worse, I think. Or would you prefer that?'

He took another step towards Flynn so he was now standing beside the camping table with the canvas rolls of throwing knives on.

'I have explained this already, so this time you really should listen,' he said tersely. 'Aethereals get migraines because of their aspects, because of their inability to control them. By learning to control your aspects, you may never get another migraine. And if you do not get migraines, no-one will know you are an aethereal.' He grabbed Flynn by the arm before he could react, and tapped him on the wrist.

'Here at The Farm, you do not wear an electronic tag. Out there, they will put one on you. You will be no more than a fucking dog to them. And you will be a target for the acid attacks, the petrol bombs through your window, the gangs who want to put a knife into your brain through your ear. This refuge is protecting you from that. So you should do as I say without trying to be a fucking clown. You do not want to be out there, wearing a tag for the vigilante gangs to see.'

He lit a cigarette with an inscribed flip-top metal lighter, all the time staring at Flynn with disdain. He took a long, deep intake of smoke.

'Aether is wasted on you,' he said, breathing it out. 'You do not appreciate it, you do not work for it. This,' he said, pointing towards the distant target with his cigarette, 'you are lucky, I am here to show you.

'Imagine throwing a knife fifty metres, and still have it reach its target. Most people cannot shoot a pistol accurately that far. Or imagine throwing it up in the air, out of sight, and have it come down on target like a guided missile. Being able to swerve it around obstacles, or go round corners. Throwing one with each hand simultaneously, so while one might be stopped, the other is a direct contact. All these things you could learn to do. If you were not so fucking lazy.'

That riled Flynn. No way was Flynn lazy – he'd worked part-time jobs from a young age while at school and doing gymnastics, being pushed hard by his coaches to squeeze out every drop of talent and never complaining. He just didn't want to do any of the things Hagen was talking about. And he didn't want to be here. But he could tell Hagen was getting angry, losing his wafer-thin veneer of calm.

'I am grateful you helped me,' he said as sincerely as he could manage, 'but I'm planning on going back home tomorrow, electronic tag or not. My mum needs me.'

The last text he'd had from his mum, before he'd arrived in this place which seemed to have no phone reception whatsoever, had said:

I told police he was drunk and fell when we had a row and said you were away with girlfriend I didnt no name or address. Your dad is still in hospital still in comer xx

That was good, Keel being in a coma. It meant he wasn't talking to the police, telling them how his son was 'one of them headcases'. But he wouldn't be unconscious forever. So now Flynn had regained his strength he needed to get home, to warn him off and protect his mum.

Hagen took a drag from the cigarette, then jabbed it towards Flynn.

'Back home? You are still not thinking,' he said. 'You go home now, you bring violence with you. Because of aether. I know the violence that comes when people fear, the way they fear now,' he said, taking another drag.

'The violence I have seen, Flynn Dallas – too much for just one eye like yours. I have seen men drowned in cages. Women with their throats cut, raped as they bled out. Babies thrown onto fires. Whole villages bombed to dust and bone. Whole cities sieged to starvation. Always the same story: the strong attacking the weak. Because they wanted something the weak had, or just because they could. No other fucking reason. But most often because of fear. I have seen these things, with my eyes,' he said, actually tapping under his eye with his left index finger. 'And now it is happening with aether. Today you are the few, feared by the many.

'But as you say, you have only one eye that works. Perhaps that is why you do not see the danger too clearly. Of course, we know where you live, you told us when you first arrived – barely conscious until we brought you back to health. So I will give you a card and you can write to your mother on it, let her know you are ok, not to worry. I will make sure the card is delivered to her. And then, she will not worry.'

He swapped his cigarette into his left hand and picked up one of the throwing knives with his scarred right, examining the blade as he spoke.

'But you Flynn Dallas, you should worry. About the people out there who want to kill you – and your family.'

He turned sharply and threw the knife with a practiced ease. It arced through the air without any PK help. And hit the target thirty feet away, an inch inside Flynn's last, best throw.

Hagen turned to Flynn.

'Think of those people who want to kill you. And remember: someone does not need aether to be dangerous.'

He gestured for Flynn to pick up another knife.

'Again,' he commanded.

13: FUGITIVE

I am still alive. Yay.

So that's something. And there really is a farm, kinda. Though they don't have any animals, not that I've seen. And I haven't yet seen Noolie yet. Or met Jane's son or any other aethereal. And maybe it is Jane's farm, I don't know – but it's Hagen who's running the show, that's for sure.

And not once have I had a single bar of phone signal. It's the first thing I do when I wake up, like now – get my phone and check it. But there it is again:

No service

Just like Hagen said.

Piper nuzzles me, licking my face, delighted that I'm awake – which means game on as far as she's concerned.

good morning! hello! yes i love you too yes!

...I emote to her with animus.

So. 8:22am. The twelfth of August. I've been here a few days now. I've wanted to leave every single day, I tell them I want to go, but... they just don't listen. They say soon, soon, you just need to stay one more day, it's too dangerous to travel right now, a couple more days, wait for things to settle, wait for some news...

In a way I suppose they're right, I did leave in the first place because my mum thought it was getting too dangerous. Hopefully she's got the red card Hagen gave me to write to her. I did another for Jazz too, so fingers crossed they're not too worried. But I can't stay here another night, I'm *totally* homesick. It's lonely here being so isolated, away from everyone I know, unable to reach anyone on my phone, being told no all the time.

The food's ok, now at least. The first morning they brought me cornflakes with cow's milk and I said I can't have that, I'm vegan. Jane actually laughed. This is a farm, she said, what did you expect. Which is totally bogus BTW, there aren't any cows, I'm sure of it. After that they did start bringing me vegan meals and even some supplements, but, well, I never thought I'd say it but: I'm missing my mum's cooking.

In fact, I'm missing my parents full stop – who'd have thought that. My mum's hysterics, always emotional about something. My father's rational, logical explanation for everything, like the world is a crossword and he knows all the answers. I even miss being in his study, the beeswax smell of the red leather swivel chair I sit in as he tries to coach me in aether, to stop my migraines.

The only reason I'm able to keep it together at all, to not be constantly breaking down in tears, is having Piper here with me. She is my fabulous furry rock.

I sit up, the swirling mass of heavy, mismatched blankets pulling at me. I'm in… well, it's a portacabin. Is it? I want to say one of those garden pods you get, but it's not as sleek as that, it's more… garden shed I suppose. A garden shed on wheels. It's a bit weird, TBH. It's the width of a small bed – the small bed I sleep on, in fact, wedged into the end furthest from the door.

The walls are horizontal planks of wood, it's got a bare lightbulb and a double socket which I use to charge my phone. And, to the side of the door is basically a cupboard that has a flushing toilet, a shower over that (weird!) and a tiny sink you can barely fit both hands in. There's a letterbox-size window above the rickety bed and a slightly larger one across one of the two longer walls, and a small, not-working TV up in the corner. There are some hooks screwed to the wall, one with a grey-white towel, the others with my clothes. The metal bed has creaking springs that keep me awake – well, that and the musty blankets which work themselves off in the night, so I wake up cold and Piper gets dragged onto the floor by them, poor thing.

On the floor are my shoes, a bowl of water for Piper and another for her food. They only have 'normal' dog food, not vegetarian. The annoying thing is Piper loves it – the 'normal' variety, I can tell. Which makes me feel bad for giving her veggy all these years.

Oh, and there's a small wooden chair which I've covered in the bits and bobs from my rucksack.

And that's it. Not exactly homely.

I reach under the bed and grab Piper's favourite toy, a blue and orange rubber ball. She jumps up excitedly, ready to pounce.

I dummy, then throw it out. It bounces on the floor then up against the 'bathroom' door then – catch – Piper has got it.

good piper clever piper!

She brings it back, I take it from her and throw it again, this time at a different angle. It bounces off the wooden walls and spins off at a crazy angle, but it's no match for Piper who catches it every time, then leaps back onto the bed to give it back to me. Over and over I throw it, and I'm watching the ball closely, summoning my PK to take hold of it. My PK is pretty lame, but a rubber ball I can manage.

And then – whoosh – I starting making the ball swerve a bit with my PK, and Piper's loving it, this test of her agility in a small space, darting about and turning sharply. And then after one big bounce I make the ball hover in the air.

I'm trying not to laugh as she looks totally confused but then she barks and jumps up gamely, trying to grab it as it wobbles up and down – and then she *does* get it with a tremendous leap and she practically does a somersault of excitement and jumps up on the bed with the ball and I laugh and pet her and cuddle her up to me and everything feels alright for a moment.

And then the TV turns itself on! I look to see if there's a remote I've missed, that I've now just accidentally leant on and turned on, but there's nothing.

The picture is covered in static and distorts every so often like it's struggling to get through. It's… the news, I think. I don't recognise the studio or the newsreader, a blonde woman in a grey suit jacket. It must be regional. She's holding a tablet and standing, talking to camera:

> Aether continues to dominate the news headlines tonight, with reports of at least eight more petrol bombings of homes where suspected aethereals live.

As she talks, behind her a giant screen shows footage of thick black smoke billowing out of the smashed bay window of a house, cordoned off by yellow police tape. Oh frick, this is hard to watch – it doesn't look that different from my house.

Then the screen behind the newsreader changes to an ankle having an electronic tag fitted.

> But first, we understand that the government has just concluded an emergency Cobra committee. We are being told that as part of the ongoing state of emergency, the government is accelerating the aethereal register and electronic tagging programme.
>
> Anyone under the age of twenty-two who has ever experienced chronic migraine must register for a tag at their nearest police station in the next twenty-four hours. Anyone failing to do so will be considered an 'aether fugitive' and will be arrested on sight.
>
> We go now to our reporter Michael Barbiross who is outside Downing Street with further details.

And then the TV turns itself off and Piper and I are left in silence.

OMFG. So… wait, let me process that for a second. They're saying… what? I've got twenty-four hours to go register for a tag or I'm a fugitive and I'll be arrested? And if I go home, my family might get petrol bombed? Is this for real?

I really don't know what to do, I'm just a bit stunned. Piper, sensing my sudden change of mood, barks at the dead TV, blaming it for upsetting me.

It feels like this is news I should be dressed for. I put on my plum-coloured A-line corduroy skirt (Top Shop), and an emerald v-neck tee (Asos) and my black ankle boots. I take the brush off my chair to attack the worst of my hair's tangles, and Piper jumps up, barking once as she stands on the bed, staring at the door as I pull my hair back into a loose pony tail.

There's a knock on the door and Jane comes in. Oh yeah, whatever, don't wait for a reply.

'Ah good morning dearie, did you see the news?' she says brightly.

'The TV?' I say. 'That was you?'

'Mm, yes, well we have an old-fashioned aerial on the farmhouse, we don't get picture often but if the wind direction's just so, it comes through and we have it set to record. Mostly rubbish, kid's programmes, re-runs, that kind of thing. But sometimes we get the news, in which case we pump it to all the TVs.'

'Oh, right,' I say. Wind direction for TV signal, is that a thing?

'And terrible news, isn't it?' says Jane. 'Oh it's a worry, all these bad things happening to people with aether. But don't you worry dearie, you're safe here, and your family knows that – your postcard has been delivered. Now, come out into the sunshine, I'll bring breakfast for you and the little dog in a bit, but first Hagen's got something to ask you.'

Well fine, I guess I'll mope about my terrible life later then, when it's more convenient for Hagen. I wink at Piper and she follows me out, down the wooden steps.

Outside the world is glistening from an early morning shower. The Farm is like this totally random collection of stone buildings and wobbly low walls, all scattered over quite a few fields. It's all really old, pretty ramshackle and mossy and crumbling, and you don't always get a sense of it because there are humongous trees obscuring bits of it.

There are also long reels of flapping orange tape on tent pegs – marking the anthrax quarantine areas I can't go in. And there are bits that look newer – brick garages, tall metal poles with floodlights and loud halers attached, some actual portacabins, plus clusters of the shed-on-wheels I'm in, shepherd's huts Jane says they're called. There are also quite a few dark green metal units that hum away, making an awful noise and smell. Black cables snake out of them and Jane says they're diesel generators. I don't know why they have to use them rather than solar panels or something out here, the generators really ruin the place.

Weirdest of all are all these camo screens they have up, along the low drystone walls and between wide apart trees or connecting odd outbuildings. It means you often can't see from one part to another, they're all hidden in a warren of camouflage netting alleys. Like some kind of maze for stag weekend paintballers. It's pretty freaky.

And that's it, basically. Beyond that it's open moorland, big lumps of stone, clumps of trees and featureless sky stretching out forever. It feels bleak and gives me a kind of vertigo.

But what am I going to do? I don't want to stay here, but if I go back I'll be tagged and I'm at risk and so is my family… and if I don't go back I'm a fugitive. Which if someone had said to me six months ago I'd have been like, an outlaw? Cool! But now I'm much more frick oh frick oh frick.

Jane has led me to Hagen and Rasputin, standing in front of one of those camo screens, next to a dilapidated barn with a rusting corrugated roof. Rasputin is dressed pretty much the same as always – plain black t-shirt, jeans and combat boots. He is shorter than Hagen but a little broader, his dark buzz-cut contrasting with Hagen's slightly greying side-part.

Rasputin is more animated, often smiling (not a nice smile) to reveal the gap between his two front teeth. Hagen is much less animated, tall and tanned, and with his hair and his confident posture he's almost handsome, like some kind of famous Danish actor or something. He's smoking as per, with an irritated expression like I've been keeping him waiting for ages, as per.

'You have seen the news, yes?' he says abruptly. No good morning, how did you sleep.

'Yes,' I say.

'Good,' he says. 'Bad news, but good. You have brought the dog I see,' he says, looking down at Piper.

'Piper comes everywhere with me,' I reply.

'Rat dog,' says Rasputin scornfully.

'What did you say?' I ask, feeling my cheeks flush.

'That dog, they are bred to catch rats,' says Rasputin. 'It will like this.'

Oh, right.

'Come,' says Hagen, stomping his cigarette butt under foot and opening the barn door.

'See you later, dearie,' says Jane, and she walks off as Rasputin follows Hagen into the barn. I need to talk to them about the news, about what to do. So... ugh. I look down at Piper, roll my eyes and follow them in, her trotting alongside.

The barn is pretty big inside. Mottled concrete floor, vaulted roof and running the length of both sides are all these stalls behind grey metal gates. Like milking booths or something I guess.

In the middle are two large, open, wheeled metal trunks. Like the ones bands use on tour.

'For the rats,' says Rasputin, pointing at the trunks. Now he says it, I think the gap in his teeth and his furry head make him look a bit ratty.

'It is infested with rats,' says Hagen, circling a finger in the air. 'It will be accommodation for aethereals. You will be all together, out of the huts, out of the cold as winter comes. You would like that, yes? But we need to get the rats out. When we went through your aspects, you said thiriokinesis was your strongest. So, let us see. Try and get the rats into the boxes. All of them. Apart from any your dog kills, of course.'

He says it as a challenge, like he knows it would be pretty impossible. Yeah, whatever. I straighten my ponytail and look around. I can't see any rats, or hear any. Frick. Eight petrol bombings of 'suspected aethereals' homes, is that what the newsreader said?

'Well?' says Hagen. 'Do you have any ability or not?'

I mean… totally. I got this.

stay piper stay

…I tell her. She comes right to my side and sits down.

good girl good girl love you

And then I show them what I can do.

I blink slowly, alternating between seeing the barn and visualizing it. And I call out with my mind, I whisper and coax. Nothing happens for twenty, thirty seconds. A minute.

And then there's scratchy movement – from the rafters, in the eaves, behind the wood panels, in the dark and dirty corners.

A twitching nose appears from inside a broken bucket, then another.

And then they come. I see Rasputin's eyes go wide, and even Hagen starts to watch me intently… as rats begin to appear in their dozens, running along beams, appearing from behind dusty straw bales and old tractor parts, from under holey milk urns and running along slimy lumps of discarded iron. They begin swarming towards us and it's a pretty freaky sight and Rasputin actually looks uneasy which is funny AF as I try and do two things at once – guide the rats while also gently telling Piper no, don't go for the rats as she jumps up excited, barking and delighted to have so much to chase.

I manage to hold her back, I have to squat down a little to stroke her, calming and soothing her excited brain as I create this river in my mind, this rushing torrent of…

food food food

…for the rats, I am thinking peanut butter, I'm sure that's what they like, the metal roadie trunks are filled with peanut butter and the rats swarm towards them, their glossy brown and black bodies bumping up and down as they scamper along. God I don't know how many there are, forty, fifty? More? And they all surge towards the trunks and climb up the sides effortlessly, pouring into the top, making a real echoing thumping noise as they bang around the trunks looking for the peanut butter, piling on top of each other and screeching and scratching in a frenzy, ready to gorge on the food they can smell, the food they know is there, until at last every single rat is in one of the trunks.

Mic drop!

Rasputin, his face a picture of disgust, slams both lids shut. Piper barks at the trunks and I bend down properly now to stroke her. My head feels woozy, full of rat chatter and it's almost as if I'm drunk.

'Acceptable,' says Hagen.

'Thank you,' I reply, rubbing my forehead. I feel like going back to bed, but I can't, there's the news, I need to think. Poor Piper too, she's gutted not to have got to chase the rats.

'There, there,' I tell her. 'Don't worry about the rats Piper, we can have more fun just you and me.'

I stand up dizzily and Hagen is looking at me.

'Piper?' he says, like I've never used her name before. 'She is Piper. And you are the Pied Piper, perhaps?'

Oh, ha ha. It's probably the closest he's ever got to telling a joke. Or smiling.

'So where do the rats go now?' I ask.

'I drop the boxes in the pond and they drown,' says Rasputin.

'What? No, you can't do that,' I exclaim suddenly, 'they're living creatures!'

'Not for long,' Rasputin replies with a gap-toothed grin.

My nose itches, I put my hand to it and realise it's started bleeding. Oh wow it's quite bad actually, I tip my head back as blood really starts pouring out of my nose, it's running down my fingers and hand, down my forearm and then dripping off my elbow onto the concrete floor. Jeez, this is ridic, it's just pouring and pouring, I don't know why.

Hagen looks at me like I've done this deliberately, to annoy him.

'Bleeding. I see,' he remarks. 'That was a satisfactory demonstration of thiriokinesis, you should go back to your room. Clearly as you have seen on the news, the situation with aether is escalating and you need to remain here for the time being, for the safety of yourself and your family. Jane will bring you breakfast in ten minutes. No milk I know, no milk, probably why you have the nose bleed.'

I stand with my head back as I wait for the blood to slow down or stop. Apparently no-one's going to give me a tissue or any help. Piper is jumping up and up to comfort me and from the corner of my eye I see Rasputin grab the handles of each trunk and start to drag them on their wheels towards the open barn door. I mean I know they're only rats, but they're living creatures and I can't believe they're just going to drown them, it's so cruel and it's my fault.

'Wait!' I call out as they start to leave, my voice echoing in the barn. Hagen pauses for a second, glances at his expensive watch and then looks at me, frowning.

'Up there.' I point with the hand that's not holding my bleeding nose, to the nearest boxed-in end of the roof. 'There's something in there, looks like a big fan, lots of electrical stuff. They've chewed through the wires, but you could probably fix it. I think it might be a wind generator.'

Hagen looks up to where I'm pointing, then back at me.

'They... you saw that? Through the rats?' he asks.

'Well, yeah, sorta,' I say.

He looks up again, then nods almost to himself. 'Interesting.'

'Don't drown the rats, please,' I plead. 'Set them loose in a field or something at least, give them a chance.' Frick, my nosebleed isn't slowing down any, I am actually losing quite a lot of blood here. I don't like to see it spotting the ground this this, these dark, angry splashes of crimson. I am a vampire that hates the sight of blood.

Rasputin laughs at my suggestion, a bark-laugh. Hagen sighs slightly; he's had enough of me, this silly little girl, and he just walks off, Rasputin dragging the trunks behind.

So I'll just stand by myself in this spooky deserted barn and bleed to death then. I needed to talk to him, about the news, and where is Noolie, and the horses, when will I meet another aethereal... but he's just left me here, feeling faint, blood pouring out of my nose onto the floor, making the place look more and more like an abattoir. Ugh.

You know what they say: The more I learn about people, the more I love my dog.

14: SUICIDE

"Some years ago there were reports of live organ harvesting, do you remember?

"Stories that people in China who practiced a spiritualism called 'Falun Gong' were being taken as political prisoners and operated on. Livers, kidneys, corneas and other organs were surgically removed while they were still alive. Their body parts sold to the highest bidder.

"Now consider aether – the greatest advance in human capacity since the birth of language – and ask yourself this:

"How much more valuable is the brain of an aethereal than the liver of a Chinese peasant?"

– From the TS Interviews with Doctor Magellan-Jones

He was gone, he was outta there, he was history.

That had been the plan. Just one more night, after his first knife-throwing session, then he was going to slope off, no matter what Hagen said.

But then he'd seen the news, beamed from the TV on the wall in his hut.

Some random newsreader saying that if he went back he'd have to register for an electronic tag straight away or be arrested. But then, once people saw his tag he'd either get drain cleaner thrown over him or a Molotov cocktail through the window of their flat.

So he'd stayed another week. Another week practicing PK: guided knife throwing, trying to lift rocks out of the moor, unlocking doors by manipulating a key on the other side. Always while being barked at by Hagen or smirked at by Rasputin. And another week building his strength back up, hoovering up the pretty decent grub and using old farming gear as makeshift gym equipment. Old milk urns, with a length of pipe attached, became barbells. Rotting winch cables were perfect for battle rope exercises. And a huge tractor tyre was the apparatus for his own bootcamp regime.

Because while he was here he might as well train brain and brawn. For the showdown with Keel.

Suddenly an alarm screamed, making him jump.

Bloody hell! What the – ?

It was so sudden and so loud, he dropped down from the rusty bar he'd been using for pull-ups and grabbed his t-shirt off the empty milk urn, pulling it over his sweat-slicked body.

From every direction it howled, an angry, urgent air-raid siren.

What was going on?

He'd peered out of the old cowshed. The alarm was coming from the tannoy system hooked up to metal poles which carried the floodlights.

He heard shouting, and through the camouflage netting screens he saw shapes moving. The Farm often gave the impression of being deserted, but now and then he'd see people moving about, obscured and fleeting, but there.

He dashed out of the dilapidated cowshed into the open, veering away from the aggravating blare of the siren, running along a low dry-stone wall towards the main farm building. He'd never been there, now might be his chance.

More shouting. What the hell was going on? He ran around the corner – and almost smack bang into a rangy, long-haired man he didn't recognise, dressed in black and holding a walkie talkie. He said something into his walkie talkie while holding an arm out to indicate Flynn to stop.

A second later another man appeared – Rasputin, with an absolutely huge, sandy-coloured dog on a thick lead.

'You,' he said, like he was disappointed. 'Come,' he said, then signalled to the man in black to go in a different direction. Flynn followed his gaze and saw a third man in the distance, wearing a backpack and pointing a space-age rifle at the sky. He didn't have time to ask, as Rasputin put a hand on his shoulder and pushed him forwards to run. Flynn ran, keeping Rasputin between himself and the huge canine beast that loped alongside. They veered away from the main farmhouse and started down a slope where he could see a crop of more shepherd's huts. To the right was a smallish old barn, its wooden boards grey and silvered with age. Rasputin turned and ran to it. He lifted the latch and opened the door.

'In here,' he ordered, pushing Flynn in. Flynn turned, annoyed at being pushed again, but Rasputin was already gone, taking the enormous, muscle-bound dog with him.

'Hi,' said a voice behind him.

He looked around – and there was a tall guy in skinny tan chinos and a band t-shirt, maybe just a couple of years older than himself. Flynn guessed he must be another aethereal.

'Hi back,' said Flynn. 'I'm Flynn.'

'Rabbit,' came the reply. 'Do you know what's going on?'

Flynn shook his head. 'No, no idea. I was just in another barn and suddenly,' he raised his palms up, indicating the wailing all around him, 'this.'

'Well, good to meet you, dude,' said Rabbit, walking forward. He had a long, sandy fringe brushed to the side and bright eyes that looked out under it above a strong jaw. He looked vaguely familiar.

'You too,' said Flynn. 'Ah… how long have you been here?'

'On The Farm? I guess… well, getting on for three weeks,' said Rabbit. 'You?'

'Two,' said Flynn. 'You must have arrived just before me.'

'Sure,' said Rabbit, nodding his head. 'But up until now, you're the first other, ah – visitor – I've met.'

Flynn grinned at the expression, 'visitor'. In other words, aethereal. 'You too,' he said.

He looked around. The barn was furnished with faded rugs across the wooden floor and a large, old farmhouse table in the middle, scattered with chairs. There was an old TV sitting on a wooden crate, and next to it a pile of swollen paperbacks and unloved board games. There were two battered leather easy chairs, a faded green sofa, a wall of pigeon holes filled with more books and glass jars and cans and metal junk, plus all manner of random farm-ish jumble sale items lying all over. There was also a wide stack of what looked like sandbags that stretched to the ceiling and a stack of cardboard boxes of chemicals in big five litre containers. And, at one end, there was a rusting, dust-covered vintage black car, like something from a black and white movie.

'What is this place?' he asked.

Rabbit shook his head, and brushed his fringe to the side. 'I dunno really,' he said. 'I came here for the first time yesterday. To try…' he paused, and looked at Flynn as if weighing him up, 'to see if I can scry.'

Huh. That was honest of him. 'I can't do scry,' Flynn replied. 'Other aspects… but not scry.' It was the first time in his life he'd ever willingly told someone other than his mum that he was aethereal.

And then the alarm went silent as suddenly as it had started. He'd got so used to it that the silence felt super-silent, like he'd gone deaf. Rabbit looked around at the smeary, discoloured windows that lined one side of the barn.

And then Hagen came in, holding a walkie talkie like the man Flynn had seen earlier.

'Oh, fucking great,' Hagen snarled. 'You two, having a nice chat here alone, wonderful. What did you talk about? You should tell me the truth now.'

'Nothing, I've only been here two minutes,' Flynn said. 'We've just said hi, that's all. The alarm's off I see. Or rather, hear.'

'Fucking drone,' said Hagen, clipping the walkie talkie to his belt and taking a pack of cigarettes from one of his khaki-green shirt pockets. 'Snooping. Dangerous for you. For all aethereals here. Cameras,' he gestured wildly, all around, 'taking pictures, video,' he finished. He lit a cigarette, which irritated Flynn.

'A drone?' said Rabbit. 'Who would have a drone out here?'

Hagen shrugged dismissively. 'Kids,' he said. 'For certain. On holiday. But we have taken it down. We have a drone gun.'

That must have been what Flynn had seen earlier – the strange black rifle with three long barrels aimed at the sky.

'Is that a bit hardcore, taking some kids' drone?' he said.

Hagen strode up to him, the way he liked to stand over people to dominate them, then lean back slightly as if they were invading his personal space.

'You want to be recognised and police come and arrest you and you are seen again who knows when?' asked Hagen. 'I have seen some things with police, let me tell you. All kinds of police. You think they are the good guys, the people who keep the law? You should know: they are the ones who break the law. More than anyone, a hundred percent. I have seen.

'The gentle times, when they attend a burglary, there is an old lady. They say have you checked what is missing and the old lady says no. So one of them keeps her talking while the other goes upstairs to look around and take whatever they want.'

He took a long drag of his cigarette and blew it up, over Flynn's head, before jabbing it at him the way he often did to punctuate a point, Flynn always a little mesmerized by Hagen's burned, scarred hand.

'That is the gentle. The rough I have seen, you would not like to know about. So many suicides in police custody, you notice? Really, they are suicides? I can tell you, it is easy to hang a man with his own belt when you already have him in handcuffs. You should believe that. Oh, you would not like the police to come here and arrest you, you would not.'

Flynn wanted to say And what about you, they'd arrest you too you miserable bastard but he kept quiet, Hagen really was in one.

Hagen stared at them both, from one to the other like he was deciding something.

'Since you have met, we will adapt. Show me if you have wispr. You – sit over there, you – over there, with your backs to each other. Come,' he said, holding the cigarette in his mouth and clapping his hands together in a reverberating boom, 'show some fucking urgency!'

Christ. The drone had really pissed Hagen off, that was for sure. Fine, ok – Rabbit gave Flynn a reassuring wink and headed down the end of the barn. Flynn got up and looked around. He stared back at Hagen and then walked to the opposite end, brushing past the spotted chrome bumper of the old car to where there were half a dozen wooden crates, like apple boxes. He turned one on its end and sat on it, a makeshift stool.

Right. So… now what. Wispr. He'd never tried it in his life. He had no idea how it was done. He sat there feeling like an idiot. What was he supposed to do? He just started thinking… hello, hello Rabbit, hello is this working. Nothing.

He realised he also didn't know whether Rabbit was trying to send him a message or waiting to receive one. Bollocks. He tried again, just calling out with his mind, concentrating on the words, really aiming to fill his head and make the words resonate and carry:

can you read me

go ahead

over

Still nothing. Maybe talking like he was on a walkie talkie wasn't the right approach. He tried to project his words, pushing them out like the tannoy alarm to ripple through the air. He felt a moment of light-headedness, and a shiver went across his shoulders and down his spine.

hello hello

is there anybody there

…he sent. Because that's what it felt like, like he was at a séance, trying to contact a ghost. And then after a few seconds a voice appeared in his head, so strange it made him jump for the second time that day:

how are you doing this

why are you in my head

am i going mad

He could 'hear' the words even though there was no sound, like they were his own thoughts, rather than someone else's voice. It was like getting a message from an unknown number. And then he got:

its this place driving me crazy isnt it and

wait

is this wispr

Rabbit seemed to be freaking out. Flynn didn't blame him. It felt unnatural having someone else speak inside your skull. It was like wearing ear buds you couldn't feel. He replied, repeating the same blossoming wave of mental energy, projecting his voice without opening his mouth:

yes its ok this is wispr

i think its working rabbit

There was a pause, and then:

what do you mean

rabbit

im not a rabbit

What? Flynn was bewildered. It was weird enough anyway, but the fact that the voice in his head was confused was… well, even more confusing. And then:

can you really talk to rabbits

…flowered in his mind. It was bloody strange. Was it one of Hagen's tests?

Unless this was Rabbit's sense of humour? Flynn sent a message back, radiating out into the air:

i am flynn

who is this

Silence. The seconds dragged on and he thought that was it.

But then a reply swept across his brain, strong and clear:

i am echo

15: MAGIC

My nose stopped bleeding *eventually*. It was ridic just how much blood poured out. Like I'd strained myself or something, doing too much aether. No sympathy from Hagen, obvs. I had a crusty-blood nose for days afterwards.

And I've started messaging Jazz. I know it's stupid – there's no signal so she won't get them, but I miss her sooo much. My funny, sassy BFF. I don't think we've ever been apart this long, not since juniors. I feel terrible about what she must be thinking. She must think I've been abducted or something, because she hasn't heard from me since I got in the van. Sometimes it gets too much and I find myself in floods of tears. I want to see her so much.

But I can't. Because I'm still stuck on The Farm.

And that's because the news out there is horrendous. Basically, the only time the TV goes on is for the news, and the news is always about aether and the news about aether is always bad. Yesterday there was another report, the same woman newsreader as always, this time in a bright red dress suit, but the same severe hair, same severe words:

> This morning armed police teams around the country launched dawn raids, rounding up around thirty untagged suspected aether terrorists for questioning, with unconfirmed reports of fatalities in Manchester when one suspect resisted capture.
>
> With an estimated three hundred aethereals still unregistered, the government is today introducing new laws as part of the state of emergency measures

commonly known as The Witchcraft Act. Effective from midnight, any public act of aether will be a criminal offence and carry a sentence of six months' imprisonment.

Can you believe it? They really are arresting aethereals who don't have a tag (ie people like me) as 'suspected' terrorists. And if someone accused me of a 'public act' of aether, I could be locked up for six months. I mean, frick. It's a nightmare. 'The Witchcraft Act' is so unfair and cruel, it's keeping me from Jazz and from my family. Christ, what must my parents think?

I have nightmares where they make one of those TV appeals, like Noolie's parents did when she went missing. My mother, she'd be hysterical, screaming blue murder and ripping the cops a new one. My father, he might actually come out of his study or miss one of his conferences to make an appearance. I can imagine him holding court, correcting myths about aether, ice to my mother's fire.

I've tried asking Hagen about me speaking to my parents, maybe going out in disguise to somewhere with signal, but he's all kinds of mean about it. He just says 'write it on a card, we will deliver'. I'm tense around him the whole time. His temper, the vile stories he tells. The way he exudes this fake calm while actually you feel like any second he might grab you by the throat and pin you against the wall. I don't know what the deal is here, but he is definitely in charge. I see other people – mainly Rasputin and sometimes Jane whose farm this supposedly is/was – but Hagen's always at the centre of it all, commanding, insulting, smoking.

He says practicing aether helps stop you getting migraines – which is actually what my dad believes too. But Hagen uses that to make me practice aether every day, over and over. It's exhausting, non-stop do this do that no you can't don't ask questions do as I say you should listen to me now do this now do it again. And he just ignores me when I ask about Noolie, he just waves me away like I'm speaking another language.

Sometimes it feels like being in an end-of-the-world post-apocalyptic movie. Barely any people here and you look out and for miles and miles and there's like *nothing*. No other people, no animals, no buildings. A world on mute.

But somewhere out there, we know terrible things are happening.

So… yeah. It's totally bleak and I was starting to feel just lost TBH. Piper could sense it, she kept trying to cheer me up, bless her. But then, just as I was losing the will…

hello hello

is there anybody there

…popped into my head. Wispr. And a few hours later, I was introduced to two other aethereals. Finally, after being here over three weeks! Rabbit and Flynn. OMG, I think meeting them saved me.

I don't know if Hagen actually wanted me to meet them; they've been on The Farm for a bit longer than I have and he'd never mentioned them once – just as he never mentions Noolie or Jane's son. But that day he was trying to get them to use wispr, only I think Rabbit can't do it, because instead of him hearing Flynn, I did. It was the day the siren went off, which Hagen said was a drone, spying on The Farm, putting aethereals at risk he said. That was all quite scary.

Anyway, basically I heard Flynn's wispr and after that Hagen decided to bring us all together and so now I know two other aethereals. Yay! Rabbit and Flynn.

I recognised Rabbit straight away, he's like actually famous. Well, famous-ish. I've seen videos on YouTube, he's this amazing street magician, he's got like two million followers or something. He's tall – six three maybe? – and twenty years old, which makes him one of the oldest aethereals around I guess. He's got a fair-haired comb-over and he's just like he is on YouTube – chilled and easy-going, usually in just a long-sleeved tee and chinos. I've noticed he seems to walk with a hint of a limp and I've seen him rubbing his leg a few times but I haven't asked him about it yet.

Flynn looks very different, dark hair, intense eyebrows, much more brooding. He's shorter than Rabbit, broader too. He looks like he's from Love Island or something. Well, not all super-groomed and tan – just, you know, shredded. Hot, I guess. Jeez, I'm making myself blush. He used to be a gymnast and a swimmer he says, so that's why the muscular bod and focus I guess. When I first met him there was something I couldn't put my finger on, something sort of otherworldly about him and then – boom! It's his eyes. One's green and one's blue! It's kinda cool I guess. He's also sarky AF which makes a change from everyone else here who's always sooo serious.

So yeah, it's cool finally meeting people who aren't total douchebags like everyone else here. We met in this place we've started calling Flint Barn – it's this grey wood barn, not so large, and made sort-of homely. It's got a big table and chairs and stuff (like an ancient car which is pretty random), and these oil heaters which we might need soon because it already feels like summer is over, like the weather is turning and there's a chill in the evenings.

And trying wispr – apart from playing with Piper it was the closest thing to fun I've had here. At one point I said:

so this is what its like in your head

theres not much to see

its very roomy

...and he sent back:

that explains why I can hear an echo

...which is as Echo jokes go isn't *so* bad. Then we got talking about Hagen and about how arrogant he is and Flynn said:

yeah he doesn't say oh em gee he says oh em ess

...which actually made me laugh out loud and Hagen saw and said that's enough wispring and later he made us see if we could wispr from our two shepherd huts but they're in different parts of The Farm so we couldn't. Which was a shame.

But they are letting me and Rabbit and Flynn do our aether sessions together now at least, which is better. And sometimes we get to go to Flint barn with its old rusting car and the table and battered sofa and chairs and just hang out for a bit and pretend things are way more normal than they really are.

Scry was weird the other day. Hagen has been really pushing us to do it, to try and read emotions, but it's an aspect none of us have got. Except that... well, Rabbit is this awesome magician who told me and Flynn that he used aether in his magic.

That's how he got famous – people couldn't work out how he did his tricks, because he was using aether.

One trick he did, for instance, was guessing which cup the ball was under.

He'd use an outside café table or the bonnet of a car or the top of a brick wall or whatever, and put five cups along it. Without him looking, someone would put the ball under one of the cups. Rabbit would open his eyes and touch the top of each cup, asking the person each time Is it under this cup? Is it under this cup? and so on, and the person would have to say no every time. And Rabbit would guess right every time which cup had the ball. Which, when you think he's aethereal, you'd guess must be down to scry, don'tcha think? With scry he could tell when someone's heart beat a little faster when they said no to the one that did have the ball under.

Well, that's what I'd think, except that he hasn't been able to do scry here at all, he's been useless. Now I don't think Hagen spent much time on YouTube, he doesn't know Rabbit's famous so he didn't *seem* suspicious. But I don't know. I want to ask Rabbit about it, when Hagen's not around. The thought of Rabbit lying to Hagen scares me, Hagen would go abso-frickin-lutely ape.

Anyway, there's that. Life sucks: I miss my BFF like crazy, I keep bursting into tears like a five year-old and I even miss my folks. It's frightening and stressful on The Farm, it's like being in prison in a foreign country… but I'm also terrified of what's out there.

But at least – finally – I've met some others who are like me. And they seem pretty ok. Yeah, they're definitely ok. I feel like meeting them has saved me from total despair and given me a smidge of hope.

So thank you, Reuben 'Rabbit' Rake and Flynn Dallas.

16. SHOCK

"Aethereals sometimes get called vampires, you've heard that I assume? Because if you get migraines, you can have a sensitivity to light. And if you're having a migraine, you certainly should stay out of the sun. So: vampires. Also because aether can seem magical, perhaps.

"It's interesting to me, because ancient vampire mythology is based on two very real conditions: porphyria and catalepsy. Porphyria affects the blood; if you have it then sunlight causes terrible, itchy rashes... so sufferers stay out of the sun. It also makes the gums recede so teeth look more prominent – like fangs.

"Catalepsy puts someone into a catatonic state with no discernible pulse. So someone with catalepsy would seem dead... and might get buried alive. Days later, they would awake and start scratching on their coffin, moaning and groaning. On occasion they would be heard and dug up – whereupon, mad with fear and hunger, they would bite themselves and those around them.

"So: vampires. A superstition created two and a half thousand years ago as a reaction to misunderstood human conditions of the time. And resurrected now in reaction to a new, misunderstood and terminal condition: aether.

"Aethereals are today's fragile vampires."

– From the TS Interviews with Doctor Magellan-Jones

She was one of those girls who said sweater instead of jumper. Posh. They'd discovered by chance that they both lived in the same town – though very different parts of it; she lived at the smart end, as middle class as balsamic vinegar and organic toothpaste. In fact, it turned out she knew the aethereal from their town who'd gone missing before he'd left, a girl called Noolie. She was one of the reasons Echo had come to The Farm, but so far Echo hadn't seen her.

She was also one of those girls who shortened words all the time, obvs, which was pretty ridic. Quite tall, vegan slim, long, deep chestnut hair, hazel eyes, freckles, always dressed like she was 'off to do the festival thing at Glasto with Camilla and Cressida and Charlie'. And pretty in a way that was quite irritating, just because she pretended not to know.

She also had a small, bouncy white dog that followed her everywhere and which growled at him every time for the first twenty minutes or so which was a pain – made more annoying by Echo saying something along the lines of 'And the thing is Piper's a really good judge of character so, you know, just saying,' every time.

And yet. Flynn liked her. (A bit.) She had a positive energy, could be quite witty sometimes and most of all she was a good person – kind, thoughtful and empathetic. He didn't need scry to tell that. She was also frightened and appalled by this place and – like him – wished she was back home. On balance, he was glad that when they first met he hadn't immediately made a joke about her name, Echo.

Though he'd been bloody tempted.

'Does the dog really go everywhere with you?' he asked her now, as it growled at him with all the menace of a child with a Nerf gun.

'Of course she comes everywhere with me,' Echo replied indignantly, crouching down to stroke her. 'Don't take it out on her just because she's knows you're a wrong 'un. She's homesick, is all. We both are,' she added.

'Yeah well Toto, I don't think we're in Kansas anymore,' Flynn said to the dog.

'Wizard Of Oz,' said Rabbit with a nod. 'Highly appropriate.'

'Enough talking,' snapped Hagen. 'I regret the day the three of you met. Always talking, always just shit, endless fucking drivel. You should listen.'

They were in a former pig-shed, one of the bigger farm buildings he'd seen, long with a pitched, corrugated roof. Echo had been there before, she said, pointing out a dark stain on the cracked concrete floor from a monster nosebleed she'd had a couple of weeks ago.

God knows how many pigs the place had once housed. It had stalls running down both long sides of it, still covered in sawdust and rotting straw and with forgotten cast-iron pig troughs in them.

'Probably full of rats,' he'd said when they first came in.

'No, I don't think so,' Echo had replied with a faraway look.

Hagen and Rasputin made them line up, looking down at some new props assembled down the central walkway. Hagen was wearing sand-coloured combat trousers and a twill lumberjack shirt plus a brown and white snood now the days were getting cooler. He also had a new yellow and black handheld device hanging from a holster on his belt, as did Rasputin. Hagen's sleeves were rolled up to just below the elbow, showing his tan, sinewy forearms, his scarred right hand and the fancy watch he had – an IWC chronograph worth about four grand, according to Rabbit.

Rasputin was dressed in his usual jeans and black long-sleeved t-shirt and he was holding a large remote control with a long antenna extended out. They both stood near something that looked for all the world like a photocopier, only with more buttons. It was hooked up by a snaking cable to one of the buzzing outdoor generators.

'Today you will be trying psynaptic shock,' said Hagen.

'Snapshot,' Flynn, Echo and Rabbit all said in unison. Then they grinned at each other. It made sense, it was the only aspect they hadn't yet practiced.

Hagen, Flynn could see, was not amused.

'I know you delicate souls would not want to try psynaptic shock on a human, so you will see we have some puppets for you to practice on,' he said, pointing.

They looked. Ten feet down was a freestanding chicken-wire screen, about six feet high, attached to two metal poles across the width of the shed. Like an industrial scale tennis net. Obscured behind it were three chairs facing them, each about four feet apart, and each with a lifesize scarecrow dummy sat on them. Grey lumpy boiler suits, presumably filled with straw, gloves for hands, big clumpy boots, and fancy dress shop plastic masks – one clown, one Spiderman, one a scary movie mask.

'To make it convincing, they have animatronics,' said Hagen. And sure enough, now that Flynn looked closely, he could see that on the other side of the chicken wire the dummies were moving slightly, just slight twitches and judders.

'Why?' said Rabbit. 'Why do you want to make it convincing? That's got nothing to do with our actual ability, has it?'

'Yeah, oh my god,' said Echo. 'They look creepy and it's a horrible idea. I would never do snapshot on someone in real life anyway.'

Hagen stepped forward, holding a hair net from a science-fiction film in his left hand.

'Oh really, would you fucking not?' he spat. 'You have aether but you would never use it, how stupid. I have an arm,' he said, lifting his right arm up theatrically, 'which I choose not to use as a weapon. But I could, oh yes. I could, Echo and Flynn and Rabbit, if I needed to. Because I have trained this arm of mine. I have used it as a weapon before, so I know what it is capable of, my right arm.

'If I needed to, I could bring my elbow down hard on your collar bone, shattering it,' he said, miming the motion while staring at them, unblinking. He took another step towards them. 'If I had to, I could gouge out your eyeballs with my fingers. If I wanted to, I could palm strike you on the nose, angled upwards to drive the septum into your brain and kill you. Or if I so desired,' he said, taking another step forward and curling his gnarled, scarred hand into a tight fist of sharp knuckles, 'I could punch you in the throat so your trachea collapses and you suffocate to death as you cough up blood.'

'Perhaps you forget that there are people out there who want to kill you? Maybe everything is too good on The Farm, we look after you too well, the food is too good and we are too soft and you are soft and you think oh, everything is not so bad.

'But you would be fucking ignorant to think that. Out there, people despise you, they want you dead. If people like that came after me, I would use my arm as a weapon, I would kill them. You, you are lucky. You have aether. With psynaptic shock you could stun them, no real harm, while you escape. If you needed to. If you had to.

'So,' he said, 'put these on and we will see if you can do anything useful.'

He handed the hair net he was holding to Rabbit, and indicated to Flynn and Echo to pick up the other two which were resting on the humming white photocopier.

'It's an EEG cap,' Echo said, picking up a blue cap with dozens of wires coming out of it. 'To measure brainwaves. My dad has something like it at home.'

'Wow,' Flynn said, 'he sounds like fun.'

'No,' Echo admitted, 'not so much. Yours?'

Flynn frowned. 'No,' he replied. 'Definitely not that.'

'Quiet,' said Hagen. 'You should be concentrating, always with the yapping, you are like the little dog.'

yeah no talking

...Flynn wisprd to Echo.

oh you are such a smart arse

…came the reply a second later, Echo narrowing her eyes at him as they both pulled on their EEG caps.

well

your halfway to being a smart arse

…she continued.

the second half

Hagen plugged the end of the ribbon of wires coming from each cap into the photocopier thing.

'You,' he said, pointing at Rabbit, 'the horror mask, you the clown,' he said to Flynn, 'and you the spiderman,' he finished, pointing at Echo.

ive always hated clowns so this works out well

Flynn wisprd to Echo.

and ive never liked spiders so yay

…she wisprd back.

just make sure you stand well back from my snapshot

…she continued

i dont want to be covered in brain

'Well,' she said out loud to him now, looking him up and down, 'not that I'd be *covered*.' He rolled his eyes.

'Ok dudes,' Rabbit said to them, 'shall we do this? I mean, they're just dummies,' he said, looking sideways. Flynn smiled. He had a feeling Rabbit wasn't talking about the scarecrows on the chairs.

They lined up to face their targets, ten feet away. A slasher flick baddie, a red-headed circus clown and a rather overstuffed Spiderman who looked too fat to swing from building to building. Each twitched and jerked occasionally under Rasputin's remote control.

'Good luck,' said Rabbit, giving them both a thumbs up. Echo smiled back.

And so, they were into it. This could be, as Echo would say, awks. Flynn believed Rabbit and Echo when they'd said they hadn't done snapshot before – Rabbit never, and Echo only in her dad's study to register brainwaves, never at a target.

Whereas Flynn… Well, only once, and only from a distance of a few centimetres, but still. If he did it too easily now, everyone would start asking questions.

So for the next two minutes he did nothing, while in the background Hagen urged them on, a non-stop stream of coaxing and criticism:

'This is for your benefit, not mine. I do not choose to stand around with the smell of pigshit in my nose.'

'Aethereals who can control their aspects do not get migraines, you should think on that.'

'Which of you is best? Let me see you giving it your all, every fucking ounce of your effort should be going into this. Are you even trying?'

'You want to go home soon? They can test for migraines, they can prove you are aethereal, a menace. Prove them wrong, stop your migraines, master your aspects.'

Flynn could feel himself being wound up by Hagen and by the memory of the other time he'd done snapshot. On another bully, in fact. One who'd tormented him and his mum for years, who'd blinded him in one eye and gaslighted his mum, breaking down her confidence and making her feel like his temper and violence were her fault.

'Now!' Hagen roared at them.

And Flynn snapshotted the clown at the same time Echo and Rabbit went for their targets. He didn't know if it was his imagination, but it felt as if the air around them went a little hazy like it could sometimes in the heat of summer.

And then three things happened.

Rabbit exclaimed 'Agh!' as if the effort of it had caused him pain.

The three dummies all spasmed more violently as if Rasputin had put new batteries into his remote control.

And the feet of Flynn's dummy, the clown, suddenly plunged down hard onto the concrete floor and the chair tilted sideways and toppled into the scary movie mask dummy and they both crashed to the ground with a reverberating clatter.

Which was when Flynn and the others realised the truth.

They weren't dummies.

He reacted just slightly more slowly than Echo, who ran to the chicken wire screen with him and Rabbit just behind, Rabbit running with a limping lope.

They couldn't get to the chairs, the chicken wire which had made it hard to see things clearly blocked their path, but close-up it was obvious they were three real people, taped and bound to the chairs, with straw stuck into the ends of their clothes to make them look like scarecrows. Spiderman's head lolled to the side, presumably stunned by Echo's snapshot, while Flynn's own clown didn't move at all. Most tragic-looking was the scary mask person, who bucked and writhed on the floor, stuck to the chair and looking like a fly caught in syrup, desperate to escape. Echo was sobbing.

'They're people!' she screamed. 'They're not dummies! You lied to us!' she yelled, whirling to face Hagen who was striding towards them.

'The remote control… misdirection,' said Rabbit softly.

'Sick bastards,' Flynn said.

'Help them!' Echo said, tears streaming down her face, 'those poor people, you just got us to snapshot real human beings!'

Hagen came up to them.

'You overreact, as always with you fucking snowflakes,' he snarled. 'They are volunteers. Who do you think you are, you think your untrained aspect can cause any real pain at this distance? We thought you would not be able to concentrate if you knew they were real people, that is all. You should calm down.'

The next ten minutes were chaotic.

Rasputin had put down his useless remote control and was on his walkie talkie. A minute later two men came in, the two Flynn recognised from the day the siren had gone off – one he'd nearly run into, and the other one, who'd had the drone gun. They had the same black and yellow plastic devices holstered on their belts as Hagen and Rasputin.

Between those two and Rasputin and Hagen, they'd separated Flynn and Echo and Rabbit, Hagen and Rasputin doing most of the talking. Rasputin with his slimy, needling voice, Hagen with his gruff, dismissive manner, both saying over and over that the people had been volunteers, measuring the output on an EEG was one thing but if they didn't know if the psynaptic shock reached its target then it was meaningless.

Echo was still sobbing and her dog was barking away in the large empty space, snapping at Rasputin as he pulled Echo away to take her back to her shepherd hut, telling her to calm down and think about the danger out there and what The Farm was protecting them from. Flynn could see from her tear-stained face that she was in shock at what she had inadvertently done.

its not your fault its not your fault

…he wisprd to her as the three of them were pulled apart and taken to their separate shepherd's huts. But she didn't answer.

There was another thing that bothered Flynn. The new black and yellow things Hagen and the others had on their belts. He was no expert, but he was pretty sure he'd seen them on US cop shows. They weren't legal in this country, not for civilians, but it looked like Hagen and the others were carrying their own form of snapshot.

They were now all armed with Tasers.

17: WOLVES

The most awful thing has happened.

Last week… Hagen made me snapshot someone. A real, innocent person. I mean, I didn't know it was a real person at the time, but really, it was just so bogus, and Hagen said they were volunteers but we never saw their faces or got to talk to them so who knows he's just such a total bullshit artist I just don't know. And that was it, I was just going, never mind the electronic tag or the curfew or being arrested or whatever –

– but then when I got back to my 'shepherd's hut', crying, the TV came on and it was the always-bad news again but literally this was another level of horror. It was amateur footage by vigilantes and it was just a girl in a field, a girl like me, same sort of age, long hair tied back. They had her hands tied back and a gag in her mouth and she was chained up against a metal pole, just in this gloomy field. They were pouring liquid from metal cans on the branches and logs around her just in the middle of nowhere, in some random field just her by herself, the two people pouring stuff had balaclavas on so you couldn't see their faces and then OMFG they just lit it, they just got a match and lit the liquid on a log and it all caught instantly and there was tons of black smoke and her screams went so high and extreme and it was the most disgusting, horrific thing I've ever heard or seen and I was hitting the TV trying to turn it off but I was close-up to the screen as I hit it with my hands just trying to make it stop but it didn't stop and I'm right up close to the screen seeing it happen and the flames didn't stop and –

– they just burned her to death.

Burn the witch. OMFG.

It is sick AF, I can't believe it, really I can't. You just can't reason with people like that. Where would you even begin with someone who thinks it's ok to set fire to someone – who's completely innocent – and burn them to death just because they were born with a terminal condition they didn't ask for and don't understand?

I'm just like… I can't take much more of this. My soul feels like it has a slow puncture. And poor Piper, she can sense I'm unhappy and that makes her sad which makes me feel bad so I'm more unhappy. Everything just feels so hopeless. As bleak as the landscape that surrounds The Farm.

The only bits that make it even halfway bearable are in the morning when they let me go out to walk Piper (though not near the anthrax tape which is *still* up) and evenings in Flint Barn when they let me and Flynn and Rabbit eat dinner together.

Like now, we've just finished eating and Rabbit is cutting Flynn's hair. Badly. With some hopeless scissors Jane gave him.

Flynn and I have both been here about six weeks now so, you know, it's time for a haircut apparently. Rabbit's offered to do mine too and I said yes absolutely, just after hell freezes over. While Rabbit cuts, Piper is at my feet begging for scraps – I know she wants the meat from the guys' plates now that she's got a taste for it but there's no chance I tell her.

'Are you sure you know what you're doing?' I ask Rabbit.

'Yeah I'm sure,' says Rabbit, not that confidently in my view. 'I've cut my own hair for years,' he says (which to be fair is a decent comb-over with a brushed-forward sandy fringe).

'I learned from my mum, she works in a gent's salon,' he adds.

'Oh, cool,' I say. 'I wish I had a practical skill. I'm an ok-ish in-line skater, but I'm yet to discover what that's good for.'

'Delivering pizza?' Flynn suggests, brushing cut hairs off his shoulders.

'You're a skateboarder, dude,' Rabbit says to Flynn, grinning. 'You can't throw shade at another skater!'

'Yes, thank you Rabbit,' I say. 'Give him one of those monk's bald patches. 'Your mum still cut hair?'

'Yeah, yeah,' he says. 'When I was little I used to help her pull out the splinters.'

'Splinters?' I say.

'Yeah,' Rabbit replies, finishing off Flynn's hair, 'hair splinters. In the feet.'

'What?' I say. 'C'mon, you're making that up.'

'No, honestly,' Rabbit replies, shaking his own mop of hair. 'Men's hair is the worst because it's usually short. The hairs get onto your clothes when you're cutting hair, and over the course of the day they work their way down and they get into your shoes. Then as you walk about they burrow their way into the soles of your feet. Hair splinters.'

'Wow. No offence to your mum, but that sounds pretty gross,' I reply.

'It is,' says Rabbit. 'At the end of the day she'd put the TV on, put her feet up… and I'd have to pull out the hairs with tweezers. They can become infected too, I used to always think that was the real reason they wash your hair in a salon. So they know at least the hair splinters are clean.'

'Reeeeally?' I say. 'I wish I had scry so I could tell if you're making this up!'

'I swear,' Rabbit says laughing, 'when we get out of here look it up, it's – oh shit, what the..?' he says, looking shocked.

Flynn and I turn and see... a hellhound.

Ok I'm exaggerating, it doesn't have hot coals for eyes and it isn't dripping flames, but OMG it's *huge*. It's like the size of a lion or something. It's sandy coloured too, really powerful-looking, with a black muzzle and ears, and a tail that curls up and forward like a scorpion's sting. I've never been frightened by an animal in my life, but frick, I'm definitely uneasy. It sees Piper and it starts to growl – the sound of someone waving a chainsaw.

It pads towards us like we're its prey. How did it get in? Where'd it come from?

i saw rasputin with it a couple of weeks ago

...Flynn (presumably) wisprs.

I grab Piper. She's gone into protector mode but this lion-dog could swallow her whole.

'Let's just slowly move back,' says Rabbit. He and Flynn are more round the other side of the table than me.

But then Piper, in my arms, yaps at the huge dog and it barks back. It's the sound of concrete tearing, a brutal, menacing noise as it comes towards us with murderous intent.

'Echo!' Flynn shouts. I'm closest to the doorway – and so to the dog – as Flynn jumps up and hefts over the big solid farmhouse table, sending it slamming to its side – a shield – as our plates and cutlery and enamel mugs crash to the ground. So now Rabbit and Flynn are behind the table, which, on its side is chest height.

The dog barks again and advances towards them. Flynn has got its attention.

My worry is, I bet it can clear the table in a leap.

'Get ready to run,' Flynn calls over to me. 'You can get help, get Rasputin – I think it's his dog.'

He wants me to escape through the door while the dog focuses on them. The dog is past me, I could take Piper out now to safety, I could get through the empty doorway.

'Yes, go Echo, now!' urges Rabbit softly. Bless them both, they're trying to protect me.

But I think it can clear the table in a leap. And frick, it's just so massive and powerfully-built – they'll be shredded like rag dolls. It barks again savagely, its teeth biting through the air as spittle drips from its jaws.

And it jumps up, front legs over the edge of the table like a killer whale appearing out of the water to claim a seal and its muscular neck thrusts forward to clamp its jaws around Flynn's skull!

– but the merest fraction before it does, it freezes. Like someone's pressed the pause button.

Me.

The dog recoils slightly and closes its jaws. Its teeth are still bared, it's still growling in a rage, but it doesn't savage Flynn.

I walk further into the room, towards the rusty black car they have in here, and the dog pulls back off the table, back onto all fours and moves towards me.

no no no no no no

...I get in my head.

I put my palm up to Flynn to stop, I need to concentrate and I can't do it with a voice in my head. The dog is looking at me and Piper in my arms, just a little chew toy to this huge creature... and then I slowly bend my knees... and sit down on the floor as it comes over to me.

'Oh my god,' says Rabbit faintly.

Frick. This dog probably weighs more than me, and it's all muscle. Apart from the teeth. It's actually kinda beautiful. The wide, strong face, velvety drop ears that are black like its muzzle, then the rest a pale gold.

And I love animals. All animals. There are no photos of me as a baby or toddler 'cos they were all burned up in the house fire – but there is one video. My mum showed it to me. She'd put it online, but my dad took it down, said it would draw attention to my aether. It's of me when I'm about four, at a play farm where they've got all these baby lambs. And there's me and a few other kids in this pen with all these lambs and the usual thing is the kids toddle around chasing the lambs, trying to hug them.

But in the video clip, all the lambs are following *me* around. They're just all over me, nuzzling me and rubbing against me and surrounding me and I'm giggling away and after a few more seconds they knock me over, they're so over-friendly, and I'm so little and laughing so hard I can't get up as the lambs all crowd round me desperate to touch me and be with me.

It was taken about ten years before aether even happened, so go figure why my dad thinks anyone would connect it to animus, he was just being super-cautious I guess. But even at four, I was never, ever frightened of animals at all.

And I am firm with this dog now, as it comes to me to investigate, to eat Piper out of my arms or bite my head off:

you not leader. one of the pack.

And I tell it:

no fighting.

I tell it those things again and again with my mind, with animus.

respect you. respect us. calm. welcome. you are with us. our pack. no danger. no threats.

The dog is looking at me, with its mouth open. It's stopped barking but there's still an agitated gurgle in its throat.

I kneel up, staring back into its black face, blinking slowly and sometimes glancing away.

i am glad you are here. friend. whats your name?

The dog steps forward again and my heart almost stops. Its head is bigger than mine. Its jaws are just a few inches from my face. No plastic surgeon could save me if this sculpture of canine muscle turns on me now.

'Oh heck,' says Rabbit softly. 'Echo, get up, get up…'

I can smell its breath… I can feel its breath…

And then…

koji.

…I hear in my mind. And now, slowly…

…it sits down and lowers its head.

I take one hand off Piper and reach out, past the bone daggers, past those soul-piercing golden eyes, past its black face. And… I stroke it.

'Jeez…' I think I hear Flynn say.

Then there's a noise at the doorway and the dog suddenly turns its massive head, knocking my hand out of the way like a swatted fly and making me jump.

Two men stride in. Hagen and Rasputin. Rasputin is holding what looks like a bright yellow gun.

He whistles: short, sharp and high. The dog gets to its feet. It looks at me with its soulful eyes and everything around me feels trapped in a frozen moment. I feel connected to this force of nature. I can almost hear its heartbeat in my head.

Then a second, more urgent whistle cuts through the air.

And…

…it's over. The dog turns to Hagen and Rasputin and goes over to them. Rasputin puts the yellow pistol away and puts a lead, a really thick chain, on the dog.

'Ok,' says Hagen. 'Your thiriokinesis is improving,' he says to me as Flynn and Rabbit scoot over, squeezing my arm in congratulations.

'What happened?' Rabbit asks Hagen. 'How'd the dog get in? How come it's unattended?'

'You ask a lot of questions,' Hagen replies, his eyebrows touching. 'It is fucking irritating. Focusing on the past, always complaining. Just be glad that the girl can do something useful. A Kangal has the strongest bite of any dog. It can break any bone in your body, no problem. I have seen.'

'A Kangal,' I say, ignoring Hagen's gore talk. 'I've never heard of them.'

'Type of sheep dog,' says Rasputin, gripping the lead firmly.

'A sheep dog?' says Flynn. 'You use that for rounding up sheep?'

'No. Not herding sheep,' spits Rasputin. 'Guarding them.'

'Guarding them from what?' Flynn asks.

'Wolves. Bears,' says Rasputin darkly. 'The Kangal is from ancient Turkey, bred to stand up to the greatest predators.'

Wow. A dog that can take on wolves and bears.

'Yes, it is fascinating,' Hagen says sarcastically, rubbing his smooth throat around his snood. He waves his hand around at the cutlery and enamel mugs and shattered plates all over the floor.

'Tidy this place up,' he says. 'Just because this is a farm does not mean you can make a fucking pigsty. You have ten minutes. Then Jane will come and take you each back to your quarters. Good.'

What he thinks is good I don't know. Maniac. But with that he turns heel and walks out, his usual abrupt exit. I've never once heard him say 'hello' or 'goodbye' come to think of it. Rasputin frowns at me. 'You were lucky today,' he says. Again, WTF that's about I don't know. Douchebag.

Rasputin goes to leave too, but the huge dog is stronger than him, and it holds its ground. It looks back at me for a moment, just staring at me.

i liked meeting you koji

…I say with animus.

Then Koji turns back and follows a cursing Rasputin out into the evening air, and we are alone.

Piper scampers over to the empty doorway and barks at it twice, in a 'And stay out!' kind of way. Like she's warned Koji off.

She turns to look at me, her tongue out, tail wagging.

I roll my eyes. 'Oh really?' I say to her. 'You've scared the big dog off?'

She yaps again.

'She just wants to protect you,' says Flynn. I've never heard him stick up for Piper before.

'I was trying to help too,' he adds, shaking his head, 'but in the end… it was you that protected us.'

'Yeah, you were pretty amazing,' says Rabbit. 'You totally bossed it.' His tone is downbeat though, distracted.

Together, they lift the big farmhouse table back onto its legs with a clatter.

'Maybe knocking it over was a dumb move,' Flynn says. 'You ok?' he says to me.

'Koji,' I say. 'The dog, the Kangal. He wasn't happy.'

'You're telling me,' says Flynn. 'You hear people say "Don't bite my head off", you think it's just an expression, you don't think it might literally happen one day.'

'No, I mean… they made him unhappy,' I say. 'They don't treat him well.'

Rabbit looks unhappy too.

'What's up?' I ask him.

He shakes his head slightly. 'The dog,' he said. 'The Kangal. I'm sure you're right, that it's unhappy – I think maybe they sent it in here deliberately all riled up, to test you. See what you could do. That's why Rasputin had his Taser out, in case it all went south.'

'Bloody hell,' says Flynn. 'No way! That's sick.'

Rabbit, he's taller than Flynn and I, he bends his head a little to us.

'It's not the only suspect thing going on,' he says, his voice almost a whisper. Because of course he can't actually wispr.

Flynn gives Rabbit a questioning look.

'This whole thing,' Rabbit murmurs, his face deadly serious. 'It's bogus.'

Flynn pulls a huh? face.

'I think they're lying to us,' Rabbit says. 'About pretty much everything.'

He lets out a sharp breath, like this is difficult to say.

'I think we're caught up in some really bad shit.'

18: LIES

"How do I explain it to you people? Here's a simple riddle: Deepak is looking at Rachel, but Rachel is looking at Oskar. Deepak is married, Oskar is not. The question is: is a married person looking at an unmarried person? You have three choices: A: Yes, B: No, C: Impossible to know.

"Most people choose option C. They reason that because we don't know Rachel's marital status, the answer cannot be known.

"But the correct answer is A: Yes, a married person is looking at an unmarried person. Because while you don't know whether Rachel is married or not, you do of course know she is either married or unmarried. So:

-If she's unmarried, then married Deepak is looking at unmarried Rachel, so the answer is A: yes.

-If she's married, then married Rachel is looking at unmarried Oskar, so the answer is still A: yes.

"Do you see? It only takes a moment to try both possibilities and realise that either way the outcome is the same. Most people don't bother. The ones that do, the ones with curiosity and determination... they're the ones who will see, eventually, what's really going on in the world. And no offence, but it's not idiots like you."

— From the TS Interviews with Doctor Magellan-Jones

It was like someone had flipped a switch. One that had turned all the lights to red, slanted all the walls, made every sound jarring and painful. The world had become more oppressive than ever.

Flynn barely slept. His body coursed with adrenalin and stress. The drama of snapshotting real people in masks had been bad. The nightmare with the giant dog had been worse. It had been just about to tear out his throat when Echo managed to stop it with her on point animus.

And then… then Rabbit had dropped his bombshell. They were being lied to. One hundred percent. The Farm was not what Hagen claimed it to be. Bloody hell.

But the thing was… if the bastard was lying, if it wasn't the refuge for aethereals he made out, then what the hell was it?

But in the days after the incident with the Kangal, Flynn and Echo and Rabbit barely got chance to talk.

There were snatched wisprs between him and Echo.

A few hurried words from Rabbit. (But only when they passed the diesel generators, the noise shielding their treason.)

Maybe two minutes outside. (But only when Hagen left after a session and if Rasputin was distracted.)

The best time would have been in the evenings, in Flint barn. Sometimes he and Echo and Rabbit got an hour alone together while they ate. But they couldn't talk then either, because Rabbit thought the barn might be bugged.

So instead they spent meal times making awkward, fake small-talk, while their eyes darted around wondering where a bug might be hidden.

It turned out, the reason Rabbit thought something was going on was that he could do scry. Just as Flynn had originally assumed. Rabbit had kept his aspect from Hagen because he was scared what Hagen would do if he knew that Rabbit could tell real from fake.

'Actually, Hagen's the hardest to read,' Rabbit had told them. 'So I've been asking Jane and Rasputin different things at different times, in moments when they're not with Hagen.'

One theory was – since Hagen and the others had a military air about them – maybe the government was training up its own 'aethereal army' for covert operations around the world. Maybe Hagen worked for the government and it was his job to get them into shape. It would explain the relentless aether sessions and the way that although Hagen shouted at them and treated them like shit, they still got fed properly – even accommodating Echo's veganism – and got enough sleep and even let Flynn exercise.

And, if it was all government, it would explain where Hagen and the others had got their Tasers. Maybe.

One thing was for sure – they never let up with the training. The early October weather was getting colder, with mist starting to roll in off the moors some evenings. So Jane had got them fleeces so they could keep practicing outside or in the freezing farm buildings, always being cajoled and criticized to do better.

Hagen continued to say it was for their benefit, it would stop them getting migraines – and since Flynn had been at The Farm, not one of them had had a migraine, so maybe. But the nonstop training... it felt like they were gladiators being trained for the arena.

There were other things too – the warren of camo net screens they had to run through, at times strictly prescribed by Hagen's fancy watch. They were being shielded and separated from anyone else who might be on The Farm. Flynn occasionally saw glimpses of people but generally the security was pretty insane, even in the circumstances.

And then there was the anthrax. Or was there?

'I don't think there's any anthrax,' Echo had whispered yesterday.

'Me neither,' Rabbit had agreed.

Yet the quarantine tape was still up. Faded from the sun and flapping in the wind as the weather worsened and winter began to creep over the moorland with the mist. And Hagen continued to tell Echo no, she couldn't see Noolie, she was still being kept apart because she might have been exposed to anthrax.

'So why don't we just bounce?' Flynn had suggested a few hours ago. They'd been practicing PK deflection – kind of the knife-throwing exercise in reverse. They'd stood outside in the cold drizzle, behind bullet-proof Perspex screens like riot police used.

Rasputin would stand twenty feet back and throw stones at them, hard as he could. The task was to deflect the stones away with their PK before they got hit (or rather, the Perspex screen in front of them). It was pretty unnerving and Echo had made Piper stay inside out of harm's way. Flynn had made his suggestion about leaving during a brief break while Rasputin picked up more stones to hurl.

'Yes, great idea,' Echo had replied with a hint of sarcasm. 'Let's just go wait by the bus stop.'

'She's got a point. Where would we go?' Rabbit had said. 'We're in the middle of nowhere, we've got no transport, no GPS, no supplies. And it's getting pretty cold at night now.'

'We'd be ok,' Flynn had replied. 'I'm sure we'd get by until we found a village or something.'

'Well, sure Bear Grylls,' Echo had said, 'but what if they catch us while we're stumbling around the moors in the dark? Besides, the news... where would we go?'

She was frightened, Flynn could tell. The 'witch burning' news report had really shaken her up and he didn't blame her. It had been pretty sickening.

'Ok, so what's the plan?' Flynn had asked.

Rabbit shrugged. 'Dude, I think we need to find out what's going on. If there's no anthrax, then maybe the tape is just to keep us from finding out what's on the other side.'

'So we need to cross the tape,' murmured Echo.

'But if the anthrax is real... we die a slow, painful death,' Flynn pointed out.

'Stuck here, I feel like I am dying a slow painful death,' Echo had replied.

'Well ok then, I'll do it,' Rabbit had said.

'No, you can't!' Echo had exclaimed. 'Your... your leg, your limp. It would slow you down. Besides, what if Koji sees you?'

'Who's Koji?' Flynn had asked, confused.

'The dog, the Kangal, I told you,' she'd replied. 'It will start barking – or worse – and give you away. I'll go.'

'What?' Flynn had said, appalled. 'No way! No, you can't go!' he'd said to her.

'Why not?' Echo had replied.

'Because... well, because...' he had stumbled.

'Cos I'm a girl?' she'd replied, hands on hips.

'No! No, not that, it's just – I'll go, I can say I was out for a run, Hagen will believe that. He already thinks I'm an idiot.'

'I'll go,' Echo had reiterated. 'I'm the only one who can calm Koji, and he's bound to be guarding the farmhouse.'

And so it had been settled. So now Flynn felt more tense than ever.

He wanted to find out what was going on, they all did. But he hadn't wanted Echo to go. Not because she was a girl, but because... well he couldn't say, put on the spot like that, but, well...

...he supposed the real reason he didn't want her going, risking herself and putting herself in danger was because...

...because he thought maybe he just might possibly be falling for her.

19: LOBOTOMY

Oh frick.

The thought of sneaking out in the dark to creep around The Farm gives me the heebie jeebies. All by myself, out there past curfew, risking being caught by Hagen? Christ.

But I've got to do something, I've got to try and find out what's really going on. Like with the anthrax tape – in theory Noolie is here somewhere, but they haven't let me see her, not once. As Jazz would say – and OMFG I miss her so much – this shit is not legit.

And it finally stopped raining today. Which means tonight is the night. Frick!

It's October the fourteenth and it feels like winter is here already. In the unheated, not-at-all insulated shepherd's hut I wake up cold, my fingers and feet numb despite sleeping in my socks, with the blankets mummified around me and Piper on me like a beautiful, furry, hot water bottle.

We've got these Primarni fleeces that Jane brought us and some acrylic jumpers (bad for the environment) but mainly we're just recycling the few clothes we brought with us, washing them in our showers, but now the weather's so cold you can't dry them outside or inside really either.

Today my outfit has consisted of an ASOS vest top, then the floral shift dress I wore on the first night I arrived here, a flannel Superdry shirt over that, a pair of black leggings with a pair of black ripped skinny jeans over the top (and I'm not loving the rips in this weather BTW) plus the black fleece from Jane.

Basically I look like I fell into one of those clothes recycling bins for charity you see in supermarket car parks. But hey, it just about stops me from freezing to death. Anyway, three things happened today:

1.	In the morning we tried to do pre-cog with this nasty routine Hagen had devised. We had to guess / predict whether – while standing on empty milk urns – Hagen (on our left) was going to push us off with a broom or Rasputin (on our right) was going to push us off with a broom. None of us could do it (I'm pretty sure pre-cog doesn't work that way anyway?) but that's why I've got bruises all over, from being pushed off a milk urn with a broom over and over, falling into piles of old straw bales.

2.	In the afternoon we did snapshot again, but this time only with the headsets, no 'dummies'. We just aimed at an apple (which didn't seem bothered). But the thing is, towards the end when I was trying really hard I got *another* nosebleed. That's twice now after doing aether here, the first time was with the rats. I don't think this place is very good for me.

3.	And then, before dinner… there was another news report. It's just… so gross. Inhuman. The first 'aether terrorist' in the UK has been convicted. Because he's considered so dangerous and impossible to imprison safely, he is going to be given a lobotomy. A. Lobotomy. I mean it, that's what they said. They will literally lobotomise you – carve a chunk out of your brain so you can't do aether any more, or basically do anything anymore. OMFG. Like, what the actual frick is happening?

So yeah, there was that. And all day, I've made out I wasn't feeling too good. That's an important part of the plan. Maybe the nosebleed helps. Go me.

Jane's just left, after bringing us dinner in Flint barn (lentil dahl, flatbread, actually quite nice) which means we have about an hour, ninety minutes tops, to ourselves. Flynn and Rabbit and I have been playing with Piper, she's like the fourth member of our crew and she totally loves the attention. And all the time I've been connected with her, sending out vibes with my animus that **i am leaving but then back, only gone for a little while, you will stay here and guard these two while I am gone and then I will be back and everything will be good and happy.**

So now I've got her sat on the old sofa, looking totally amaze-balls with her beautiful white fur really popping against the shabby emerald velvet, her happy pink tongue out and paws perfectly placed over the end of the seat like she's posing for a home interiors magazine.

And so this is it. OMG. Deep breath.

'I'm still feeling a bit ill,' I say to Flynn and Rabbit. 'I didn't sleep well last night, and what with the nosebleed earlier… I'm just going to put my feet up on the sofa for a bit and close my eyes, ok?'

This is to cover for why I'm not going to be speaking for the next hour or so, for Hagen's benefit in case he really is listening in.

'Ok Echo,' says Rabbit, 'you do look a little under the weather.'

'Yeah, I'm not being rude but… to be honest you've looked ropey all day,' adds Flynn, winking at me. I narrow my eyes at him. Really not the time for bants, Flynn.

good luck youll do great

…he wisprs to me. Rabbit gives me a thumbs up. I smile back, remind Piper to stay and I open the door super quietly, then step out into the frozen ink of night.

Ouch, it is *really* cold out here.

Oh, I can see the moon. A clear night. And there's a mist, seeping malevolently across the fields. Darkness, moonlight, mist – this is something from a horror film.

Get a grip I tell myself. I start down the long slope to the outbuilding that's surrounded by the quarantine ribbon.

I'm walking slowly, but my heart is sprinting. I keep looking, left, right, for someone patrolling around, praying I won't be spotted. As I walk, I start to bend my knees and back, getting lower to the ground, trying to create a smaller profile against the moonlit sky.

This is already horrendous. My legs are shaky AF and I've only gone twenty metres!

I step, tiptoe, step, placing each foot gingerly as if I'm walking through a minefield. A tree: I stand up against it, using its cover to get a better look around. Is that someone? I'm not sure. They're not moving. No… I don't think so.

I make it to the low stone wall that runs the length of a field to my left. I'm flattening myself against it as much as I can to shield my outline. Plus it's a bit of shelter against the wind which is sooo cold on my legs and hands and face.

There it is. One of the out-of-bounds. Single-storey, pitched roof, white stone walls. Small windows on two sides, modern wooden door fitted with a brushed steel handle. It has a small patch of grass next to this wide pathway I'm walking down. And the outbuilding and grass are all cordoned off by the anthrax tape.

Ok, you got this. I try and calm my breathing. Uh – what was that? A noise, just over there. From the car shed where they keep the Land Rovers. Its doors are wide open and there's a light on. Frick. If I get caught now I'm pretty much screwed.

I wait for the right moment to dart across the open path to the outbuilding then do my best attempt at a 'silent run', avoiding any crunching stone chippings.

I make it! Hashtag winning. But am I sure? Like, am I really, *really* sure there's no anthrax? Ok, ok c'mon Echo, you got this. Sooo... I hold my breath...

...and step over the rippling tape that marks off a quarantine zone.

I'm still holding my breath. Waiting to dissolve from the feet up as the anthrax starts eating my flesh.

Ok, nothing yet. Breathe. I'm sure there's no anthrax. Besides, standing still just lets the cold seep into me further. My legs already feel like two Calippos.

I step forward up to the door and put my ear against it. I am totally owning this spy stuff.

Nothing, not a sound. I reach out and grip the door handle. Wow, that's a whole new level of cold. Locked. I sidestep over to the window. There's something black up against it, paper or card or fabric. I can't see anything at all. It doesn't have any kind of latch.

Over to the next window. The same.

Great. I mean just phenom. I've failed before I've even started. Then another noise! From the car shed again, I think; a clank. Something being dropped or moved or hit, I don't know. I can't hear any voices, it's spookily quiet in this part of The Farm actually.

What am I going to do? I can't go back, not with nothing. I mean, what an anticlimax that would be. I agreed with Flynn that he wouldn't wispr to me in case it distracted me at a bad moment. But I could wispr to him though? Or… could I get the key from somewhere? It would be… well, it would be in the main farmhouse, wouldn't it? Somewhere? Where Hagen will be.

My heart is in my throat, choking me. I don't know… can I sneak in without them seeing me? I mean, if Hagen catches me, his rage will be off the charts.

I hug myself to try and calm my rattling heart and rub some warmth into my limbs. Then I step back over the ribbon, and start back up the track, ready to turn left, down the main path, past the car shed. Frick! Someone's coming!

I duck down low to the ground and shuffle sideways to get against

the stone wall. My boots crunch against some stones in my rush. They must have seen me, mustn't they?

I wait, not daring to move. There's no sound. Are they watching me? I wait a few more seconds, then lift my head slowly. There! A dark shape moving against the sky. It's definitely a person.

They're not coming towards me. They've turned right, down the main path where I was going to go. I stay squat down, shivering, watching them melt into the mist, then disappear completely when they move behind one of the camo screens that pepper The Farm. OMG I am so cold from just waiting here, I've got to keep moving. Here goes.

I tiptoe along like a pantomime villain creeping up behind someone. When I get to the car shed I duck down in front of the Land Rover that's parked, then sprint past. I don't even dare look sideways as I go past, as if looking at them will make them look at me.

And then because I'm not looking where I'm going and it's dark and misty I run into something solid and waist high and go flying head over heels. It's Koji!

I am lying sprawled on the ground, I've grazed my palms and widened the rip in my jeans at the knee. I look up and Koji comes towards me. I hear his chain chinking on the ground as he pads over. Oh jeez.

Calm, calm, I must radiate calm. I pour out emoticons of peace, but then there's movement on the path and several voices talking. I'm trapped!

I look about, I'm desperate, I'm going to get caught, what will I say, oh crap – wait –

There's an overturned, rusted metal pig trough. I try to send out soothing waves at Koji as I scoot over to the trough. The voices are bearing down on me, coming from round the corner of one of the other dilapidated farm buildings.

I grab the rough edge of the trough, it is freezing, like my hands might stick. I haul it up, expecting it to scrape across the stones but it's ok. I have only a second to spare and I scooch under, sliding my body onto the freezing hard ground, dropping the trough back over me.

OMG this is grim, it's sooo gross under here. I feel sick, for real. Maybe it's the anthrax, ha. My heartbeat is bouncing around this metal coffin.

I hear the voices. Two. Three? All male. One is Rasputin, I'm sure of it. Oh god I'm screwed. I can catch odd words. There is a harsh laugh. A jangling noise... what's going on? I'm going to be bonded to this concrete floor in a minute. Like when something gets left in the bottom of a freezer drawer too long.

Then – some movement, shuffling boots, a few more words, I don't know, I can't tell if it's even English, a slam and... silence.

Are they waiting for me, pretending to have gone?

Do you know what, I don't even care, I'm so cold. I've got to get up or I will die for sure. I have to bring my knees in and use my back to push the trough up enough to get a chink of gloom and squeeze my fingers under. The trough does scrape this time, but clumsily I manage to wriggle my way out.

I am filthy and freezing. But there's no-one standing there – apart from Koji staring at me with those golden eyes. I have just barrelled into him, my knees smacking against his ribs, but he's not baring his teeth or growling or anything. He remembers me, I can tell that much.

calm calm. friend. everything is ok. you are good. good quiet. stay. sit. quiet. good.

Squatting down, I shuffle over and stroke him. He is so big and powerful, he's just incredible. But there is a chain on him, he's chained to a metal bootscraper cemented into the ground by the door. Chained up outside like this, it's not right. He likes being stroked I can tell, he doesn't normally get much affection. He is not happy here. He is obedient. But he does not like these people.

Yeah, I'm with you on that Koji. Me neither.

I give him a last rub between the ears and emote see you soon would be good to him and stride over to the door. I must be quick. This is a newer, single-storey extension built onto the backside of the farmhouse, and the small rectangle of opaque glass in the door is black, suggesting there's no-one on the other side. I turn the handle.

It's locked, obvs.

I mean, what is up with these people? They lock every door, every time? They have some serious trust issues. I look about. There's no other way in. Unless..?

Quickly, I step up onto the pig trough. Forcing my frozen fingers – which feel like they're shot with arthritis – to clamp around a wooden strut that goes up the side of a wall, I haul myself up.

I wish I had Rabbit or Flynn with me. Not that Rabbit could actually get up here, with his bad leg. But he gave me this great tip about moving around in the dark.

He said if you're moving from dark to light, when you go into the lit room, keep one eye closed. That way, when you go back into the darkness, you've still got night vision in the eye you kept closed. It could be a useful advantage, he said. Course I haven't bothered to do it, but still, pretty clever.

Anyway. I can see the spread of buildings, all shapes and sizes, and the scatter of shepherd's huts as well as the maze of screens with camouflage netting. Maybe Noolie is in one of those huts. I can also see the fields and the lines of quarantine ribbon marking off the no-go areas, I can see the floodlights, I can see Flint Barn, I can make out a circular stone building peering out from a copse of trees. Beyond I can see the moorland, dark and secretive, the low-lying areas hiding in pools of fog.

Then... closer to the farmhouse I can see shapes, moving about.

The tiles are covered in damp moss. It might only be ten feet up but I'd break something if I fell off. But I creep as fast as I dare over to what I'd seen from the ground – a skylight. Not a modern, double-glazed, triple-locked one, but some rotting sash-window thing set into the roof.

I push... and it does kinda wobble in its frame. But it doesn't slide up. Of course not. FML. Won't just *something* go my way?

There's a broken bit of roof tile, a triangle shape. I grab it and run it up the gap between the window and the window frame, trying to loosen it, prise out the moss and twigs and whatever crap has built up, while wobbling the window with my other hand. I work like this for a few minutes, breathing life into the idea of this being a functioning window.

And then at last the window gives a little and I'm able to force it up with a shudder. I look through; there's no light on but the drop doesn't look too bad and there's nothing but the floor to land on. So I twist onto my belly, poke both legs through and, gripping onto the sides, drop down.

See, this bit Flynn couldn't do – his shoulders are too broad to fit through!

I dangle… then let go. It's about a four foot drop I guess and I land badly, but I'm ok. Jeez, I'm breaking in!

I'm in… I don't know, an office? A short corridor – literally about three feet – leads to a bigger room with a couple of doors going off it. This room has cardboard boxes, metal cabinets and a desk against one wall. That's promising. There's a computer on it. Without internet, I guess.

It's too risky to put the light on so I have to peer up close at everything in the gloom. Checkerboard lino floor. Wall-mounted shelves with all sorts of random things – packets, old tools for god knows what, a camcorder, tins, a couple of books. The locked door – it's just on a Yale lock, so although I couldn't get in, I can get out. I grab the chair at the desk and move it to under the skylight. No, not high enough. Ugh – I've got filth and slime on it from my boots. A pile of books is on a stool – like an old milking stool, maybe. I put the books on the floor, put the stool on top of the chair. My mother would not approve. But I stand on top, wobbling precariously as I heave the skylight shut. That stops the freezing draft and hides my actions.

I drop down and put the stool back with the books on top to cover the footprints, and I wipe the chair seat roughly with my arm. And then I notice there's a metal key box on the wall – at last!

Oh, frick. I can't believe it.

It's not just a key box, it's a lockable key box. Keys protected by a key, jeez. I bet banks aren't this hard to break into. Voices! I slide down under the desk and pull the chair in front to hide me.

No, after a few minutes they fade away, I'm ok. But as I got under I saw a small key sticking out of one of the desk drawers. I get it open: nothing very interesting. No other keys, no clues. Just a pile of papers. I guess with no internet they have to print stuff out if they want to share things. I pull some out, I've got to find something of use, something to tell us what's going on.

Here's a sheet that looks like… well, something businessy. Like a balance sheet or a stock take.

My eyes are adjusting to the gloom and I can make out seven labelled columns. The first six are PK, PS, PC, Te, Th and W. I know what they are straight away – the six aether aspects. PK is Psychokinesis, PS is Psynaptic Shock (snapshot), then there's Pre-Cognition, Telesthesia (scry), Thiriokinesis (Animus) and Wispr.

Down the side there are eight rows, each with a pair of initials. Names? Not me, Flynn or Rabbit though – maybe another group? There's a number for each, so the first row, CP, has PK2 PS1 PC? Te2 Th4 W5. It's a ranking or a score I guess. And… WTF?!? The seventh, final column has –

– voices again, much closer!

I panic, shoving the papers back in the drawer, scrunching them, pushing the drawer shut and sliding under the desk. I pull the chair to – just as the door opens and people come in.

It's… a man and a woman, talking in serious, urgent tones. I recognize one voice straight away: Hagen. Oh god. I can see his thick-soled boots and the legs of his olive combat trousers. The other, the woman, she sounds familiar too, though I can't place where from. It's not Jane. Someone younger, wearing a skirt, with shapely calves. And a voice I've heard... where? From back home? No, I don't think so. It's weird.

I can't even concentrate on what they're saying, I'm trying not to breathe, trying not to move a muscle even though this is uncomfortable and hard and cold. I'm terrified. Something sketchy is going on here, those papers... and if Hagen caught me now, oh god. What if they smell me, covered in god knows what from lying under that pig trough? Plus of course there's –

– oh frick! I've got it! I've worked it out! I almost cry out when I realise, I have to put my hand over my mouth.

That voice. It's not as clipped and proper as the other times I've heard her speak. But I definitely recognise it.

I've heard it before at The Farm. On TV. In a TV studio that neither I nor Flynn nor Rabbit had seen before we came here. But it's her alright: the voice of doom, always delivering bad news.

She's the newsreader.

OMFG.

As my BFF might say, shit just got real. Especially on top of what I've just seen on that piece of paper.

The final column, past the six aether aspects had a pound symbol. And underneath, next to each person, an amount, as if each aethereal had a price, based on their aether scores.

A valuation.

20: GENIE

"Are you even listening to me? You can't put the genie back in the bottle. And from the earliest days it was obvious that with aether, the genie was well and truly out.

"I know what people will say, I can hear their sanctimonious voices already: the role of a scientist is to observe, study, understand – but not to interfere. And yes, when a naturalist is taking footage of a baby elephant that's become separated from the herd and is dehydrated and dying, they don't put down the camera and give the calf a bucket of water. They film it wandering around helplessly, calling for its mother, succumbing to thirst and sunstroke until it topples over and dies.

"But aether is not a baby elephant in the savannah. It is a bull in a china shop. And aethereal abilities are too dangerous to simply document the chaos.

"That's why A9 was set up. An unprecedented alliance of five governments – the UK, the US, Germany, France and The Netherlands – creating the A9 taskforce to mediate the development of aether. To harness its potential for just purposes. And yes of course, to identify ways to neutralise aethereal abilities, should the need arise. You might call it interference. I would call it imperative."

– From the TS Interviews with Doctor Magellan-Jones

Four minutes since he'd last checked his G-Shock. Thirty-three in total.

Thirty-three minutes since Echo had slipped out the door, into the night.

'Echo's quiet,' said Rabbit as they sat at the farmhouse table, having finished their dinner. 'I think she's fallen asleep.' They were making out she was with them in Flint Barn, resting because she wasn't feeling well. Just in case there was a listening bug hiding somewhere.

'Yeah, I hope she's ok,' Flynn replied.

Rabbit smiled. 'Dude, she'll be fine,' he said. 'She's tougher than she seems. Like a willow tree. They bend but don't break.'

Flynn smiled back. 'Yeah, for sure. You're right.'

'Game of cards?' said Rabbit, producing a pack.

Flynn shook his head. He wouldn't be able to concentrate.

'No, it's tempting to mysteriously lose to you for the ninety-ninth time in row, but not tonight.'

'Fair enough,' said Rabbit, slipping them back into his chinos.

'When did you know?' Flynn asked him now, sitting forward at the table. 'You know… that you could do things? And that it might be good for magic?'

Rabbit sat up a little and slid his chair back, the legs scraping on the wooden floor and making Piper perk up for a second on the green sofa where she'd been slumped, waiting for Echo's return.

'Good question,' said Rabbit. 'I'd been all over magic for years. Some of it's so simple, that's how people are fooled, they overthink it. Other times a magician needs amazing physical dexterity, and you're fooled because you never realise they could do something so difficult. But often it's just clever misdirection – psychology really – and I loved that too. And always there are people with amazed faces, lit up with the wonder of it. I grew up in this small seaside town, and there were always street entertainers, tourists being blown away at the things they did. I got so jacked, seeing the reactions they got.'

Flynn nodded.

'Anyway, I was seventeen when I first realised I could do something unusual.' Rabbit got up and walked over to the pigeonholes, his limp barely noticeable. He picked something up and brought it back to the table. It was a ten pence piece he must have seen there before.

'I was at the arcade,' he continued. 'Like I said, I grew up in one of those touristy seaside towns with a pier, fish and chips and arcades – video games, fruit machines, ghost train, dodgems. And those coin pusher games, you know, where all the coins are piled up overhanging the edge, looking like they're about to fall?'

'Yeah, I know,' Flynn replied.

'I was there with a few mates. We'd got pretty good at going round and knowing which games were ready to pay out. You hang around an arcade long enough, you get to know its moods. I had a pile of ten pees,' he said, spinning the one he'd just picked up on the table with a flick, 'and I found a coin pusher ready to drop a load. So I feed it with a pounds' worth of ten pees, dropping them at the right time to nudge up and push over my winnings.

'Except, it didn't work. They piled up but nothing went over the edge. I was so sure they should have tipped over, it really got on my wick. And I was just looking at the coins through the clear plastic top, staring at them and willing them to tumble over the edge because that's what they should have done... and suddenly they did. They jolted over in a big crashing wave of coins, paying out ten times what it would ever normally do.'

'PK,' said Flynn. It reminded him of his less successful attempt to get migraine drugs, back at Boots all those weeks ago. He checked his watch again. Forty-two minutes.

'Yep,' said Rabbit. 'All my mates congratulated me, they were like woah, 'cos they'd never seen anything like it before, said the machine must have developed a fault. I didn't say anything. I was too confused I guess.'

He started making the coin dance across the back of his fingers while he spoke, just his fingers rising and falling like his was playing piano, making the coin tumble across his hand, then under and round and across again, over and over.

'A couple of days later it gave me the idea: maybe I could do tricks differently. You go on YouTube, you'll see every trick any magician has ever done get explained. Spoiler after spoiler. But I thought, what if I do classic tricks in a way people can't explain?'

'Like what?' Flynn asked.

'Well... like a famous illusion that magicians do is the "coin passing through a glass table" trick,' Rabbit said. He put the ten pee on the farmhouse table. 'The magician puts a coin in the middle of a glass table, and asks an audience member to cup her hand under the table, underneath where the coin is. The magician then puts his own hand over the coin, concentrates for a moment… and wow! The woman feels the coin fall into her hand. The magician lifts his hand away and sure enough, the coin isn't on the table anymore, it's travelled through the glass and is in the woman's hand.'

'Oh yes, I think I've seen it on TV,' said Flynn. 'Pretty cool. How's it done?'

'Well, I shouldn't really say,' said Rabbit grinning, 'magic circle rules and all.'

Flynn raised his eyebrows.

'Ok dude, look, just between us,' said Rabbit, 'you have two identical-looking coins, both magnetic, and a gold ring that's also magnetic. You can get it all on eBay.

'It's pretty simple – the magician rests their hand with the gold ring at the edge of the glass table. On the underside of the table, held in place by the magnetic gold ring, is one of the magnetic coins, hidden from sight. In the middle of the table, on top, is the magnetic coin we can see, with the audience member's hand underneath the table, under where the visible coin is.

'When the magician slides their hand across the table, the coin that's underneath slides along too, pulled by the magnetic ring, hidden by their hand. That's why the punter has to cup her hand, so there's a gap between her hand and the table, so when the magician moves his hand over the top of her hand, the hidden coin slides between that gap.

'As the magician moves their hand with the magnetic ring over the coin that's on top, that coin sticks to the ring. It blocks the magnetism that was holding the hidden coin under the table in place. So now that hidden coin falls into the woman's hand. And when the magician lifts his hand, the coin on the table stays stuck to the ring, so you don't see it. You see a coin in the audience member's hand under the table and it looks like the coin on top has travelled through the glass.'

'Got it,' said Flynn, nodding. He checked his watch again. Forty-nine minutes. Echo would have to be back in the next ten minutes or so, or Jane might turn up and realise she wasn't there.

'Yeah, but it's just magnets ultimately,' said Rabbit. 'And if you see a magician wearing a ring on his middle finger, you know why. So that's where I'd come in, doing it with a twist. I'd do a trick like that, exactly the same, except I wouldn't need the ring – I'd just hold the coin in place with PK.'

'Way more clever,' said Flynn.

'Thanks,' said Rabbit, picking the ten pee back up. He let it lie in his open palm for Flynn to see.

'And now, people watching videos of me doing the trick in slo-mo, analysing every move… they couldn't work it out. Magic.'

He closed his hand around the coin and turned his hand over.

'I have to say, seeing you and Echo doing wispr, that would be awesome for magic. All the tricks where you're blindfolded or have your back turned – I could have an assistant who could see what was going on, like what card someone picked, and wispr the answer to me. Shame I can't wispr. Although… I guess none of that matters now anyway. With all the news about aether, everyone will have worked it out by now and the only subscribers I'll have left will be the trolls.'

He opened his hand to let the coin fall to the table, but it didn't drop. He turned his hand back over to reveal an empty palm – the coin had gone.

He gave Flynn a small smile. Flynn hadn't thought about it before – for Rabbit, aether was more than just a curiosity, it was basically his profession.

'It'll work out,' said Flynn, now trying to reassure Rabbit. 'In the end. Things can't be this crazy forever.'

Rabbit brushed his fringe to the side.

'Maybe,' he said. 'I hope you're right. But in a country where they've just started lobotomizing aether criminals, there's probably a long –'

Piper barked suddenly and jumped off the sofa, running to the door.

It opened… but it wasn't Echo – it was Rasputin and Jane. Jane looked tired and agitated, wearing a holey blue jumper, lots of wiry grey hair escaping the band she had it tied back with, and her lined face looking even more weathered than usual. She smelled of smoke.

Rasputin wore a snide look. 'So, Echo is not with you?' he said.

'She wasn't feeling very well so she went to bed,' said Flynn instantly.

'Yeah, she had a nosebleed earlier, remember? I know she's supposed to wait for you Jane, but she just felt terrible,' added Rabbit.

'Yes, that makes sense,' said Rasputin, 'because I have just found her collapsed outside.'

'What?' exclaimed Flynn, pushing his chair back. He felt angry that Rasputin was telling him this news, and so calmly too.

'Yes. Perhaps she fainted, after her nosebleed. Blood loss,' said Rasputin. 'Or it could be she just slipped, from creeping around in the dark, which do you think? What we know for sure is, she has hit her head against a wall. A cut and concussion – we have taken her to the hospital room.'

'What? I want to see her!' said Flynn, jumping to his feet and making Piper bark again at Rasputin. Jane went to stroke Piper but thought better of it as the small dog growled at her.

'No, not tonight, said Rasputin. 'She has a concussion, are you listening?'

'She wasn't making much sense, dearie,' said Jane, shaking her head at Flynn. 'You know, bit delirious. From the bump.' She stared down at Piper like she wanted to kick her.

'You must wait a couple of days,' said Rasputin. He adjusted his belt which had the ever-present Taser hanging from it. 'Then we'll see. Ok, time to go. I'll take you,' he said to Flynn, 'Jane will take you,' he indicated to Rabbit.

'Great, back to the shepherd's hut with a scratch like a shepherd's crook on the door,' said Rabbit, shaking his head wearily.

'What about Piper?' Flynn said.

Rasputin looked blank.

'Echo's dog, Piper,' he said. How many times?

Rasputin shrugged, looking indifferently at Echo's Westie. 'It's not hygienic to have a dog in the hospital room,' he said. 'You take it if you want. Or I can give it to my dog to play with.'

Bloody hell. Flynn went over and scooped Piper up. She knew him well enough after all these weeks, she'd go with him for now – at least until she realised Echo wasn't there.

He looked at Rabbit. 'Echo's fallen,' he said flatly.

Rabbit looked back at him as Jane stepped between them, reeking of fags, and he made a tiny, subtle gesture, tilting his head and screwing up his mouth slightly.

A tiny gesture which said they're lying.

Flynn felt a fire ignite inside him and his eyes flashed back at Rabbit. He wanted to push Rasputin aside and go find Echo, go see where she really was.

'Yes,' said Rabbit. 'Sounds like she's hurt herself. We just need to wait a short while for her to get better, I guess.'

A short while. Yes. Flynn understood. Rabbit knew they were lying because he had scry… but they didn't know he had scry. So Flynn and Rabbit could play dumb for a moment and then regroup. Flynn knew exactly where to find him.

Flynn looked around the barn, at the rusting vintage car they sometimes all sat in, pretending they could drive off into the sunset, the table they'd laughed and joked at, the stacked boxes of chemicals and the pigeonholes of farmyard knick knacks and dusty glass jars and musty paperbacks.

And as Rasputin led him away, Piper nestled in his arms, something occurred to him. Echo and Rabbit and him had been acting as if there might be a bug, listening in. But what if there wasn't.

What if there was a camera?

21: INTERROGATION

It's filthy, under this desk. My mum would freak, being where I am right now – she's a total OCD germophobe. She's always telling me gross stuff, like 'one in five office coffee cups have faecal matter on them'. Or 'free nuts in bars have an average of four different men's urine on them'. The one that really shocked me was that in a hotel room the most germ-ridden thing is the TV remote. Way more than anything else, because unlike stuff in the bathroom, it never gets cleaned.

I wish I could see her right now. Oh god, I'm missing my mum, things must be bad. What have I done? What happened, that I ended up bent under a dusty desk, holding my breath, terrified of giving myself away?

'Well something should be done,' says the female voice – the newsreader. 'Staying in this dump day after day, it's unbearable.' She's angry, but there's a wobble in her voice I've not heard before. Scared, I think.

I can see Hagen's right foot tapping up and down, and his right hand, the burned / scarred one, clenching.

'I have something urgent to deal with,' he says, 'so I am even less interested in your fucking whining than usual. Totter off to your quarters and give my ears a break from your mindless screeching.'

He flicks his hand out to wave her away. Her stilettoed feet move round.

'But… oh, this place, you people. How did I ever get involved?'

'I would hope you can remember,' says Hagen. 'Or am I fucking wrong, do you need a reminder?' There is a tiny pause.

'You're sick, all of you! Sick monsters!' There's an angry drumbeat of kitten heels on lino as she storms off down through the hallway. I see her shoes and calves, then a midnight blue skirt with large white flowers, then a red cardigan or sweater and blonde hair held up by a large hair clip. My heart is thumping and my muscles, all twisted and squashed, are groaning.

'Fucking actresses,' says Hagen to no-one in particular. 'She is a stupid fucking bitch. And what about you?

'Are you a stupid fucking bitch too, Echo?'

Oh, shit.

I don't move, I'm frozen. Then he squats down and I realise he's not bluffing. Did he see my muddy prints on the floor?

'Come out. Now,' he commands, looking straight at me with his Scandinavian movie-star face.

I feel paralysed, I really have to will my muscles to move. I'm shaky AF as I crawl out from under the desk and get achingly to my feet.

'I was just... I was seeing if there was a computer anywhere I could borrow,' I say, flushing at the lie.

Hagen makes a dismissive tut. 'It does not matter,' he says. 'Why you are here, what you were trying to do. What we should discuss is what happens next.'

'Ok,' I say, standing straight, looking up at him and trying to sound way more together than I feel. 'And what's that?'

The door opens – it's Rasputin, holding a metal tin like a pencil case, which he hands to Hagen with a nod before giving me his full-on unhinged death stare.

'You are not ready,' says Hagen, opening the tin, fiddling with the contents from behind its lid. 'To leave here. Soon you will go, yes. And then you will look back at your time here with tearful eyes and realise how lucky you were. How nice it was here.'

'What – what do you mean?' I say, backing into a corner as Rasputin's menacing face looms in at me. Even his buzz cut looks angry. 'The woman, the newsreader – it was all fake news, wasn't it? You've been lying to us!'

And then Rasputin just grabs me, his fingers squeezing down hard on each of my arms. He twists me so he's got his right arm around my neck and mine are locked behind me in the crook of his left arm.

And then – ugh – WTF? I've been jabbed! Hagen – he's injecting me with a syringe from the little tin. Oh frick, oh god this is bad, this is so bad –

'What are you doing?' I yell, struggling in Rasputin's pincer grip. 'Get off me, you bastard!'

'Yes, struggle,' says Hagen. 'It make the blood pump, helps things take effect more quickly. You are going to cooperate, and I will tell you why. But until you understand what the fuck is what, this is necessary.'

I'm almost in tears, Rasputin is being so rough; I can feel his strong, unyielding frame pressed against me and I have been injected with god-knows-what and no-one knows I am here and I just want to go back home and see Jazz and my family and forget all this and oh god –

'Ok, take her to noncom,' says Hagen. And then, I think, I faint.

Uh. Ugh.

I can't think, my brain is shorting.

Fzz. Pfss. Fffz.

It's just a blurry picture, darkness, then another out-of-focus picture.

Again and again.

Rasputin is dragging me; a sack of potatoes.

Into one of the Land Rovers?

Faces staring at me.

Driving… where?

Along, around. Up.

Black.

Just blurry pictures.

Trees.

Cold, outside again.

Half-dragged, half-carried by Rasputin, Hagen in front. Oh god, what are they going to do to me?

Someone, please!

Help. Help me.

I don't understand.

My head is throbbing.

Pulsing, pushing, swelling.

Like a hangover.

Or...

...no...

...like a...

migraine.

I think this is the roundhouse, curved walls. The one I saw from the roof. It is cold. Help me, someone, please *please*. I'm – oh frick, what is this? They're strapping me down to a metal hospital bed, oh god, I'm struggling, but Rasputin is too strong, too vicious, he's strapped me to this bed and my head is pounding. Then something like a belt goes over my forehead and my head is strapped to the bed too!

'Ah, how delicious, how simply delicious,' says a wet, menacing voice.

'Mmm, let's have a look. Now, this is going to hurt you more than it hurts me!' It allows itself a disgusting chuckle.

And then – oh shit, WTF – they're doing something to my eyes, oh please god, are they blinding me? My body turns to ice, I can't bear it, I think they're taking my eyeballs out! I want to die, I want to just frickin' die –

'You should try and stay calm before Ezra plucks out one of your eyes by accident,' says Hagen voice. 'They are just eye clamps, no lasting damage, provided you stop wriggling like a stuck pig. Hold her, grab her chin,' he says to someone.

Oh god, this is the absolute worst moment of my whole life. I am sooo scared and there's a horrible screaming sound coming from my mouth and my head is being thumped over and over from the inside.

And, Jesus, I can't close my eyes! I can't blink, I can't shut it out, I'm being forced to see – they've clamped my eyes open! Oh dear god.

Aaargh!

Aaaaaargh!

Bleurgh –

Help me, dear god, help me!

I am going to hurl. They're off, they're off, the blinding lights are off! My chest is heaving, big wracking sobs, my eyes are streaming, my nose is streaming, my throat is screaming.

Oh, oh, Christ.

Frick, I'm in so much pain. They just blasted me with insanely bright lights, like floodlights. Blinding white light and I couldn't blink or look away. They have scorched my eyeballs and burned my brain, fried it in my skull.

'Probably no permanent damage to the retina,' says the new voice again, in a high, fake soothing tone. The eye clamps come off as a flabby slab of hand strokes over my head, on my hair, over the belt that's pressing into my forehead, over my wet, tortured eyes, it's so, so disgusting.

My brain is convulsing inside my head, throwing itself against the walls of my skull, trying to escape and smashing itself to pieces in the process. I feel godawful sick.

'Just a little light therapy, my pretty little bird,' says the voice again.

'Enough, Ezra,' says someone else – Hagen, I think. 'Can you hear me? Hey? Echo, wake the fuck up. Can you hear me?'

'You frickin' maniacs,' I burble between snot and spit. 'You evil bathtards, wha' have you done?'

'Open your eyes,' Hagen says. 'The floodlights are off. Look at me right fucking now, or the clamps go back on.'

Oh Christ. I try and relax my screwed up eyelids, try and ignore my vibrating heart in my throat, choking me, and gradually I open my eyes, blinking away streams of tears.

Everything is smeary, like I'm wearing dirty glasses. But… a small room. Frick, there really are floodlights, like the ones they have on poles dotted around The Farm. Metal tables. And… three men gathered around the metal bed I'm strapped to. Hagen, Rasputin and the new voice I'd heard – I think Hagen called him Ezra? I look him over, which he seems to find amusing. He is grossly fat; I can see his huge sagging moobs under his faded striped shirt, the buttons straining to contain him. A shiny, oily face and even oiler hair, thinning and slicked over his scalp. He has black goggles hanging on elastic around his neck.

Hagen steps forward to look down at me. I try and turn my head to look at him directly but the brace around my head stops me moving. I see the shiny fat bastard – Ezra – flick his tongue out over his lips. He's a toad that some black magic has recast in soggy human form.

'Until you realise you need to behave, migraine symptoms will stop you doing aether,' says Hagen. 'You have a reasonable psynaptic shock, after all.'

What? WTF? He's saying… they're deliberately giving me a migraine, so I can't do aether?

'Your thiriokinesis and wispr are valuable. And your psynaptic shock could be,' he continues. 'Which makes our current situation all the more fucking unfortunate.'

I feel woozy, I feel out of it – but behind it all, I feel mad as hell. When I was younger I'd be terrified of getting a migraine – it meant missing school, missing out, it meant being in a living hell of inescapable torment… and they're making me have a migraine deliberately? That is so not ok.

'Wha…' I mumble. I have that feeling of being at the dentists, of my jaw being semi-numb so I can't talk right and there's that pink mouthwash gargle that dribbles everywhere when the dentist says spit because your mouth's half paralysed.

'Why… why you doin thish?' I stammer, my tongue lolling around in my mouth.

Ezra giggles. 'Ah, what a pretty, innocent little bird you have brought me, Hagen,' he says, practically wringing his hands. Hagen casts him an irritated look. Then he turns back to me. I am twisting my arms in the cuffs that tie me to the bed, the abrasion – the pain – distracts me from the agony between my temples.

'Stop that,' he says. 'I have just told you why you are here, if you paid attention once in your snowflake fucking life. Your aether, your aspects, they have value. We,' he says, gesturing around at himself and Rasputin and Ezra, 'are part of an organisation interested in human value. Human resources. Here on The Farm, it is aethereals.'

A noise comes from my lips, a moan. Ezra grins and scratches one of his disgusting sweaty breasts then turns to one of the metal tables, moving things around with scratching metallic scrapes that go right through me.

'Sometimes this part of the business, it is called… what do they say?' Hagen asks Rasputin.

'Headhunters,' he replies.

Oh Christ. Headhunters. Hunting for people whose heads can do aether. New tears start to race down my cheeks, their slick path made easy by the tears that went before. Of course I know it's true – I've already seen the valuations on that piece of paper from the desk. So they… they literally sell aethereals, like pieces of meat? I mean, WTF? My head is swimming. Drowning.

'I juth wan'ed to fine a compuber…' I stammer, spluttering through my tears.

'Stop all that shit,' says Hagen sternly. 'You were snooping around. I knew it was a bad fucking idea to bring the three of you together. But the magic geek met the blind one when the drone came over, and then we saw that you and him could wispr. But when you are a group you just talk and question and think you know everything and it is so exhausting listening to your shit. And the three of you came up with this little brainwave together, that is for fucking sure.'

'Oh, naughty girl!' says Ezra in a camp, high-pitched voice, his back still to me as he fusses with his metal trays. He is so disgusting and greasy and gross. I just want to die, right now, I just want to die and blank all of this out.

'Wha – wha you gonna do?' I beg through my tears and spit and snot.

'With the others?' asks Hagen. 'We will leave them for now. One fucking problem at a time.' He turns to Rasputin.

'Go tell them you have found her outside, she had fallen over or something, concussion. We are looking after her in the hospital room. They can stew on that for a few days and keep training, and we get them ready for sale.'

Rasputin nods and looks at me with a sneer, then leaves. Hagen reaches into his pocket and takes out his cigarettes and lighter.

'Wha do you wan?' I say, pulling at my bonds with my last strength.

Hagen lights his cigarette and takes a drag before waving his hand patronizingly at me to suggest I should calm down. Oh Christ, what a prick, if I ever survive this, I swear if I ever get out of here –

'You could be an asset or a liability,' he says. 'My job is to make sure you stay the right side of that line. So until we can be sure you will cooperate, Ezra will keep your migraine ticking over. Enough to suppress your aspects.'

Ezra chuckles and lifts the goggles from around his neck and puts them on his pink, oily forehead in readiness.

'When I know you will behave, you can complete your training and then oh so exciting, new life begins. You should know, you have had it easy here on The Farm. Oh yes you have, don't squirm like that. I have seen what comes after. Life will be harder for you, not like the holiday camp this has been. I have seen. The girl you are always pestering me about..?'

'Noo-ee?' I say.

'Yes, that is it. Noolie. We put her with new owners just after we got her to send you that text. I am sure she wishes she was back here. The people who buy aethereals, they are not so fucking soft as I have been.'

The fat man turns around. 'Oh yessss, they are bad men,' he says solemnly, nodding his head up and down. What do they mean? OMG, Noolie, poor Noolie!

'And you gonna keep torture-ing me...' I sob.

Hagen looks annoyed. 'You cannot train like this,' he says. 'That is why you come as volunteers to The Farm. It is easier when you choose to be here, with just a little nudging. Just kept apart, quarantined so you do not start your little gossips, your little theories, it all works well.'

The anthrax tape. To keep us from meeting other aethereals... wait, maybe ones who are getting different fake news rom us, depending on what Hagen thinks they need to hear to keep them compliant?

I want to pass out. I can't see Hagen clearly any more, there are bright dancing spots of light around my eyes.

'Ok, I am going to leave you in Ezra's experienced hands,' says Hagen. Oh Christ, no, dear god no. 'Ah, pretty, fragile flower,' Ezra says, his voice gargling through drool.

'There is one more thing. Concentrate,' says Hagen. 'In the future, we need your complicity all the time, without migraines. That is why we always have this,' he finishes, taking something from the side pocket of his olive green trousers.

What is it? I can't see, everything is like looking down the wrong end of binoculars. Blurred fairy lights are draped around the edges of my vision. It's... something red. I don't know. What is it? What can it be? I mean it just looks like a red square, like a piece of paper or card…

Oh, wait, a red card…

OMFG.

I remember now. Even in my drugged-up state I remember it. I stare at the card as Hagen waves it at me. OMG. Like… when I first arrived. Before, even – in the car on the way in, I remember.

I wrote my home address on a red card.

'The men here, ex-military, not at all squeamish. I will send one, Elgar I think, to visit your family,' says Hagen, his voice soft and menacingly calm. 'You should know, Elgar was thrown out of the army. Too violent. Can you believe that? He is a maniac. Too violent for the army. When he goes to your family home, he will hurt them.'

'Nooo!' I scream.

Hagen's face is just inches from mine. 'Yes. He enjoys wet work. He will make a video to show you. Just so you understand the seriousness, and the need for your absolute fucking cooperation.'

I am properly sobbing now, shaking in my restraints.

'Pleathe!' I scream. 'Pleathe no, an'thin, an'thin, pleathe!'

'Now now,' says Hagen, folding his arms across his chest. 'We will talk again soon. I will show you Elgar's footage. Nothing too bad, not this first time, provided he remembers not to get carried away. And also I think that rat dog you have. We can bring that in here. Ezra would enjoy some live dissection.'

The big fat slob shrieks excitedly, literally rubbing his hands and I am screaming, screaming no, stop, listen to me, whatever he wants, I'll do it, just no, I am screaming and retching and drowning in my tears as I beg him to listen but he ignores me and opens the door and leaves.

And now it's just the bloated toad, Ezra grinning and closing the door and turning to me and he wheels something forward, like a coat stand – it's a, oh god, it's a drip, like from a hospital on a tall metal pole on wheels, there's a bag of some foul liquid, oh god, oh god he's got a needle and I almost pass out as he bears down on me –

– and I think of my family. And I think of Piper. And I think of Flynn and Rabbit back in Flint Barn not knowing what's going on.

We've been stupid, so naïve. OMFG. Thinking we were learning new skills to stop us getting migraines. Christ. We've been living on a farm, but we weren't the farmers. We were the livestock.

Being fattened up for sale.

22: HULK

"You're just not getting it, it's like talking to children. And not bright children. Where's Constantine? I need to speak to Constantine. What? Just... look, compared to other animals – even primates – human brains have much greater plasticity. You understand? From birth, the human brain is shaped by its environment and experiences much more than any other brain on the planet. As a for instance, the brains of digital natives are wired differently to those born before The Digital Age.

"So: the plasticity of the human brain... in an environment that's more sophisticated than at any other time in history... with growing experience of using aether. You see? It means that, as far as aether is concerned, this is just the beginning.

"Stop worrying about where aether came from. Start worrying about where it's taking us. A9 exists to ensure the answer to that question is not the 'end of humanity'."

– From the TS Interviews with Doctor Magellan-Jones

Flynn took a deep, calming breath and pulled on his Nebraska jacket. He checked his watch: 8:13pm.

'Ok little dog,' he said. 'I'm going to go get your owner, k?'

The small white dog sat patiently on the floor looking up at him.

'Echo,' said Flynn. The dog cocked its head to the side, as if looking at something it couldn't quite get the measure of.

'Just stay here, don't eat my socks, and I will be back ASAP. With Echo,' said Flynn.

Piper made a little whine. Maybe Flynn did have some animus after all. He squatted down to stroke its soft, wiry coat.

'I will come back,' he said. 'But I won't come back without her. You understand?'

Piper nuzzled him with her nose. She understood. Maybe.

So, time to go.

Time to raise hell.

But first: time to find Rabbit.

He pulled open the sticky, ill-fitting door on his shepherd hut and slunk out into the night.

It was bitterly cold, he could tell, with a biting wind that had brought in the mist over the black moorland which surrounded The Farm. But he could tell it was cold in a detached way that didn't touch him. He could sense it on his skin and see it in his clouds of breath, but it didn't make him shiver or want to rub his hands together or get out of it. Because inside him was a raging furnace.

What the bloody hell was going on he didn't know. But they had caught Echo and then lied to him and Rabbit about it.

Another nickname he'd had at school: usually it was Cyclops. But occasionally he totally lost his shit – a temper he'd inherited from Keel. And that temper, combined with the physique of a gymnast who'd spent hours on the rings and pommel meant they'd sometimes given him another nickname: Hulk.

And Flynn could feel himself turning greener and meaner by the minute.

Dotted around The Farm he reckoned he'd seen maybe a dozen of the shepherd's huts. Now he ran to them one by one, trying to avoid the floodlights on poles that intermittently lit large areas of The Farm.

Rabbit had told him where to find him, just before they'd been pulled apart. The hut with a shepherd's crook scratch on the door.

And there it was! He knocked on the door quickly – too quickly and loudly, adrenalin making him careless.

A few seconds later the door opened outwards, and there was Rabbit, a beanie pulled over his head and his black fleece on.

'Hey, dude,' he said, coming down the steps. 'I knew you'd get it.'

And then, with the emotion of it all, they had a real bro moment and hugged on the steps.

'Ok,' said Rabbit. 'Before we rush headlong into chaos… do we have a plan?'

'No,' said Flynn.

Rabbit did a face-shrug. 'Fair enough,' he said. 'Let's just go find our girl.'

'If they've touched a hair on her head…' Flynn said, swallowing back the emotion.

'I know dude, I know,' replied Rabbit, putting a hand on his shoulder. 'But she's a willow, remember? She won't break.' He brushed his dirty blonde fringe across, poking out under the beanie. 'Now, let's go give them the benefit of all that aether training.'

'You going to be ok?' Flynn asked, nodding towards Rabbit's bad leg as they came down the steps.

'Sure,' said Rabbit lightly. 'I might not be able to manage much of a sprint, but I can do a pretty convincing impression of a jog.'

The night sky was clear, pricked with specks of light. Before them lay a dark movie set: hints and shadows shrouded in mist that was thickening to fog, rolling in from the surrounding hills; a mysterious guest come to see how things played out.

'Ok,' Flynn said. 'I reckon the farmhouse is a good place to start, don't you? I'll wispr to Echo every few minutes.'

They ran across the path, past the generator, around the corner of the shower block, along a ribbon of quarantine tape and –

– marching towards them were two men. Already. One about six two, wiry, with long hair under a black baseball cap. Flynn recognised him from the night with the siren and the drone, the guy he'd almost run into. The other was shorter and stockier, in a long-sleeved heavy metal t-shirt and black jeans.

'Where's Echo, you bastards?' Flynn called into the night.

'Flynn, watch out, Taser!' said Rabbit. Oh shit, he was right – the shorter guy was pointing one at his chest. The other held a telescopic metal stick with a black rubber handle – like a police baton – in one hand, and in the other, a small can aimed at them. Pepper spray?

'Hey headcases, you know it's against the rules to be out at this time,' said the dumpier one in the long-sleeved tee, Battle Demon emblazoned across his chest in fiery gothic letters.

Rabbit had gone completely still, prepping for aether. Flynn let his body sink down into his legs, imagining the muscles inside his thighs and calves were winding up like springs.

What happened next was a blur.

After the tiniest confirmation nod from Rabbit, Flynn launched himself at the big guy with the baton and pepper spray. It was a kamikaze dive forward as if he were back in gymnastics, about to somersault off the vault.

As he leapt, heavy metal t-shirt guy fired the Taser and two darts shot towards him on wires carrying fifty thousand paralysing volts.

But that was the moment Rabbit sent out a PK blastwave. The two darts were fast but very light…

…and instead of hitting Flynn they careered off at weird angles, repelled by Rabbit's momentary shield.

Flynn slammed into the tall guy and let fly a close-range snapshot. He hit him with such force the man's baseball cap came off, and Flynn felt his body go slack as they both fell to the ground, the baton and pepper spray falling limply from his hands. But a second later, heavy metal t-shirt was on his back trying to get him in a headlock.

Flynn rolled his head in, tucking his chin under. Then he snapped his head back, smashing the back of his head into the man's face. There was a cry of pain and shock and the man fell back…

…but then scrabbled for the police baton lying on the ground. He held it up – as blood poured from his nose – ready to brain Flynn.

But Rabbit held out an arm towards the body on the floor… and the small can of pepper spray flew up to his hand.

'I wouldn't,' he said, stepping forward with the can held out. 'I'm guessing this isn't deodorant.'

The man stopped dead as blood dripped down onto his Battle Demon t-shirt.

'Let me say it again, dickhead,' Flynn said. Where's Echo?'

'You thtupid bastardth!' the man said through his broken nose. 'You don't have a clue. You'll be thorry, you wait!' He backed off, still clutching his head, then turned and ran, not in a panicked way, but purposefully fading into the gloom, taking the baton with him.

'Bollocks,' Flynn said.

'How were they on to us so fast?' said Rabbit, rubbing his leg.

'I dunno,' said Flynn, looking around into the night. 'Way to go with the PK though. Top timing.'

'Top tackle,' said Rabbit, checking the unconscious body. 'I think you just knocked him out,' he said. 'He seems to be breathing normally.'

'I snapshotted him,' said Flynn. After the incident with the dummies-who-turned-out-to-be-people, he wasn't sure how Rabbit would feel about it. He wasn't sure how he felt about it.

'Meh,' said Rabbit indifferently. 'He deserved it.'

Behind them an engine kicked into life, then another.

'What's that?' said Flynn.

'Run!' said Rabbit.

And they did – they legged it from the high, throaty engines that roared and snarled and came at them in a rush. Flynn briefly looked back as they turned down a long path, a snatched moment to see two bright white eyes bobbing up and down, closing.

They ran between a couple of the camo screens, then up, along a low stone wall, away from the farmhouse now, heading in the direction of the pig-shed where they'd done several aether training sessions. They were motorbikes, like dirt bikes, that was the noise and the white eyes, hounding them, going out wide to drive them one way, revving and accelerating to cut off another route.

Rabbit began to struggle, his cheeks puffing in discomfort, and Flynn had to slow down to help him.

'C'mon Rabbit,' he said, 'you can do it. You're doing great. Let's get out of the light,' he said, hauling Rabbit in another direction away from the floodlights.

'Leave me,' panted Rabbit, 'go without me, you can't help Echo if you're caught.'

'No!' breathed Flynn. 'We can make it, let's get into a building and –'

– holy shit.

They had turned a corner, and lit by one of the floodlights was heavy metal t-shirt, looking unhinged with a river of blood from his nose all the way down his front, his laboured breathing making clouds in the freezing air, still holding the baton he had taken. And next to him was Jane. Innocent farmer Jane Brown in a lumberjack shirt, old Barbour jacket and wellies… pointing a gun at them.

'Hello dearies,' she said coldly.

And then the nasal whine of the bike engines snarled in victory as they appeared out of the mist like wraiths, two motorcross dirt bikes, one blue, one orange.

Heavy metal t-shirt wiped away crusted blood from around his mouth as the two arrivals pushed out the kickstands and got off their bikes.

'Four of uth, two of you,' he said. 'Now who'th the dickhead?'

'Just you stay nice and still,' added Jane, both hands on the revolver she had pointed at them.

'Jane, you wouldn't shoot us. Come on,' said Rabbit. 'This is all getting a bit extra, don't you think?'

She pulled back the hammer on the gun.

'Well I wouldn't kill you dearie,' she replied through her uneven brown teeth. 'You're worth too much for that. But one in the gut or the kneecaps would be just the job.'

The two who'd been on the bikes strode up – it was Rasputin with another guy… maybe the one who'd had the drone gun that time. Close-up he seemed to have a tear tattoo at the corner of one eye, and another of a small crucifix on his forehead.

'What are you kids doing still up?' said Rasputin, flecks of spittle from his mouth dancing like sparks in the glare of the floodlights. 'You were tucked up an hour ago. This is way past your bedtime.'

'Where's Echo?' Flynn said.

Rasputin ignored the question, fingering the Taser at his waist. 'You have been violent, I see. You do that?' he said, pointing at heavy metal t-shirt's face and staring at Flynn.

'Yes,' Flynn replied, staring straight back.

Rasputin nodded. 'Well, it doesn't look too bad,' he said.

'Well, I'm not done yet,' said Flynn.

Rasputin laughed, a cold, empty sound in the open air.

'You cocky thit,' said heavy metal t-shirt. 'You thould apologithe before I wrap thith around your fuckin' nut,' he said, brandishing the baton.

Flynn turned to face him.

'And your brain should apologise to your mouth,' he replied. 'It's making it say the thtupidest things.'

Someone tapped Jane on the shoulder. She turned… but there was no-one there. Just a stone the size of a paving slab, floating on Rabbit's PK. It had tapped her on the shoulder and now her gun wasn't pointing at them – and the stone fell. It landed on her ankle, foot and toes with a bone-crunching thud and she shrieked, collapsing to clutch her crushed foot, and the gun was down.

Flynn ran again at heavy metal t-shirt. But this time the wild-eyed thug was ready, and as Flynn leapt, he whipped the baton down, striking him right across the ribs; there was a flare of sharp pain across his side, but Flynn ignored it and punched down hard onto t-shirt's jaw with his left, followed by a vicious uppercut with his right. The man, already with a broken nose, crumpled and screamed in a strange, muffled way as if the uppercut had made him bite off his tongue.

'Told you I wasn't done,' Flynn said, standing over his groaning body, as next to him Jane howled in agony.

…And then Rasputin fired his Taser…

It hit Flynn right in the back…

And that it was it, game over

Except…

…this was pre-cog.

Flynn twisted, buckling his knee as he fell back, and instead of hitting him in the back, the Taser darts shot past him, just missing his cheek.

The dirt bikes clattered into each other and toppled over, felled by Rabbit's powerful PK. Then he shot out a second swoosh into the ground, pushing a tidal wave of mud, leaves and small, sharp stones over Rasputin and tear-tattoo guy, hitting them in the head and arms as they tried to shield their faces.

'Run!' shouted Rabbit. 'Split up – find Echo!'

And this time, Flynn did run – as fast as his protesting ribs would allow.

There was shouting, and a couple of seconds later a whistle, sharp and piercing in the clear, black night.

Then from another spot on The Farm, a booming, savage bark replied.

And Flynn ran with everything he had, crashing down the long path, away from the direction of Flint barn, past the shower block again and down towards the farmhouse as crunching boots pelted after him and the bark of a huge devil dog got louder every second.

He clutched his screaming ribs as he half-ran, half-tumbled clumsily downwards, past the garage… no wait, not past, into the garage.

Round the side, out of sight. There was a door on a latch. Locked. Holding the latch up, he shoulder charged it. Argh – his ribs, oh shit. But he had to do it again, harder. The door buckled but the noise had given his location away to Rasputin.

He smashed the sole of his foot at the latch and it gave way. Inside, he pulled over a metal cabinet, blocking the door and sending bouncing reels of cable and tools everywhere. Now the dog had caught up and it thumped savagely into the door, butting its head against the gap at the base.

'Pray I reach you before Koji!' shouted Rasputin from the other side of the door. Oh yes, that was its name. Koji. If only Echo were here.

He ran across the garage, around a couple of Land Rovers to the door on the other side. There was a key hanging on brown string by an alarm box. Stacked up next to the door were chickenwire crates. The top one contained rolls of black nylon – the throwing knife rolls they'd used in PK training.

There was a screech of metal on concrete – and the other door was open! Shit, shit! Flynn tried to use the key but the lock had shrunk or the key had swollen. The Kangal barked, echoing in the garage and it was over to him in a second, Rasputin just behind.

The key went in, the lock turned and he pulled the door open and got through as the dog leapt at him. Flynn pulled the metal door shut just in time to avoid losing an arm, but his Nebraska jacket bled white stuffing as the dog's teeth caught it.

Across a small courtyard, down a path: the farmhouse, ignoring his sore, sore ribs. The door was open again, the dog, Rasputin! Flynn grabbed the underside of a doorframe to pull himself up, twisting his legs to get his feet up onto a rough granite windowsill. He stood and grabbed the zinc guttering to pull himself up.

Then he was running across the ridge of the roof. The dog was barking, barking and jumping and trying to claw its way up the wall. And then Rasputin was up on the roof too. No sign of Jane or drone-gun guy, perhaps they were chasing Rabbit.

And now – jump – Flynn leapt into darkness, from one rooftop to another, smashing down on the edge of a single-storey extension to the main farmhouse like a parkour novice. Uh – it stung like hell, his ribs felt like they were scraping over each other.

Bringing his arms in, he rolled down the roof side, his hip slamming into a sharp, jagged corner of zinc guttering as he let his body roll, then he twisted down to land on the other side of the building. He took a couple of sharp breaths, trying to block out the pain flooding his body. He vaulted over a low wall marking out a field and was running across it in an instant, away from the barking, melting into the fog and black.

He could hear motors revving and angry yelling and the dog barking wildly, but none of it was closing on him. He slowed, he couldn't take any more. He had a cut by his hip from the zinc gutter and searing ribs, maybe cracked or worse by the baton strike.

And now he'd stopped running he could feel the freezing fog clawing away at his body heat, greedily sucking it from his bones.

He had escaped.

And his pre-cog had saved him again, like all those weeks ago at the skate park, with... Maxen, that was it. Bloody hell, that seemed a lifetime ago.

So he had escaped, but as Echo might say: woo fricking hoo. He didn't know what had happened to Rabbit, if he'd escaped or been caught. His ribs were murder. And he still had absolutely no idea where Echo was. He hadn't had chance to wispr to her and he'd be out of range, out here. How had they been on to them so soon? And where was Hagen? There had been Rasputin, Jane, that horrendous devil dog. But no Hagen. Was he with Echo?

And Jane... when she'd been standing there with the gun, she'd said they were worth too much to kill. He didn't want to think about what that might mean.

He zipped his jacket up as high as he could to keep out the fingers of fog, tried to push back some of the loose stuffing into the arm where the dog had ripped at him and pressed the light on his G-Shock to check the time.

9:19pm.

Only then did he realise he had something clenched in his hand. It was the garage door key. The garage that was full of throwing knives. Could be useful.

Because somewhere on The Farm they still had her. And she really was worth too much.

'I'm coming, Echo,' he said softly.

23: DECEIVED

It was a couple years ago I realised: real life has no plot.

It's not like the movies. In fact, I think maybe the biggest way movies are different from real life isn't the special effects or the fact everyone's good looking or the emotional music. It's the fact that movies have a proper storyline.

But real life isn't a neat story arc with a happy ending. Real life is just shit happens.

I feel beyond awful, BTW. Like, sooo wretched. I don't know what time it is. Or what day it is. Hell has neither windows nor clocks. My head throbs and pounds, too small for the angry snake inside which lashes out at random, sinking its poisonous fangs into the walls of my skull.

Sometimes I hear screams and torments through the walls. In another room, I think there's someone else going through what I am. Hearing someone being tortured, it's worse than going through it yourself, I can't bear it, I really can't. And Noolie, oh jeez, sold on to god knows who.

The greasy toad – Ezra – has been pulling on his black-out goggles and blinding me with the floodlights again. He doesn't use the eye clamps now, he prises my eyelids apart with his fat, sweaty fingers. There's a camera above the door, but he shields it with his body when he forces my eyes open and presses as much of his disgusting, sagging body against me as he can. It is a second torture. I think it's only the camera that stops him from doing much worse. God help me. It takes me back to the boy from Noolie's party. Holding me down, treating me like just a thing. Only then I had aether and now I have nothing.

And the drip in my arm, oh Christ I want to rip it out. WTF is in it?

My brain keeps crashing, rebooting. It's just a series of error messages. I forget things, remember things and get muddled between what's real and what's a nightmare. What's real is a nightmare.

At some point – I don't know when, some time after the pain gets too much and I vomit all over myself – my chief torturer comes back. Tall, tanned, terrible. To check on his product, I guess, make sure I'm still going to be worth something. I am crying again. I hate the fact that he has made me cry, this total douchebag. If somehow I do ever get out of this, I swear to god.

'I was just thinking I wish you'd go to hell – and here you are,' I manage.

'Oh, with the fucking jokes now,' says Hagen. 'Perhaps the light therapy has been a little too… light. Oh, now I am making a joke.'

Ezra is on the other side of the bed now – what's he doing? Rubbing something – Vaseline? – into my sore wrists.

'How can you do this?' I plead with Hagen. 'How can you live with yourself? All of this… like the news reports, why would you make all that up? The girl, the girl who was burned at the stake, how did you even fake that?'

Hagen frowns as if struggling to remember. He smoothes down the collar of his shirt.

'The... oh, her. I do not know what you mean by fake. She was not a witch, if that is what you mean. Just a runaway. We get them sometimes. They call the number, pretending to be aethereal. But she was just a homeless girl from a bad background. So she did not have aether, but she was still able to be useful. By being in the video. No-one missed her.'

'You're evil!' I scream at Hagen in horror. 'You are just fricking sick!'

Hagen tuts dismissively.

'Young people,' he says. 'So fucking dramatic, all of the time. She lied, she was an imitation aethereal. But you are the real thing. And we treat aethereals well, you should know.'

I start to protest but he talks over me, waving his big hands, one covered in the scars he's never mentioned. 'Oh yes, you are treated well. You have had a few bright lights, sometimes it may be necessary to stun someone. But generally, you are cared for as prized assets. No-one dies. You are too valuable for that.

'You do not like the idea of being trafficked for your mind? There are much worse fucking things, I have seen.'

He nods with a wild-eyed calmness as I sob. 'Oh yes. You should be grateful your mind has value. Otherwise... I have seen such things that would make you shudder. Human resources. What someone wants, we get them. People will pay anything to satisfy their urges, to live out the sickness of their dreams. I have seen, you should believe me. Such things that would make you vomit up your stomach.'

Hagen seems amused as he watches me recoil in horror.

'So you are lucky. Count your lucky fucking stars. And you should think about how you are going to be a well-behaved aethereal when we remove the drip. Because otherwise…'

'Oh yes, she would be popular!' wheedles Ezra excitedly.

I am trying to shake my head, but it's strapped to the bed, oh god oh god.

'You are worth more as an aethereal, so we have the other thing to help you remember to behave. Your family. Elgar is visiting your home with his hammer and his knife. You and I will watch his video together, we will see some things.'

Oh god, no! Just kill me now. I am just a mess, just a dribbling jelly. I can't think any more; I'm in too much anguish.

I doze, pass out, murmur and hallucinate. I don't know how much time passes, how long I am left alone in this windowless hell. I want to give up but my ravaged body stupidly clings on.

And then the door opens suddenly, making me jump in my bindings; I think I almost rip the drip out of my arm. Frick, my wrists really are sore, despite the Vaseline.

It's Rasputin. Looking pissed off, as always. He stalks in, hunched, eyeing everything suspiciously. He ignores me completely. He pushes Ezra's trolley of crap to one side with a discordant jangle.

He does look at me eventually. He has very dark irises, almost as black as his pupils. It makes him look evil. Which of course he is.

'Your friends,' he says with disgust. 'Silly, stupid kids. Their aether tricks. Tah.'

What's he on about? Nutjob. He leers in close to me.

'And the one-eyed boy,' he hisses. I can see spittle at one corner of his mouth, bubbling angrily. 'He won't last the night. He'll be gasping with hypothermia by now.'

WTF? Like, for real: what is going on? He's talking about Flynn? This probably all makes perfect sense but my brain is totally fried, I'm just sick, sick about my family and I –

The door bangs open again, this time with such force I hear it smack against the wall.

'What?' barks a voice at Rasputin. It's Hagen. Christ, he's *seriously* pissed, I can tell.

'The two boys came looking for this one,' replies Rasputin. 'We have the magician, but Flynn Dallas is out on the moors somewhere.'

What? Oh my god, what is going on? This is ridic.

Hagen ignores Rasputin and pushes past a bemused Ezra to bear down on me, claustrophobic and menacing.

'Who the fuck are you?' he shouts, right in my face. He is mad as hell.

What? Who am I? What kind of question is that? He's really hyper, it's just overwhelming. None of this is making any sense.

'I'm… you know who I am,' I mumble. 'I'm Echo.'

'No!' he barks. 'No, you are not who you say you are. You have deceived us, you have lied to me!'

What? I'm Echo, my head is spinning my wrists are sore my stomach is sick and my eyes are raw. I am broken, I don't know, I don't know. I'm just me, just ordinary Echo. Oh dear god, I wish my brain wasn't so fried so I could wispr to Flynn, tell him where I am. Maybe he could... oh I don't know, maybe something.

'Please, just let me go,' I beg weakly.

'Who fucking sent you?' he shouts, his hands gripping the hospital bed next to the chafing leather cuffs that bind my wrists to its metal frame.

I just – really, who does he think I am? I can't think, I can't, I don't know, he's literally gone crazy. I'm just ordinary Echo Jones. But Christ, he actually seems almost scared. Wait... is he scared of me?

In fact, he literally checks my bound wrists and pulls at my eyelids, examining my eyes.

'Your father send you here, to spy on us?' he asks.

I am close to passing out now, this is overwhelming – the shouting, the press of bodies in this small room, the weird questions. There are some major deets missing from this conversation, I just have no idea what he is banging on about.

'I don't know what you're saying,' I plead. 'My father? He doesn't know I'm here, does he. Who do you think I am? I am Echo Jones, I really am, I promise you.'

'No,' asserts Hagen. 'That is not correct. That is a deception. That is not your proper name.' He draws himself up to his full height, a picture of contained fury.

'You are Echo Magellan-Jones.'

I can feel tears running down the side of my head to my ears again, my eyes are stinging where he has pulled my eyelids around, letting too much light in. My head continues to pound.

'Yes,' I say, 'Echo Magellan-Jones, that's my full name, I don't use it cos it's a mouthful.' I am exhausted. 'Why does it matter?' I ask.

Hagen peers down at me furiously. He is twitching with rage and it's terrifying.

'What does it matter?' he shouts. 'What does it fucking matter? It matters a great fucking deal that you have lied to me this whole fucking time!

'You are not just "Echo Jones", You are Magellan-Jones – the daughter of Doctor Virgil Magellan-Jones.'

'Shit!' barks out Rasputin, suddenly animated. I totally have no idea what they're on about. Yes, my dad is a doctor – of neuroscience, he lectures at a university, he also does research and works in a lab. Yes his name is Virgil, FFS. But there's nothing special about him, nothing major league – I don't understand what they're freaking out about.

'A nine...' says Rasputin quietly, shaking his head once at Hagen.

'Yes, thank you,' snarls Hagen, sounding intensely irritated. 'I have just had a call from Elgar. Military watching the house, a fortress, no way in.'

'We've got to get the one-eyed boy...' says Rasputin.

'Yes, you fucking must,' Hagen says. 'In the morning, when the fog has cleared, take the dog and find him,' he says. 'But right now, deal with this,' he says, pointing at me. 'We cannot, under any circumstances, have a nine looking this way.'

This is like, sooo confusing. Why do they keep saying 'a nine'? Or is it 'A9?' What does it mean? And who do they think my father is? The only thing I'm clinging to is he said no way in. No way in to the house, so they haven't done anything bad, thank god, oh thank god for that. And Hagen hasn't even mentioned Piper, so I'm hoping she's safe somewhere – although not with Flynn by the sound of it.

'Are they tracking her?' asks Rasputin.

Hagen shakes his head slowly. 'I do not know. Perhaps. Ezra has pawed over her,' he says, looking at the fat slob of jelly. 'Have you seen a scar or bump that could indicate a chip?'

Ezra shrugs, his greasy face blank.

'Maybe the signal jammer has blocked it anyway,' adds Hagen. 'Or perhaps they have just been waiting. Either way, her father is Magellan-Jones, part of A9 and she is a fucking liability!'

He slams his hands down on the metal bed frame with a fury. What does he mean, signal jammer? Is that why we've no mobile signal? And what is this about me having a chip? I'm not a pet dog. I can feel my body start to shake, like I'm going into shock or starting to fit.

'You want...?' says Rasputin enigmatically to Hagen.

'Yes,' says Hagen abruptly. 'Put it down to wastage.'

'Quarter of a mill of wastage,' spits Rasputin.

Hagen straightens. He seems to have made his mind up.

He peers at me, shaking his head. 'A9. This is very fucking disappointing. You are a devious little bitch.'

He nods to Rasputin. 'One for the moors. Unless they do a drone flyover, they will never find the body.'

Find the – what? The body? *My body?* He's saying... no no no, all that about wishing I was dead, that was just me talking rubbish, I don't want to die, not here, not like this. I mean, this is all bogus, for real, Elgar has gone to the wrong address, talking about the military, saying my father is part of some organisation they seem scared of. This is all so messed up. I mean, I just came here to escape mobs with a grudge against aethereals, this was just a temporary retreat, a place to get a handle on my aspects and get fewer migraines.

I start to protest, to jabber and sob, telling Hagen he's got it all wrong, but the glassy, final look in his eyes stops me. He scratches his throat and then reaches into a pocket for his cigarettes. 'You are big fucking disappointment to me. All the work we put in, and your thiriokinesis? We do not get many like that. Rasputin says quarter of a mill but you could have gone for three hundred, three-fifty maybe. I am going to go kick your pathetic little dog to death, just to cheer myself up.'

What? God no, no, I'm yelling and begging and shouting as Hagen storms off and Rasputin starts unbuckling the cuffs around my wrist. He's far too strong for me anyway, but in my weakened, migraine-addled state I'm just a rag doll for him to throw casually about.

Ezra has a sad expression on his face, his hands pressed together in a prayer.

'Ah, my pretty flower. Do you have to take her right now?' he asks Rasputin plaintively.

Rasputin ignores him and throws me over his shoulder, a sack of potatoes again. Ezra does a fey little wave, mouthing bye bye softly but the world is upside down and the blood rushing to my head makes it throb loudly again.

Oh Christ, it's Baltic out here, I don't know what time it is but it is black and foggy and *so cold*, it's a shock like jumping in the sea. I haven't got a coat or any shoes. They don't care about that, they're going to kill me anyway, oh Christ. I want to scream for help, but the icy air steals my voice.

I am totally, totally screwed.

Upside down, I see the curving outside walls of the roundhouse, trees, fog. Then glinting metal panels – a Land Rover parked up. My body is shaking from the cold and I'm going into shock. Rasputin hefts me around roughly as he gets the key fob from his pocket and unlocks the door.

As he does, I take my chance to escape, suddenly wrenching around and pushing as hard as I can to break free. But he just swings me up and grabs me by the throat, choking me, squeezing the last drops of resistance and life from me.

'Maybe I just finish you here,' he spits.

Then –

Hwswsh. There is a noise.

It's kind of soft like a whisper, but condensed into a fraction of a second, actually more like a train whooshing past. And Rasputin's iron grip – one hand on my throat, the other pressing into my shoulder – slackens and he stumbles. I fall to my knees gasping – and he collapses too. He twists around to look into the darkness, and there is something weird about him.

Oh, I see it.

The back of his rib cage, on the left hand side. It has the handle of a knife sticking out of it.

It looks like the throwing knives we do PK training with.

He mouths some words at me but it's like watching a goldfish; just opening and closing with no sound. A second later he collapses on to his right; I think he's trying to stop himself falling onto the knife handle. OMG.

Just as I'm about to pass out a face looms out of the black fog. I think – is it… Flynn? Oh my god, it's Flynn!

'Hey you,' he says. 'Let's get out of this shithole.'

24: VENGEANCE

"I notice you haven't once asked where the name A9 comes from. Like I said before, this whole time you've been looking in the wrong direction, obsessed with the wrong thing.

"So let me tell you. A is for Aether, of course. But the 'nine'? It's for the nine aspects of aether.

"Because, while there are six aspects most people have heard of – precognition, psychokinesis, psynaptic shock, telesthesia, thiriokinesis and wispr – we believe three more are emerging. Even rarer, but potentially more powerful too.

"And that is what should concern you – not what aether is now, but what it will soon become. And then I think you will be very glad for A9. Then you will revere us, not revile us."

– From the TS Interviews with Doctor Magellan-Jones

'Hey you,' he said. 'Let's get out of this shithole.'

She looked up with bleary, tear-smudged eyes. He recognised the exhausted, long-suffering look of someone coming through a migraine.

'Flynn?' she said, shaking with cold.

'Yep,' he replied.

'Yay,' she said weakly. 'Oh god. Flynn, it's been… thank god. How did you… I mean, I'm so glad you're…like… uh.

You know what,' she said wearily, 'the people here are very bad.'

'You're right,' he said. 'I think we should leave. Are you ok? You look terrible.'

'They gave me a migraine,' said Echo, her voice cracking. 'Some drug, a drip in my arm. And floodlights. Like, way, way bright. It was horrendous.'

'Ok… that's not too promising,' said Flynn.

'I'm ok if I don't open my eyes,' said Echo, trembling.

'Right,' said Flynn.

'Or speak,' she added.

'Finally, some good news,' he replied.

'Or move,' said Echo.

'Right,' said Flynn after a pause. Rasputin was lying sideways, hunched up and staring at him.

'Help me up, could you?' Echo asked.

'Sure,' he said. 'I hope you didn't have a big dinner,' he added, gritting his teeth from his pained ribs as he put her arm around his shoulders to half carry, half walk her.

'Luckily I threw up earlier,' she replied, 'so I'm managing to keep the weight off.'

He took her down the slope into the trees to hide their movements from Rasputin. She was leaning on him heavily, moving her feet but barely putting any weight on them and shivering violently – she wasn't wearing boots, just walking socks, and she didn't have a coat.

'Take my coat,' he said, stopping.

'No no, I'm ok,' she replied.

He unzipped it anyway, letting the icy night in.

'It's a bit dog mauled,' he said, pulling it around her. As he did, her saw her glance at the roll of throwing knives under his coat.

'Ok, maybe just for a few minutes. Thank you,' she said gratefully, her teeth chattering with cold. 'Rasputin... did you..?'

'Kill him?' answered Flynn. 'I don't know. I think he was still alive

when we left. It was just... I saw him grab you by the throat. It reminded me of something. Someone. I just snapped.'

'Christ,' said Echo. 'I mean... thank you. He was going to kill me. Christ,' she said again. 'What is going on?' She was slurring slightly, probably from the migraine.

'I dunno,' admitted Flynn. 'I was hoping you did.'

'Mmm, said Echo. 'A bit. I saw the woman on the TV news reports, here on The Farm. It's all faked.'

Flynn nearly stumbled on a tree root, invisible in the black night.

'Shit!' he said. 'Bloody hell – that was all fake?'

'Yes,' Echo said. 'There's – there's more, way more. But we've got to get out of here first. If they catch us... oh god. And we have to get Piper before Hagen does! And what about Rabbit, is he ok? What's the plan?'

Flynn frowned and readjusted his grip around her waist to help her along. 'Err, well...' he said.

'Tell me you have a plan?' said Echo, looking at him with her tragic eyes.

'Maybe I have a plan,' said Flynn.

'You don't, do you?' she said.

'Hey!' said Flynn back. 'I said maybe I do.'

'And do you?'

'Well... not so much. But that's not the point,' Flynn replied.

'It's not the point that you don't have a plan?'

'No, the point is you just assumed I wouldn't have a plan,' he said.

'And you don't have a plan,' said Echo.

'You might be right I don't have a plan but you were wrong to assume I wouldn't have a plan.'

'Am I right to assume you're an idiot?' she said.

'Charming,' replied Flynn. 'I can't believe I bothered rescuing you.'

'Rescuing me? Is that what this is?' she said, her teeth chattering.

Charming.

'Is Rabbit ok?' she asked after a few moments.

'Probably not,' he admitted. 'We split up, to find you. They were chasing us. With his leg...' he trailed off.

'...they've probably caught him,' Echo finished.

'Yep,' he replied flatly.

'Well then we've got to get Piper and Rabbit. And then... I need to get home. I need to talk to my dad.'

He pursed his lips. 'Ok.'

They walked in silence now, Echo struggling with her migraine, him with his ribs, both of them besieged by the cold. She was walking on her heels, tottering about to keep as much of her feet off the frozen ground as possible.

As they trudged on... he began to lose hope. She was right, it wasn't much of a rescue. She was still coming out of a dull migraine and he had damaged ribs and a bad scrape down his side from the zinc guttering. And the cold was eating at them both, a starving swarm of ice piranhas. She had no boots, he had no coat and if there'd been enough light he was sure he'd be able to see them both turning blue.

They were shaking and shivering, their muscles desperately spasming to generate some heat, but underneath he could feel his body starting to shut down. They were walking to collapse, a futile, badly-equipped expedition where they would succumb to the cold.

'I think I can smell horse,' said Echo suddenly.

Err... what?

'Yes, definitely,' she asserted. 'I can smell horse!'

'Well, pardon me for not having showered,' he replied. 'You're not exactly box-fresh yourself, Miss Eau de Vomit.'

'Not you, I mean really, a horse,' said Echo. 'This way,' she said, stumbling blindly into the blackness.

'What?' he replied. 'What can you see?'

'I can't see anything,' she said. 'But I can feel something. Trust me.'

He sighed inwardly but let her lead him, divining her way over the frozen ground. And then he smelt horse too – horseshit, anyway.

And then: a horse shelter! A three-sided wooden shed-thing with a roof that sloped back, hay or straw or whatever in the bottom and – a horse, an actual live horse.

'It's a horse,' said Flynn.

'You're not an animal lover,' replied Echo in a matter-of-fact tone.

'Course I am,' said Flynn. 'Chops, ribs, bacon, sausages, burgers – I love animals. Just not horse. I'm not French.'

Echo pressed herself against the horse's neck. Then Flynn saw a folded horse blanket over a beam. He grabbed it and put it around Echo's shoulders. There were no riding boots conveniently lying around, but at least she had his coat and the blanket around her now, and the heat steaming off the horse.

'Carina,' said Echo.

'Huh?' replied Flynn.

'Her name is Carina,' Echo replied. 'She told me.'

Flynn shook his head in disbelief. 'Does this mean your aspects are coming back?' he said.

'A tiny bit,' she replied distractedly. 'Probably only animus, a fraction.'

'You know what,' he said, 'I stabbed the front tyres of the four by four at the roundhouse,' he said, 'and the ones in the garage too. So a horse could work out well.'

'Can you ride a horse?' asked Echo.

'Err... sure. How hard can it be?' said Flynn, straightening up.

'Pretty hard. As in hard difficult and hard painful. There's a saddle and reins though,' she said, pointing to some leather things hanging from hooks, 'help me get them on?'

'Sure,' said Flynn, thinking of his aching ribs. Bouncing up and down on the back of a horse would be murder.

'So… how are we going to rescue Piper and Rabbit?' said Echo, as he lifted and she guided getting the saddle on Carina. Flynn looked into her pretty, hazel eyes beneath a fringe that really needed a cut.

'Well,' he said. 'Would you believe it, I have a plan.'

Echo smiled – the first time he'd seen her smile all night. It was a grim, pain-tinged smile, but hey, it was something. It made him smile too.

'Cool,' she replied. 'And, just… thank you. For, you know.'

'What?' said Flynn.

'Oh, you're going to make me say it? Thank you. For. Saving. My. Life. Literally.'

'Oh that. Don't mention it,' replied Flynn.

Now it was Echo's turn to shake her head at him.

'Hey, now I've got your coat and the blanket,' she said in realisation. 'What are you going to wear?'

'I'm wearing the smile you gave me,' Flynn replied.

'OMG,' said Echo, rolling her eyes.

Flynn grinned again. 'I'm ok,' he said. 'If I get too cold I'll borrow the blanket, k?'

'Ok,' said Echo. 'Make sure you do. Come on then, let's find Piper, and Rabbit... oh and the others too!'

'What others?' said Flynn.

'Oh god, Flynn, it was awful,' she said. 'When I was in the roundhouse I heard someone in another room, I think another aethereal being given a forced migraine like me. There are other aethereals here Flynn, we've got to save them too!'

'Ok, well my plan's not quite big enough for that...' he said. He could see Echo starting to look dejected. 'The best thing might be to just call the cops,' he added. 'Get out of here, and as soon as we've got signal, call the Old Bill, let them deal with it.'

Echo nodded fervently. 'Yes, yes that works, let's do that,' she said. 'And then... I do have to get home,' she said, not for the first time.

'Sure,' Flynn replied. 'I think we all want to go home.' His ribs were really playing up.

'No, I mean, really, as soon as – something's not right.'

'At home?' How would she know?

'When I was in the roundhouse... Hagen said some things about my father. Have you heard of A9?'

Flynn shook his head.

'No, me neither. But it had Hagen spooked. And Rasputin. In fact Hagen was really angry when he found out who my father was.'

'Angrier than normal?' said Flynn.

'A whole new level of angry,' said Echo. 'That's why I have to get home, as soon as I can.'

'So… who is your father then?' asked Flynn.

'He's my dad.' she replied. 'He's… I don't know. I – well, I just need to get back and find out.'

'Ok then,' said Flynn. 'Well, since we live in the same city and you're still a bit fuzzy… I'll come with you. Just until you recover.'

'Yay,' she said. He couldn't tell if she was being serious or sarcastic.

'Help me up onto Carina, will you?' she added.

It took about twenty minutes to get across the field, Echo doing a good job of keeping the horse calm as she rode on its back, Flynn doing his best to lead them. It was still sub zero, but at least on the horse Echo's frozen feet were off the ground and she had the blanket. He was slowly turning to ice, but he didn't say anything. Maybe it would numb the pain throbbing from his ribs.

They could hear voices and movement as they approached the farm buildings; sometimes a loud noise would make the horse shake its head and snort or stamp its hooves. But they stayed a good twenty metres back, away from the glaring floodlights that had turned the central area into sharp contrasts of harsh light and ominous silhouettes.

'Once we go in, we'll have to move fast,' Flynn said. 'I think there are cameras on the poles with the floodlights and sirens. That would explain how come they were on to me and Rabbit so quick. And you too, probably – they could see us on the cameras.'

Echo nodded faintly, stroking Carina's flank to keep her calm.

Quickly now, Flynn led them round until they were behind the back of the garage. He checked his watch.

'Why here?' asked Echo.

'There are two lit kerosene lamps by the wall, hidden behind a pile of tarpaulin,' he answered. 'And up on the roof gutter, a twenty litre can of petrol.'

'The plan?' asked Echo.

'The plan,' he confirmed. 'I reckon a fire should distract them, don't you?'

'So you're gonna… wow, you can PK all that way?' asked Echo.

'No,' admitted Flynn. 'But maybe I can get one of these throwing knives there,' he said, pulling out the knife roll.

'Right,' said Echo. 'But what's the real plan?'

Flynn's eyes narrowed.

'I'm sure people who are rescued are supposed to be more grateful than this,' he said.

'I'm sure people who are rescued are supposed to be more rescued than this,' she replied.

Ok, game face. He could see the can's silhouette thanks to the floodlights and he walked as close as he dared – about ten metres out. Sudden movements – like throwing a knife – made his ribs feel like red hot pincers squeezing his vital organs. And his numb sausage fingers wouldn't help. But he had to try – they needed some misdirection as Rabbit would call it. He calmed his breathing, slid a knife out of the black woven sheath and concentrated on the little black rectangle in the distance. He threw.

Hopeless – short and wide, the knife slipping in his frozen fingers as he let it fly. He breathed on his hands, trying to warm them to give him enough sensation to grip the knives properly.

'How's it going?' Echo half-whispered, half-called.

'Yes, very well,' said Flynn. 'I'm just calculating the angle and wind direction.'

'Oh, right,' said Echo. 'Don't forget the magnetic pull of the moon,' she added.

Hmm. He took another of the three remaining knives. He closed his eyes for a couple of seconds, visualizing the knife. The knife, the can. Coming together. Two become one. He opened his eyes, pushed out a lungful of air through pursed lips, and threw hard, ignoring the squeals from his ribcage.

The knife disappeared into the fog, arcing high, but he tried to keep hold of it in his mind, willing it to its target. At the last second it reappeared, lit up by the floodlights as it slammed into the sloping garage roof, a couple of feet from the can. Bloody hell.

'Everything still good?' called Echo.

'I should have drawn a picture of your face on the can,' said Flynn.

He took another knife and tried again – but he wasn't concentrating, his PK was all over the place and the knife just vanished.

Bollocks. Last chance. He bit his lip, took aim at the can just visible in the distance and holding the last blade, flicked it cleanly up and out. As it vanished from sight he tried to lock on like a heat-seeking missile. Then a second later – slam – it reappeared and hit the edge of the can; not with the blade, just with the handle. But… yes, the miss-hit had dislodged it, and…

…it fell, in slow motion. He hoped it had knocked over one of the lamps and the petrol was sloshing out onto the tarpaulin. Would it work? Would it just miss and pour out uselessly onto the iron-hard ground?

Then he saw a bloom of sickly yellow, shimmering in the fog. It had worked.

'Echo!' he called. 'I did it! Obviously.'

'I never doubted you for a second,' she replied drily.

They brought the horse forward, away from the fire. He could hear the flames now, crackling and spitting as they ran up the garage wall, hopefully getting inside and starting to seize on anything that was flammable. There were shouts too, barked orders, combat boots crunching on the ice crystals forming in the channels and indents of the furrowed ground.

'Quick,' whispered Flynn. 'Let's get to the huts.'

They scrambled up the stony path, away from the garage and the farmhouse, towards the cowshed before veering off to the field where Flynn and Rabbit's shepherd's huts were. They passed a dirt bike parked up on its kickstand, no rider in sight.

His hut was first and he ran up the trampled, wet grass as Echo weakly dismounted from Carina. He had just opened the door when a furry white rocket barrelled past him and down the wooden steps, bouncing over the field towards Echo. It leapt up straight into her arms, a bundle of pure excitement and happiness, little yapping noises bursting out of her as she kind-of scampered about in Echo's arms and licked her face and nudged her with her nose as Echo hugged her and whispered to her.

Flynn ran into his hut to grab his rucksack and stuff in whatever clothes were dry, and he wrenched the blankets off the bed to take with them. Ten seconds later he was back out.

'Rabbit's,' he whispered. He ran on, up the incline to the hut with the tell-tale scratch on the door. There was a wedge jammed under it to stop it being opened from the inside. Flynn kicked at it, back and forth to loosen it and called out urgently:

'Rabbit! Rabbit, you there?'

A voice called back through: 'Flynn! Get back, it's a trap!'

The warning came too late, and Piper barked – also too late, and Flynn turned, too late, to see the guy with the tear and crucifix tattoos storming out of the black, holding a machete and what looked like a walkie talkie.

'Flynn!' Echo called out.

There was a shove on the other side of the door, the wedge had been dislodged enough and Rabbit burst out.

'Don't get funny,' called out the man, advancing to the foot of the steps. 'You're not the only ones who can stun.' He pressed a button on his walkie talkie and there was a bright, noisy crackle of blue electricity dancing between pointed nodes. Not a walkie talkie: a stun gun.

'Get in the hut!' the man commanded. 'And you,' he called over to Echo, who looked unsteady on her feet. 'All of you get in. I've just paged reinforcements. There'll be five more here any second.'

Rabbit shook his head, presumably using his scry. 'No, that's not true,' he said.

And Echo collapsed to the ground.

'No!' Flynn cried out.

Rabbit had been staring straight down the steps and suddenly the stun gun crackled into life again. The man's arm whipped up sharply in an unnatural arc – and he jabbed the stun gun into his own neck, holding it there as he spasmed and shuddered and fell to his knees, then rolled onto his back, twitching.

Flynn ran down the steps and jumped over him to Echo, just as she was coming around, Piper dancing around her agitatedly. The stench of black, sour smoke filled the air now, mingling with the fog.

'I – what happened?' said Echo groggily. 'Why am I on the floor?'

'You passed out,' Flynn said, helping her up slowly. 'I think maybe you fainted.'

'Oh, sorry, sorry,' she said. 'And, what's happened to you?' she said, touching his side gently. 'I thought I noticed it before – are you hurt?'

'Bruised rib,' he replied, 'it's fine, honestly. We've got to move!'

Together, he and Rabbit managed to haul the man – dazed from the stun gun Rabbit had PK'd into his neck – up the steps into Rabbit's shepherd's hut and they barred it shut with the door wedge.

Then they ran back to Echo; surely they only had moments 'til they were spotted.

'Let's get out, get some signal and call the police,' said Flynn. 'Rabbit, can you ride a bike – one of the dirt bikes? We saw one on the way up.'

Rabbit nodded. 'Sure dude, I can ride a bike. You on the horse?'

'Yeah,' said Flynn without much enthusiasm. 'And then Echo has to get home, Hagen seemed to have heard of her dad, which is weird.'

'Majorly weird,' said Echo softly.

'I'll sort the police,' said Rabbit, 'you head home – once we work out which direction is which. Then… be in touch, k?'

'Totes,' said Echo, her voice breaking a little. She came forward and hugged Rabbit.

'It's been emotional,' said Rabbit.

'Totes,' she said again, and as they parted her eyes were wet and sparkling.

'Good knowing you, Nick Fury,' said Rabbit – a reference to Flynn being blind in one eye – as the two of them hugged now.

'You too,' said Flynn. 'It's been… magic.'

'And look after each other, k?' said Rabbit. 'The way you too can wispr together so easily… I really think that means something.'

Gritting his teeth through the pain, Flynn helped Echo back onto the horse, lifted up Piper to her then got on behind her, Rabbit passing him his rucksack and the blankets. Then Echo was able to give him Piper back, to sit on the blanket in his arms. They got down to the bike as quickly as they could, looking out for Hagen or his cronies, and Rabbit started up the engine.

'Later dudes!' he cried and he wobbled and buzzed his way over the stones towards the entrance to The Farm.

'Hold on,' Echo whispered weakly, and she nudged the horse into a trot, not super fast, but still Flynn felt like he was going to fall off any second. With one hand he held Piper and with the other he held onto Echo's coat. Well, his coat actually.

Getting faster now, dangerously fast maybe but they were on borrowed time, they began to hurtle along, bouncing roughly – he could see the garage, completely ablaze now, being consumed by fire. The flames were hypnotic, a hundred different vivid shades of yellow and red and orange and green and blue that danced and pulsed against the black sky. He would have like to have watched the flames for longer.

Then they came around a corner and a great big black Land Rover, sliding about, blocked their path.

Hagen was behind the wheel, Jane was in the passenger seat, holding her gun. And filling the entire back seats was the dog, the huge Kangal that had almost taken Flynn's arm off in the garage and his face off in Flint barn.

Hagen leapt out, opened the back door and the dog jumped out.

'Passauf!' Hagen shouted. He pointed towards Flynn and Echo.

'Passauf!' he commanded again. 'Attack!'

But the dog didn't move. It just stood by the side of the path, facing Flynn and Echo and Piper and the horse, just staring at them.

Hagen looked like he was about to kick the dog, then thought better of it.

'You fucking shit bags! You stupid fucking idiot bitches, I am going to kill you tonight,' he shouted at them. 'You should not have caused me this trouble. I have seen many ways to die in screams, I will show you, you will see!' he raged. 'You think being burned at the stake is bad? It is nothing!' He jumped back into the Land Rover…

…and it launched at them.

'Echo!' Flynn exclaimed, leaning back instinctively as the four by four charged forward; the metal tow-bar aimed straight at the horse's legs. It was the cavalry of World War I about to be crushed by the machinery of World War II.

Flynn braced in the second before the Land Rover hit them, but Echo somehow managed to get the panicking horse moving and pulling left.

And the Land Rover skidded right to try and catch them –

– but it slid past, missing Carina's back hooves by a fraction as Hagen lost control. He couldn't keep it straight, couldn't steer the Land Rover properly… because it had two flats from when Flynn had stabbed the tyres outside the roundhouse.

Flynn heard Hagen cry out, a roar of rage and disbelief as the car span past – and slammed into a stone wall with a huge, discordant crash of twisting metal and exploding glass.

And the horse let out a terrified cry at the noise and bucked and Flynn held on for dear life and saw the Land Rover's windscreen crack as Jane Brown and Hagen both headbutted the glass, turning it crimson.

Then the horse came down and Flynn just managed to stay on – just – as it bolted forward, past the watching dog that was itself the size of a small horse, and Carina galloped up the main path, away from the buildings and into the open field and – Jesus, they actually jumped the gate – out onto the unlit, tree-lined path down to the road.

Away from The Farm. Forever.

25: LIE

Flynn saved my life on The Farm. But that same night, the cold almost kills us both. It chews at our bones relentlessly, sucking out the marrow, spitting back ice.

Flynn picked up more clothes at The Farm, so he's got more layers now and a blanket, and he got another blanket for me. But we didn't have time to go to my hut, so I've got three pairs of his socks on over my walking socks (my feet *do not* smell good), but no boots, they took them off when they tied me up in the roundhouse. I've got my phone, they never took that, but it doesn't keep me warm. We have to keep off the road, so we're out on the exposed moors in the freezing mists, and without the farm buildings to shelter us from the wind the cold is menacing and dreadful.

Oh, and I threw up again BTW, twenty minutes after we got out. It was sooo embarrassing. Just gross, throwing up in front of someone like that.

Now freezing shards stab at my soul like the sharp beaks of circling vultures. Yeah, I know I sound like a melodramatic teenager trying to be poetic, but OMFG. The life is seeping out of me. I mean, it's always seeping out of me in a way: I've got aether and that's terminal. But at least whenever it comes it will be sudden. This is a slow, painful death.

And I can't fight it any more, the cold, the fatigue – escaping took the last of my strength. I just *can not* take it anymore.

I pull Carina to a halt and just slide / fall off into the wet moor, defeated by the cold.

That's it. They've won.

I give up.

I'll just lie here. And die.

Except.

Except Flynn is with me.

And Flynn does not give up.

Ever.

He's more stubborn than Carina. Than the cold, even.

He doesn't make a big deal of me falling off. He doesn't rant, he doesn't make a big show of helping and he defo doesn't panic. He's just like, whatever. I mean, yes, he thinks I'm a melodramatic teenager, for sure. But he just gets off and puts Piper down, then he picks me up, helps me to my feet and we stumble on to a rocky outcrop with an overhang that shelters us and, barely conscious, I watch as he picks giant fern leaves, shaking off the frost and piling them up on the hard ground, Koji watching too.

Oh yes, Koji is with us!

So, after we got out of The Farm, we slowed down. Hagen had crashed the Land Rover he was in, so we figured we were ok, we just needed to get out into the night and they wouldn't find us too easily.

And then – not long before I throw up in fact – Koji appeared. He'd been following us. Flynn and Piper freaked out, but… it's pretty wonderful, you know? This huge dog, this elemental force, it's followed us because it doesn't want to be on The Farm any more. It doesn't want Hagen or Rasputin or Jane or the others – it wants us. And so I stop

Carina – who's a bit skittish around Koji – and I make everyone become friends. Or at least, not so much enemies.

'You realise, Doctor Dolittle, there are now more animals in our group than people,' Flynn says at one point.

Anyway, at the rocky outcrop Flynn puts two of our blankets onto the mattress of ferns and helps me onto it. We're shielded from the wind, there's something between us and the ground, and he puts the horse blanket on Carina to give her some warmth. We have Piper and Koji, there's a real heat coming off Koji, Kangals are just massive dogs. And Flynn and I... well, we spoon.

Nothing happens. I mean it, he's in front, I'm behind and it really is not the time or the place or the temperature. We're just trying to stay alive.

Anyway. As we lie there, in and out of consciousness, sometimes I hear vehicles on the road half a mile away: maybe it's them, I don't know. It makes my heart lurch a little each time but really, I'm too weak.

I fall asleep, or pass out. My muscles twitch and wake me up. My body keeps sending warning: low battery messages to my brain; red alerts that I'm close to death.

Somehow, we make it through the night. We only get about three hours sleep, but we survive. And they don't find us.

The next day we ride slowly. We are meerkats, our heads darting around constantly, scanning the horizon for predators. I'm able to have Piper on my lap sometimes, and still hold the reins for Carina. It's so great having her back, my lovely, gorgeous dog, I missed being without her. And as my head clears, my instinctive animus gets stronger and I feel this powerful connection with Piper and Carina and Koji, it just feels amazing, like they're giving me their strength.

Koji walks alongside us tirelessly, matching the horse's pace easily. I don't know where Kangals come from, but they are clearly sooo tough. And calm too, now he's not being all riled up by Hagen and Rasputin, you can see how easy-going and tolerant he is. He puts up with Piper trying to boss him about brilliantly.

Then two things happen at once: we see a village... and we both get phone signal! We know because suddenly our phones start going ape, making us jump. They're buzzing with message after missed call after message after missed call, all coming through at once. And the ton of messages I'd written Jazz must be sending.

OMG it is so exciting. But kinda scary too.

Flynn phones his mum straight away, bless him. I'm not phoning my parents, no way. I want to see my father when I speak to him. Instead I call Jazz.

But I'm a mess, just an absolute mess when I call her. I actually feel scared to speak to her – I'm shaking when I tap on my favourites. I mean, she doesn't know anything about what's happened, she doesn't know if I'm alive or dead, nothing. OMG. OMFG.

And then we speak and it is totes emosh, just floods of tears from us both, I'm trying to explain the unexplainable and hearing Jazz's voice, speaking to my BFF for the first time in weeks and weeks... basically it's just the most traumatic and wonderful conversation of my whole life and I am a total melt as we both cry down the phone to each other.

Eventually we both calm down enough to just be normal and back to ourselves and Jazz has recovered from the fact that I'm ok and haven't been abducted or murdered or anything and she updates me on all the deets. 'The Witchcraft Act' is still full on and there's still a heavy anti-aether vibe, but not like the stuff we were told at The Farm – not lobotomies or anything like that, not witches burned at the stake. So, you know, that's something I guess.

And me and Jazz talk and talk, it's amaze balls and I love it and I love her but I've got to go, I've got to get back home and see my father so I need to stop talking but it's totally impossible for either of us to hang up, we just keep saying one more thing and my phone is getting hot against my ear and OMG.

Eventually we do manage to say goodbye one final time and end the call and she messages me immediately:

Sooooooo good to have you back wifey, never never never leave me again!!!!! #blessed (Face throwing a kiss emoji)

And I send one back:

Promise x (Sparkling heart emoji)

A few moments later she sends another:

I may not always be there with you… but I will always be there for you xxx

Followed immediately by:

Just got that off Pinterest (Face with open mouth vomiting emoji)

Oh god, just amazing. I am so jacked from talking to her – and Piper too, she's jumping up, she recognises Jazz's voice on the phone.

While I'm on the phone to Jazz, Flynn's talking to his mum, telling her much the same stuff – he's alive, he's ok, he'll be home soon and he hasn't seen the news so what's been going on with aether? I pretend not to notice, but I can see tears. His mum means a lot to him, I can tell.

After that, well, I still have mum's credit card she gave me when I left. Jeez, how long ago was that? I feel like I've grown up a lot since then. I give the card to Flynn and he goes in to the village and tries not to look aethereal. His ribs are in a bad way – he doesn't say, doesn't complain at all, but I can tell. That's why I've been trying to make Carina walk as smoothly as she can.

I get anxious while he's gone, and I distract myself by playing with Piper and getting her and Koji to play together, though Koji's not really one for games and Piper's not used to sharing me. Inbetween, Jazz and I swap *a lot* of messages.

Flynn's gone a couple of hours. He's used Google Maps to work out where The Farm must be and he's called the police, told them everything. So, fingers crossed. And maybe they can find out where Noolie was sent to when they sold her.

He's also bought me some wellies, so I can take his stinky socks off. And a coat! I think mainly so he can get his own jacket back TBH, but still. Gloves, a hat, a scarf – and food! And diet coke – it's months since I had anything like that. It tastes incredibly sweet, but I drink it anyway. And some painkillers.

I gorge myself on the food – I eat a whole giant bag of Doritos just for starters, which I would never normally do but I'm famished. And crisps are generally vegan. I also devour a pack of scones, not fresh, the ones in plastic that last forever but I don't care, I wolf it all down. Then I eat two apples. Then we wash down the tablets. Flynn's got a bag of dry dog food and water too, and I feed Koji and Piper, Koji eating about ten times what Piper does.

Then we get back on Carina. We need to keep moving.

Life is creeping back into our bones, like a shy kitten in a cardboard box coming out to explore. Carina though, is hobbling a bit and blowing too, tired and fed up. As my strength improves I try and use animus more, to keep her calm, to keep her going, but it doesn't feel right. By mid afternoon, Flynn and I decide to carry on without her.

I am sad to say goodbye. She has been wonderful and I'm worried who will find her and look after her. But we venture closer to the road, and Flynn spots a bus shelter on the other side. We leave her in the nearby field by a tree, back from the road so she won't be spooked, but in sight so someone will find her.

So now we walk. Flynn on one side, me in the middle, then Koji (as Flynn is still wary of him), with Piper walking some of the time, and carried some of the time because she only has little legs. And as we walk, we talk. I like talking to Flynn, he's not like most other guys.

I tell him what Hagen said about The Farm. People trafficking. The Headhunters. And also what he said about my father, A9, why I have to get back.

He talks about his fam too. He barely said a word about them the whole time on The Farm. But… I guess we're closer now. I mean, we did spoon, out there on the moors! Anyway, he opens up a bit now. He says his dad was in prison until recently, his second time. And he tells me about his mum. And then… he tells me about his eye. What happened to make the left one turn green. How he was blinded.

It's sooo incredibly sad and a really terrible thing to happen to a little boy just trying to protect his mum. I have to wipe away crystal tears as Flynn says it all in a flat, quiet voice. I want to hug him and maybe I should, well definitely I should but I'm so busy with my internal dialogue talking myself in and out of it that I miss the moment. Sometimes, by the time you're sure what the right thing to do is, the right time has gone.

I can't imagine anything like what Flynn's gone through. My little family, we have our fights and sure, I can think of a dozen times when I've screamed blue murder in my mum's face, but that's just normal growing up stuff. I've always felt safe with them. There was the disaster of course, when I was five, our house burning down. But I don't remember it, I've got no physical or emotional scars. Just means no baby photos.

Although now, I s'pose there is some drama in my family. Nothing like Flynn's, but something shady's going on. Hagen recognised my dad's name, started talking about A9, whatever that is. It makes me feel… odd. Like there's something going on I've been kept out of.

Flynn, ever practical, has found a car. He spotted a tripod – two people taking photos of the sun beginning to go down over the moors. Down a short lane next to a field gate is their car, a battered old red Citroen rustbucket. And OMG, our first bit of luck ever: the door is unlocked and the key is in the ignition. I suppose they didn't expect anyone to be around, it's so remote, and the car's probably not worth anything anyway. Except to us.

'Quick,' whispers Flynn, swinging his rucksack in.

'Can you actually drive?' I ask, as I get in the dirty, crumbling passenger seat.

'How hard can it be?' he replies.

'You said that about riding a horse,' I answer.

'And as I recall it was you that fell off, not me,' he says.

Frick, he's got me there.

I use my animus to encourage Koji into the back seats; he's not keen as they're small and he's huge, but he squishes in, and Piper sits with me on the passenger seat.

I check that the seatbelt, at least, is working and Piper lies in my lap and I stroke her and tickle her ears and scratch under her chin which she loves. She has a lot of mud in her fur and it's more grey-brown than white, she definitely needs a bath, poor thing. Then Flynn turns the heat up to full and as the engine warms up, hot stale air blasts at us through mouldy black grills. It's fantastic.

Flynn's driving is less fantastic, the car lurching and clanking whenever he changes gear. I start to feel pretty gross – the stale heater, woozy head and now lurching motion sickness. But at least we're eating up the miles between us and home – and after a couple of hours I see a sign for our town!

It's weird, seeing the name of it lit up like that, advertising how close home is. Only ninety miles to go. It's dark, nearly six o'clock, but Flynn wants to ditch the car before we get caught. The services are up ahead, that's a good place to stop, he says. And we can get something more to eat, then maybe hitch or get an Uber, if one will come this far out.

He turns in, the indicator loud and clicky. We go over the speed bumps and park up and all four of us get out to stretch our legs.

OMG, people!

I mean, not a huge crowd, but there are lots of people milling around, getting in and out of cars – children, adults, talking, gesturing, arguing, smiling. It's a bit much, after all this time.

Flynn looks at me. 'I know, right?' he says.

And then he does something weird: he holds out his hand. And I do something even weirder: I take it. And hand in hand, we cross the road towards the big services building, Piper and Koji padding alongside.

Just outside, there's a boy with a frazzled mum. The boy – maybe about seven? – is standing outside the automatic doors. He's – oh, what he's doing is, he keeps taking a step forward to trigger the sensor that makes the doors slide open, then he steps back. Every time he moves forward he holds his hand out toward the doors, fingers bent like a wizard. I suppose he's pretending he's got PK. He's loving it.

'Come on Marcus,' says his mum wearily. 'You are not aethereal!' she hisses, looking at us awkwardly. I smile back at her.

It's kinda nice, seeing someone who actually *wants* to be aethereal. It lifts my spirits.

Then I see there's a sign by the door.

'No dogs,' I say.

'Could be worse. Could be "No aethereals",' Flynn replies with a grin.

'I can't put them back in the car,' I say, 'it's not right.'

'Leave them out here,' says Flynn. 'It doesn't say they have to be tied up or anything, just leave them sat out here.'

'What if someone takes them?' I say. Maybe I'm being paranoid, but the last few months have given me a heightened sense of stranger-danger and kidnap threat.

Flynn pulls a face and points at Koji.

'Christ, Echo, if someone tries to take that dog away from you, poor them. It would literally eat them for breakfast.'

I crouch down to fuss over Piper and Koji.

stay here not long. stay together. wait be good not long. i will be back soon. good you are good dogs. i love you.

…is kinda what I get across with my animus.

And Flynn and I go in to the service station. There's not much choice for places to eat.

'Burger?' says Flynn.

'I'm vegan,' I remind him, as if he didn't know.

'Have the salad then,' he replies.

'Are you kidding me?' I say. 'The stuff they put on them in fast food places? They have more calories than the burgers.'

'Sounds like you want a burger,' says Flynn.

The service station has showers so we make use of them and I get money from the cashpoint and Flynn books a cab. It feels amazing to be finally clean again and I get a brush for my hair.

'What do you think?' I say to Flynn, giving him a twirl, my hair not in knotted rats' tails for the first time in weeks.

'Easy on the eye,' he says – pointing to his blind green eye. Ha ha.

We make our way through all the people milling about (no electronic tags that I can see) and go eat. The little boy from earlier is at a nearby table with his mum. He looks glum now he can't do his magic. There's also a last sachet of ketchup he wants, but his mum has put it out of reach. Flynn notices, and when the mum isn't looking, he uses PK to gently slide the sachet across the table to the boy. The little boy's eyes go wide in wonder and delight.

'Shh,' mouths Flynn to him, a finger on his lips.

'You know, when I first met you I thought you were a sarcastic, arrogant, annoying dick,' I say to Flynn.

He scrunches up his eyes at me. 'And now?'

I shrug. 'Maybe I was wrong about the dick part.'

He grins and looks at the discarded newspaper he's grabbed from another table as we eat. There's plenty in it to suggest people are still hating on aether. Like Jazz said, there's still a state of emergency in place, the so-called Witchcraft Act. And it's definitely illegal to do any act of aether in a public place – frick, like Flynn just did then. No wonder the boy's mum didn't want him pretending to be aethereal.

There's a story about a celebrity who 'came out' as being aethereal having to delete all her social media accounts because of all the trolling and death threats. And in the sports pages there's a story about a goalkeeper who's been suspended for allegedly using snapshot to put off the other team's strikers. Oh, and just before I left for The Farm all those weeks ago, there was a story about a 'gangland kingpin' who was busted free by an aether gang on his way to court. Despite a massive manhunt he is still at large, the paper says.

Oh god – I've just thought – what if he was one of the people Hagen sold aethereals to? Maybe his 'aether gang' were being forced to do it, maybe even someone like Noolie was among them, being made to do aether to help this crime boss escape, or they'd be tortured or their family killed? Frick. When we left on Carina, Hagen crashed his Land Rover. I wonder how badly he was hurt. And I really need to know just how he knows my father's name.

Flynn winks at the boy as they leave, and we finish up too. Time to go. I'm warm, clean, my stomach's full and my head is clearing.

I'm sooo tired but I don't think I'll sleep in the taxi – I'm churning up with emotion. I'm nearly home. It's nearly time.

In a couple of hours I can look my father in the eye and ask him what's been going on. And find out exactly how much of my life has been wrapped up in a lie.

26: ROBBERS

"Let me break it down for you people: with three pounds of Semtex, you can demolish a two storey building.

"With three pounds of weapons-grade uranium you could cause more destruction than the Hiroshima bomb – which in nineteen forty-five flattened ten square miles and killed more than one hundred and forty thousand people.

"With three pounds of Venomous Agent X you can kill one and a half million people. More than the entire population of Birmingham.

"But with three pounds of organic tissue you can do far, far more damage. When that organic tissue is a human brain. And because of aether, the potential impact of a single human brain has never been greater.

"And yes, that includes my own daughter. That night, that October fifteenth – perhaps her first time of really using aether in anger – showed the potential she had. Even if that incident did end rather tragically."

– From the TS Interviews with Doctor Magellan-Jones

He had cried, on the phone.

His mum had set him off. After all those weeks, wondering, worrying – it was overwhelming to finally be able to speak to her. Her fractured wrist had healed, that was good.

And the man, he had needed to ask – how was Keel? Alive but still in hospital, in a wheelchair. She had been to visit him. To check what he was going to do, that was incredibly brave of her. But he was calm, she said, sleepy, blank eyes, he didn't know anything. His memory had been knocked out of him, along with his menace.

Robbers, she'd told him. Robbers, she'd told the police. Two of them. Keel had bravely tried to stop them, to protect his family, and they had attacked him. And Keel had nodded. Yeah, he had said. Robbers. I think so. Two of them. I took them on.

And Flynn? the police had asked. Where's your son?

We had an argument, she'd told them. I blamed him for not locking the door, that's how the robbers got in, you saw – the door wasn't forced. So we had a row and I sent him away. I haven't seen him since. And then she had started weeping down the phone, and that had set Flynn off too. I'm so sorry for saying that she'd said and he'd said no, that was clever, quick thinking.

And the man was in a wheelchair. Maybe forever, his mum said. Flynn had never been so happy to live on the fourth floor of a block of flats where the lifts were usually out of order.

They'd talked for a few more minutes, Flynn had been vague about what he'd been up to the last few months. But I'll be back soon he told her. We'll be together again, a family, just the two of us. I just have to help someone first, this girl.

This girl. Here she was, sat next to him in the back of a taxi taking them to their home town. 8:42pm said his G-Shock. It was good to just sit for a while, do nothing and rest his ribs. And then he saw the city lights down below as the motorway curved right, taking them in.

Echo got quieter as the taxi – a big seven seater that was willing to take them and the two dogs – took them ever closer. Mile by mile, he could feel her coiling up. Their banter had died away. She was brooding and contained. He wanted to give her a hug. But... maybe it wasn't the right moment.

The taxi drove into town, past multi-storey buildings and car parks and the shopping centre, through dozens of traffic lights, out to the suburbs. They turned off a brightly-lit, steeply sloping street with fancy coffee shops, weirdly-named bespoke kitchen stores and restaurants flogging posh pizza. There was an Italian with flaming torches either side of the door. He watched the flames as they went past – it reminded him of the fire he'd started back on The Farm. Seeing the flickering, dancing flames felt oddly soothing now.

Then the cab turned up towards the park, past big, spaced-out houses with front gardens and manicured trees and tiled paths. Echo lived in the same town as him, but in a different world.

'Oh, what's this then?' said the taxi driver. Something ahead, more lights. Flynn craned his neck to see.

'They've closed the road,' the driver said. 'I'll have to go round the other way.' He stuck his elbow up on top of the seat and reversed around a corner. Echo said nothing.

'Ok?' said Flynn softly, nudging her. She looked at him briefly and flashed a quick smile as she nodded. There was a light tapping sound as raindrops began appearing on the windows.

They drove a couple more minutes before the taxi began slowing again. 'Hold up,' said the driver, sounding aggrieved. 'They haven't closed both bloody ends? Scuse me!' he called, lowering his window to flag down someone walking away from the new barricade of lights. 'What's occurring?'

'Gas leak,' the buttoned-up man replied, hunched into his coat against the thickening rain. 'Some idiot's cut through the main pipe. They're evacuating half the street, you can't get in.' He shrugged and strode on.

'Bloody council,' said the taxi driver to no-one. 'Sorry,' he called to them in the back of the cab, 'can't go no further, looks like your road's closed off.' He turned to face them. 'Mebbe you can't even walk in. You want me to take you to somewhere else?'

'No, thanks anyway,' said Echo. 'We'll be ok, thank you. We'll try our luck.' She opened her passenger door and got out. Luck, thought Flynn, was something they'd had very little of so far. But the two dogs jumped out into the rain immediately and he followed them as Echo paid the driver, and he pulled on his rucksack gingerly.

'Have a good night,' said the taxi driver. 'That dog,' he said, nodding down at the Kangal, rain pouring off its fur, 'it's summat else ain't it? Good as gold mind, but put a mane on it and you'd take it for a bloody lion.'

Flynn nodded in agreement as Echo began walking down the street towards the blurry lights. There was a police car parked across the road with a ROAD CLOSED sign in front. The car's blue lights were flashing. There were police standing by, watching them approach. Part of Flynn was annoyed there were cops here, worried about a paltry gas leak when they could all be raiding The Farm, closing down Hagen's sick operation. And another part of him was put on edge. Cops. Could they be the same ones who'd questioned his mum, who'd asked what had happened to Keel and where is your son?

'This street is closed,' a policewoman called out sternly. 'Major gas incident. We are evacuating all properties in the vicinity and closing the street to access while we investigate. And that dog should be on a lead. Both of them, in actual fact.'

'My name is Echo Jones,' said Echo. 'I live at number fifty-one. Could you just check if I can see if my family are still there?'

The policewoman stared at her, rain streaming off the end of her peaked cap, then she held the walkie-talkie on her lapel up to her mouth and spoke into it. After a pause, a distorted voice spoke back; Flynn couldn't catch what it said. The policewoman listened, then looked up at them and nodded once. Flynn was surprised: they were ok to walk towards a possible gas explosion? Brilliant.

what does that mean

…appeared in his head as Echo gave him a sideways look.

i dunno i dont think they should let us walk into a gas leak explosion risk though

he wisprd back.

so your saying theres no gas leak

she wisprd to him.

'What?' he said as they walked on. 'No, I don't mean that, I mean – err, well, I suppose there might not be a gas leak.'

'Which would mean the police are lying to us,' she said. 'And I think we've been lied to enough recently, don't you?'

'Definitely,' Flynn agreed.

Echo sped up a little, now with one dog either side of her, Flynn behind them on the pavement. She had a quiet determination about her. She was still fragile, they both were, but she was walking with purpose, ignoring the rain soaking her skin, the flashing police lights, the tannoy voices of cops communicating by walkie talkie. It felt more like a set than a real street, surprisingly empty of other people. But perhaps that was just because he was used to the hustle of living in a block of flats. Maybe this was what rich people's streets were like.

Fifty-seven. Fifty-five. Fifty-three.

Fifty-one. Here they were, standing outside a smart, sage-coloured door inside an open, arched porch with a tiled roof that kept the rain off. Piper was excited and making yipping noises, she obviously knew she was home. She shook herself in the porch, sending raindrops everywhere, preparing for a warm welcome into the house.

Echo raised the brass knocker and knocked, once. It echoed down the silent street as if every door was being knocked on. Flynn saw the police moving in at both ends, going up driveways, presumably telling people either to evacuate or stay inside, he didn't know. Come to think of it, he couldn't see any roadworks, or digging, or anything where a gas main might have been cut. He was about to comment on it when the door opened and a man's face appeared, bathed in warm light from a chandelier hanging in the high-ceilinged hallway behind him. He was in his early fifties, trim, with greying hair at his temples, wearing blue chinos, a dark yellow jumper, frameless glasses and a serious expression.

'Hello father,' said Echo.

27: TRAGEDY

'Miss me?' I ask my father.

Piper is hyper BTW, she's sooo excited to be back, she loves her basket and her toys and she's practically chasing her tail, skittering round in circles.

i know i know!

I emote to her. She's such a good soul, just happy to be home – never mind that home feels weird AF. Koji sits by my side, just this big, commanding presence calmly appraising the strange people in our living room. And he's right, they are strange.

'Of course, darling,' says my dad emphatically, adjusting his specs. 'We have both missed you so much.'

I have so many memories of this living room. So many hours spent on the huge Chesterfield grey linen sofa. It's basically two rooms, the original lounge and dining room knocked together, with heavy Laura Ashley curtains covering the large sash windows in duck-egg blue check. The room is plenty big enough, even for the assembled cast.

Because as well as Flynn and me and Piper and Koji and my dad, there's also a policeman – tall, senior and precise, with short grey hair, a dressed-up woman wearing a hideous shade of purplish lipstick and holding a tablet, and sat in a chair and wearing a sporty zip-up top is a slender, shaven-headed black guy who may be nineteen or twenty. I bet he's aethereal, that's why he's young. Maybe a scryer, to see if I'm telling the truth?

'It's so good to have you back safely!' my father adds a second later – and you don't need scry to see how fake he is; he's never been this jolly in his life.

'We were so worried! Thank goodness you're ok. And who's your friend? And Piper seems to have a new friend too, quite the specimen. Where have you been, my dear? When we found out you hadn't arrived at Aunt Marianne's, well, we were worried sick!'

It's like he's had too much sugar or something, he's almost as hyper as Piper.

'This is Flynn,' I say. 'I met him at this place we've been at called The Farm.' A few glances are exchanged and my father's brow squeezes into a ploughed field. The woman starts tapping on her tablet.

'You've heard of it?' I ask my dad.

'You've been on a farm?' he says hesitantly. 'Is it –'

'Where's mum?' I ask, interrupting. Piper is pawing at my leg for me to stroke her, making a little barking noise. She can sense that things aren't quite as fabulous as she'd expected. She can tell that I'm angry, but she's not sure why. TBH, at the moment I'm not sure why.

Dad looks bemused.

'Your mother? She's out... with a few friends. Peyton, Quinn, I think? They've gone to the Italian place I believe.'

'Ok... and who are these people?'

'We've been extremely concerned Echo, we've been getting help from all sorts of people – there's been a nationwide search.'

'Wow, I must be some kind of big deal,' I say. 'Or you are.'

He smiles lightly. 'Like I say, I'm just glad you're back. As your mother will be. It's great to see you. You look thin. How is your health?'

Jeez, the way he's acting, it's so cringe.

'I've been lied to, exploited, imprisoned and tortured,' I say. 'We escaped just as I was about to be murdered and then we nearly died of exposure. But other than that, totally awesome.'

The senior cop, not the type that wears uniforms with all the brocade and badges, this guy's more SWAT, watches me. My scry game is not strong but I still have a bad feeling about all of the strangers in this room.

The kid with the shaved head, slouched in one of our big velvet chairs, pipes up.

'You're a talented aethereal – apparently – so how did they hold you against your will?' he asks. Yeah, I was totally on point to dislike him right from the get-go.

'I didn't know I was being held against my will at the time,' I retort, realizing how stupid that sounds.

'The Headhunters,' says the woman with the purple lipstick and black pencil skirt suddenly, looking up from her tablet. 'They operate three cells including The Farm,' she says to my father.

'Christ!' says my father angrily. 'Err, this is Rebekah,' he adds, 'and Captain Droy. And Noah,' he adds, pointing at the one in the chair. 'Just some of the people who've been helping us try to find you. We've even had drones out.'

'Drones,' I say to Flynn.

'Well that confirms it,' says Flynn drily. 'You are a big deal.'

'Echo, we're all so glad to have you back,' says my father. He's started repeating himself, like he's run out of script. 'We need to get your health checked out, make sure you're ok – and you too, ah, Flynn,' he adds.

He's interrupted by the front door slamming – and my mum comes in through the hall and straight into the living room, her Burberry trench dripping water all over the floorboards. I mean wow, this is a night of firsts – my father acting all jolly and now my mother traipsing the wet weather through her OCD-perfect house. So now the whole family's back together.

Yay.

'Echo!' she says, dropping her umbrella on the floor – dropping her umbrella on the floor, OMG. If anyone else did that she'd go batshit. 'My god, you're back, you're ok, you're alive!'

She runs forward and embraces me, our wet clothes sticking together as she hugs and squeezes me. We've never been very touchy-feely, but it feels good and I hug her back. We are two wet sponges wringing each other out.

'Hey mum,' I say as she pulls away. 'Good to see you. I'm ok, I'm ok, k? This is Flynn, by the way.'

'Virgil,' says Captain Droy to my father. I'm pretty sure he's saying it in a this-situation-is-going-south-fast kinda way, but I may be reading too much into one word.

And my mum's look of happiness is quickly replaced with one of anger.

'Is this why you wanted me out the house?' she shouts at dad. 'You knew she was coming back tonight!'

'No no,' he replies soothingly, 'not at all.' There are tiny glances exchanged between the people I don't know – Noah, Rebekah and Captain Droy. And… I'm just throwing it out there, but has a lie just been revealed? He said mum had gone out with friends. But she just said he wanted her out of the house. Weird. I remember there was this study which found sixty percent of people couldn't go more than ten minutes of conversation without lying at least once.

And in another study, they found that well-educated people lie more than less well-educated people. And that men lie more than women. And here I am, having a conversation with a well-educated man that has just gone past the ten minute mark.

'Is it just a coincidence you have these people round tonight?' I ask. 'Or did you know I would be back? How?'

My father looks tongue-tied for a moment. Piper is getting anxious, nudging her nose into my calf, wanting me to pick her up so I can comfort her and she can comfort me. She can tell I'm edgy when this should be a super-happy moment, being back home.

its ok lovely all ok not to worry like play fight ok? like a play fight

…I say to her with animus. She darts inbetween my legs to shelter from the negative vibes and I bend down and give her a reassuring stroke.

its ok my beautiful Piper

'Well, no, I didn't know for sure,' my dad says. 'But I hoped. The authorities,' he says, gesturing at Captain Droy next to him. 'They've been monitoring if anyone used your bank card, or the credit card your mother gave you. Today it was used for the first time in months. The second time at a service station cash point. They checked its camera and saw it was you, thank goodness. I just – I didn't want to get your hopes up without being sure,' he says to my mum.

This is getting more and more sus – a few minutes ago he acted like he was totally surprised to see me, now he's saying he was half-expecting me because he'd seen me on a cash machine camera! It confirms something else I was sure of too.

'There's no gas leak, is there?' I ask.

'You were right, that is why they let us in,' says Flynn. 'At the road block.'

Yeah, Hagen said the guy he sent here, Elgar, he saw the place was crawling with police. In fact I think he said military. They've been here a while, and they're something to do with my dad, not any gas leak.

I stare straight into his eyes, looking for any sign of admission. The purple lipstick chick, Rebekah, moves over to the full length curtains to take a call. The young guy – Noah – sits staring at me as intensely as I'm staring at my father. My mother seems to be realising, in horror, what's she's done to the floor, as well as freaking out about the huge dog sat on her parquet with claws twice as long as Piper's.

'I... I couldn't say about the gas leak,' my father says. Definite lie. Well, whatever. Time for the million dollar question.

'What is A9?' I ask.

It's literally like all the air is taken from the room. The woman over by the curtains turns to stare at me then starts talking at her phone in a frenzied whisper. Captain Droy gives my father a loaded glance and then he too speaks into the walkie-talkie on his shoulder, murmuring behind his hand. Noah looks vaguely amused.

'Yes, tell her, Virgil,' says my mother imperiously.

'I – where did you hear that term?' my father asks.

'The Farm,' I say. 'Now come on dad, I answered your question, can you answer mine?' Check me out, all serious and in control. I stroke the back of Koji's head, he's so chill it calms me a bit. A bit.

am ready can kill

…is kind of the feeling I get from him. I'm just like… well, I don't know whether to be honoured or horrified.

no no all good thank you but no no no

…I emote back with my animus.

I stare at my father, in his mustard jumper and tan loafers, smoothing his perfectly styled grey hair into place. It's almost a nervous tic, like when he adjusts his rimless glasses before making a pronouncement. Maybe he can sense Koji's readiness to pounce. He glances at purple lipstick woman, who is pacing up and down as fast as her tight pencil skirt will allow as she talks on the phone.

'I – A9 is an aether-interest group,' he says. 'Aiming to understand aether better. After all, Echo dear, you have a terminal condition.'

Jeez, is that it, that's his lame-o answer? He's doing it for me? That's his angle?

'At The Farm, they knew your name,' I say. 'Doctor Virgil Magellan-Jones. They said you worked for A9.'

'I – well, yes, that is true, I suppose,' he says. 'They sponsor some of my research.'

'Research into what?' I ask. 'You've never talked about aether as part of your job before, not once. Which is pretty weird since you've been helping me with it.'

'Much of my work is confidential, Echo,' he says, falling back into his condescending I-know-best tone. 'There's nothing sinister, I just can't talk about it, even to my family. Now, we need to get you to a medical facility –'

'What? No! That's why you didn't want me here – you want to lock her away, run your tests on her!' shouts my mother. 'You are not taking her to any medical facility. Over my dead body!'

Thank god at least my mum's got my back. Flynn, I notice, is staring at the young guy I think is aethereal, Noah. I think Flynn feels the same way about him I do. We can spot a wrong 'un a mile off.

'They were bad people at The Farm, dad,' I say. 'They were people-traffickers, part of a crime gang. Like Rebekah says, they called themselves The Headhunters. And they were going to kill me when they found out I was your daughter! I'd be dead if Flynn hadn't saved my life.'

'Well to be fair, you saved mine first,' says Flynn.

'Sure, thanks,' I reply. 'So dad, please don't stand there saying you're just doing some research, because those scary bastards were scared of you!'

He shakes his head like he's confused.

'I don't know Echo dear, I don't know what to tell you.'

'Just tell me truth!'

'Aether… it's new, it's fascinating really, as a neuroscientist of course I'm going to take an interest…'

'But how come they'd heard of you?'

'I don't know, maybe they'd read an online article I'd written, I don't know…'

'What are you researching?' I say.

'Nothing, nothing to concern you, really…'

'What are you researching!?' I cry.

'You!' shouts out my mother suddenly.

Flynn and I turn to her. Her eyes are wild. 'He's researching you, Echo,' she says tremblingly.

'I don't know what A9 is, something government – they don't tell me,' she continues, sounding close to tears. 'But he's been studying you since you were little. Since… not long after your first migraine.'

'What?' I say. I turn back to my father. I mean… what? His mouth opens and closes like a guppy. I step towards him furiously. Like… this is my dad FFS. Like that very first time, feels like a lifetime ago, when we tried PK and he got me to lift that little sachet of sugar in his study. What was that? That and everything after? Parental support? Fatherly love? Or scientific research?

'You've been studying me?' I yell at him. 'What does that even mean? I'm some guinea pig for your experiments? I thought – I thought all this time you were helping me?'

'I was, Echo, I was,' my father replies, trying to get back control and gesturing at Droy that everything's ok. 'I am. Of course. But you know I'm a neuroscientist, so when you presented the symptoms that suggested you might one day show aethereal ability, I've also taken a professional interest in your development, recorded your progress. It could help others.'

My mother makes a gurgling, despairing sound in her throat. I have to pick Piper up, she's getting too distressed. She's like my own heart walking outside my body – and when I get upset, she does too. I hold her in my arms now and she's trembling like she does on fireworks night.

its ok Piper my lovely don't worry

I tell her.

'So what do you know about aether?' I ask. 'Where it came from, what it has to do with migraines, what it means?'

Noah, who has been sitting silently this whole time, smiles indulgently and sits forward, looking at my father like he's interested in what someone in the room has to say for the first time. Flynn takes my hand. I am glad of it.

'Look Echo, perhaps now is not the best time,' my father says. 'But I don't really know much more than you,' he continues soothingly, 'none of us do.'

'That's a lie!' screams my mother, making me jump. She's *really* emotional. 'Tell her! Tell her the truth! For once in your life Virgil, tell her the truth!'

He shakes his head. 'I don't know what you're talking about, Lucile,' he says, gesturing to someone out in the corridor. A policeman comes in and my father points at my mother – frick, I think he actually wants the policeman to remove her.

'You've been under a lot of stress with Echo missing, you're overwhelmed with her suddenly coming back. Take a couple of your sleeping tablets. We'll make sure Echo gets the medical care she needs.'

'No! You can't take her, don't let them take you, Echo!' screams my mum.

'What are you doing?' I say, horrified as the policeman takes hold of my mother by the arm.

'Let go of her!' I cry. Flynn steps towards my mum like he wants to help, but he's not sure what to do. Koji rises to his feet, sensing my distress and ready to act.

'Get off me, get off!' screams my mother, sounding scared. It's like a flashback to when Rasputin dragged me into the roundhouse. The policeman ignores her and starts pulling her back, her heels scraping across the wooden parquet floor.

'Stop it, let her go!' I yell. 'Please, please! Father!' I plead.

'No!' screams my mum, grabbing the doorframe with both hands. 'No Echo, don't call him that! He's lied to you too long. He's not.

'He is not your father!'

...

It is as if one of Flynn's throwing knives has thudded into my chest.

The way she says it – as she's being dragged out backwards, with nothing to lose.

The way it just spills out of her, raw and unfiltered. It's like… she's being totally legit.

My insides lurch and my back goes really cold and… I *know*. It's one of those moments when you instantly know.

I know she's telling the truth.

I feel it. I can taste its bitter truth. I can smell its stink. It's true.

He. Is. Not. My. Father.

The policeman stops dragging my mother for a moment and she gets to her feet, shoving him, ruffling his uniform as she pushes him off her.

WTF?

Flynn turns to me and looks at me with haunted eyes.

jeez echo are you ok

I hear in my head as he gives my hand a squeeze. I shake my head back to him. I don't know what to say. I came here for answers, but… I'm going to choke on my heart, or cough it up – or it's going to punch its way out of my chest. This is unbelievable.

This man who brought me up, who I've called dad all my life… isn't?

…Wait… all my life. Something's just occurred to me.

'No photos,' I say flatly.

'What?' he says blankly.

'That's why there are no photos,' I say, my voice cracking a little. 'You've been studying me since my first migraine – when was that? About five? That's why we've only got family photos from then. Because you weren't around before that. You only showed up after my first migraine. Our photos weren't lost in a house fire, it's because I only became your lab rat after I showed "aether potential"!' I am close to tears.

This just totally, totally sucks. I need to understand, I need to speak to my mum, but I can't stand this, I can't be in the same room as this man until I find out what's really what.

lets go

I wispr to Flynn.

'You got it,' says Flynn. Noah's eyes flick to him.

'We're going,' I say to my father – no, Virgil. He starts to protest but I ignore him. We start to move back and Noah stands up for the first time, the sudden movement drawing Koji's gaze. Captain Droy makes a gesture.

'Don't do this Echo,' my fath – jeez this is going to be hard – Virgil says.

'We are going,' I say firmly. 'Are you coming with us?' I ask my mum. She looks at me with red, tear-smeared eyes.

'Yes, yes I am,' she says, grabbing her umbrella off the living room floor and pushing past the policeman, who seems to have given up.

We kinda reverse out into the hallway, and Flynn opens the front door while I hold Piper. Koji is practically as wide as the whole hallway, blocking anyone from getting past us. Ugh, it's really chucking it down outside now.

'I'm afraid you cannot leave,' says Captain Droy, following us with Virgil and Noah. 'If you step outside you will be placed under arrest.'

'Arrested for what?' says Flynn. 'We haven't committed a crime.'

'You let me worry about that, boy,' says Droy. And then Koji growls at him.

'Where did you get that dog?' Droy asks. 'Unless I'm mistaken – which I'm not – you have a high-functioning military attack dog.'

'I dunno about that,' says Flynn. 'But we were told it's got the most powerful bite of any dog breed in the world. And it hasn't been fed for a while.'

Koji actually stands guard now, facing Droy and Noah and Virgil and purple-lipstick with its dagger-teeth bared, as my mother steps out with her umbrella, followed by Flynn and me carrying Piper (who is very nervous and confused).

Outside the rain is heavy. It's a grim night – and what are those circles of light?

'Bloody hell,' says Flynn.

They're torches. Torches on rifles held by… eight police, positioned on the other side of the hedge of our front garden. They are dressed in all-black outfits with helmets, goggles, lots of pockets and straps. And their eight rifles are all trained on us.

'Echo, please,' says Virgil – I'm getting the hang of it now. 'Come back inside, let's talk about this sensibly. I can help you. Your aether – you've been corrupted by the amateurs who held you. I can help you, A9 can help you. Lucile,' he calls to my mother 'don't take another step. You're not taking Echo anywhere.'

'We are going,' I say, not that I have any clue where – just as long as it's away from him.

'If you go any further, things will become more difficult, Echo,' Virgil calls, louder now, crosser now. Definitely back to his I-know-best voice.

We step out of the storm porch into the rain, and my mum opens her umbrella to keep it off us as best she can. Koji pads out alongside and Flynn is here too, ignoring the pouring skies.

I start towards the armed police. I am scared AF. We look totally screwed here. But they can't arrest us, can they? Not really? We get halfway down the drive when an unfamiliar voice calls out behind me.

'Stop, Echo.'

I turn and it's Noah, holding an arm out like he's commanding me. He steps out of the storm porch into the rain… but it doesn't drench him. I should be seeing it running in rivers down his shaved head, soaking into his zip-up top but it isn't. Instead it runs around him, making him look slightly ghostly as it shimmers and smears. How is it – a PK shield? What a show-off. But also pretty clever. I don't think my feeble PK would be strong enough to hold off the rain and still be able to talk.

Noah points a finger at me now. 'I can only warn you once.'

Flynn looks like he's just heard the most outrageous insult ever, and he strides towards Noah to give him a piece of his mind.

Noah clenches the fingers of his outstretched hand into a fist and then stabs them out. Flynn wobbles in his stride and then freezes: a Flynn waxwork. 'No bro, you're not going anywhere,' says Noah.

Woah – Flynn contorts and twitches, his arms are flicking about in a weird way, flinging his rucksack to the ground. Then he slides backwards across the driveway as if pulled hard on an invisible string, his heels digging grooves in the gravel. He stops again and twists sharply at the waist and lets out a yell.

'Let him go!' I scream at Noah.

But instead… Flynn rises up in the air! He's trying to cry out but his whole body is being gripped tight by aethereal force – Noah is using PK to lift him right off the ground.

He rises up jerkily until he's – what – ten, fifteen feet off the ground? OMG. I look at Noah and he doesn't look like he's straining at all. And he's still keeping the rain off himself. He looks back at me evenly and starts walking towards me. Oh frick, what should I do?

'Echo, it really is safer inside,' calls out Virgil. 'Noah – you can see what he can do. I can help you harness your gifts too – you could be just as powerful! Come away from the guns, I didn't ask for them, come back inside.'

'Stop it!' I scream at Noah. He stops a few feet from me, he's not even facing Flynn, who continues to twist and twitch in the air like an escape artist tied up with ropes and padlocks. Noah sighs at me slightly as if this is all a terrible bore for him.

'I can tell he's aethereal,' he says, 'but what kind? He could be dangerous for all I know.' He smiles at me. 'In fact,' he says, 'I trust him about as far as I can throw him. I wonder how far that is?'

Flynn rises up further – he must be twenty feet in the air, maybe more I can't really judge, dangling from an invisible rope, looking straight down at the ground.

'Still want me to let him go?' Noah asks, smirking.

Virgil, purple lipstick Rebekah and Captain Droy are all standing in the storm porch, watching. Captain Droy speaks into his walkie-talkie again, presumably to the armed police or SWAT team or whatever they are, lined up against us.

What should I do? I am thinking.

'How can you do this?' I ask Noah. 'Let them use you, like a tool? That's what you are – a tool.' I think of The Farm – trafficking aethereals, making them use their aspects with threats and violence.

'Doctor Magellan-Jones is sentimental about you,' Noah calls back. 'You should listen to him. This could still work out ok for you.'

My mum makes a self-pitying sob. I look up at Flynn, suspended in the sky and he looks back at me at the exact same moment.

'I'm sure this is all a terrible shock – about your father,' says Noah. 'Boo hoo hoo and all that, so sad.'

I wispr to Flynn:

use pk to break your fall get ready

'I've got some bad news for you too,' I say to Noah.

'Oh?' he replies disinterestedly. 'What's that?'

'Koji,' I say.

And Koji takes two bounds and leaps at Noah who cries out, suddenly not so cocky as Koji's front paws slam into his chest, knocking him back with massive force.

As Noah tumbles back, his beam of PK comes off Flynn, who drops from the sky like a brick and just as he's about to hit I think I see a haze between him and the ground, which is his PK pushing him back from the earth to soften the blow. I hope.

But the beam, oh god, Noah's beam of PK – it arcs through the air and shatters brittle branches of the tree out on the road. They explode into frozen sawdust.

Koji pins Noah down, fangs bared right in his face as the PK beam sweeps down across the ground, hitting the driveway and sending a grenade of gravel firing out in all directions. Then as he writhes in terror it swings back up and across – it slams into a parked car, pushing it into the road, shattering its side windows and setting off the alarm.

back to me koji come back

I use my animus to recall Koji and he springs back to me. Noah is on the ground, all his self-satisfied smugness gone, and as he squirms his dying PK beam swoops over and smashes into the cops, sending them sprawling before it suddenly stops with a loud bang.

Flynn stands up gingerly – thank god, he's alive. My mum screams. 'Echo!' calls out Virgil. Flynn comes over slowly, I watch him hobbling. 'Oh shit… Echo,' he says.

And then Piper makes a little yip in my arms, poor thing – she's cold and wet and a delicate soul not used to all this temper and noise and –

– oh god. What's this? Frick, she's wet, but... is that...

...blood?

OW OW OW

She's in awful distress I can feel it, she's in terrible pain so I am too, what is it, what's happened Piper oh my darling?

I look about, trying to understand and I see the armed cops picking themselves up after being hit by Noah's PK beam. One of them is checking his weapon.

Wait – no. Not... oh, Jesus.

When the PK smashed into the one on the far right...

...I think...

...I think it made him fire his gun. That was the loud bang.

– I am shaking –

Noah's PK beam made the cop's finger twitch on the trigger and he was pointed at me, the threat. OMFG. The blood, the blood, it's Piper's blood. It's weeping through my fingers and I can see, even through the rain, a wound, a big rip in her stomach under the ribs. Oh frick, oh Jesus Christ, no no, this can't be happening, it can't –

'Help!' I scream. 'Now! Help, help us!' My heart is beating faster than it ever has, my hands have gone all soft and strange no no no –

I try and press on the wound to stem the blood and Piper yelps in pain and anguish but she trusts me and doesn't snap even though I'm causing her pain.

its ok its ok i know it hurts but better soon just hold on

And in this moment I feel such a powerful link with Piper like I can't describe, like nothing before. It's as if our souls are fused together and I can feel her breathing in my head, shallow and erratic; she's hurting so much and I feel like I'm choking on my own blood.

She's in my head or I'm in hers, I'm experiencing the same pain she's in, it's filling me, it's agony, and everything is hazy and dark around the edges. But she trusts me and she's in my arms and she knows I would never let anything bad happen to her.

stay with me darling stay with me awake awake be awake my beautiful piper

Noah staggers to his feet, brushing some of the mud off himself, but Virgil puts an arm out to keep him away. Flynn is on his phone, trying to find an emergency vet or something maybe.

But Piper is fading, OMFG it hurts, it's unbearable, I'm holding this beautiful, pure life in my hands, I've had her since she was just weeks old, I'm all she's ever known, I'm her world and she's mine.

i love you so so much

...I tell her over and over. But my vision is dark and murky, it's like I'm going blind, everything is faint and distant and I feel incredibly tired. I can't keep my eyes open. I just need to rest, the awful pain and I'm fading – no, she's fading, and then I feel her emote back to me:

love you! completely. my best! love. always.

That's the best way I can describe her feelings coming out to me, washing over me. It's gentle and beautiful.

And then her little head, looking up at me, showing her perfect white teeth and her panting, pink little tongue, her head goes limp in the crook of my elbow –

– and she dies in my arms.

My stomach heaves and I retch to the side.

My insides are shredded with razors. This is beyond agony.

Flynn stumbles toward me, and Koji looks up at me with those sad golden eyes. He's also connected to me and he can sense it too.

She is gone.

My perfect little Piper, who never harmed a fly.

d

e

a

d

I am shaking. I am breaking. I can't contain it all.

Hagen. Virgil. Noah.

Eye clamps. Guns. Aether.

I can't hold it all in.

I just manage to wispr to Flynn in time before my grief and rage mix together and explode.

And then, as Flynn knocks my mum over, over the top of them I let it go:

Snapshot

Not at Noah or Virgil or the cop whose gun went off. At everyone. My mind just flips, I go blind for a second and the world shudders and shifts as an incandescent wave of psynaptic shock blasts out from my brain.

Flynn and my mother are spared because he's knocked her to the floor, but everyone standing…

I am a rock thrown into the pond.

Noah, Virgil, Captain Droy, Rebekah, and the eight police out here with their guns… they all collapse. They just crumple like they've been unplugged. Falling away from me like bowling pins.

And I drop to my knees, still holding my beautiful Piper. Great wracking sobs consume me.

I am vaguely aware of my mum. 'Oh Echo, oh god,' she's saying, sobbing. We are surrounded by bodies and she is wild-eyed, staring at them in horror.

'Piper,' I sob, my tears knocked aside by the rain. It's all I can say. Then my mum does something – she kisses me on the cheek.

'You have to go,' she says, as Flynn looks on hopelessly. 'Let me take care of Piper,' she says, holding out her arms.

Take care of her. She means bury her. Sobs are convulsing my whole body; I think I'm going to be sick again.

'Please,' she says. 'Please, I know you loved Piper. But don't give up now. You can do something Echo, you can do something about this, about A9. I know I should have told you, but it's been so hard, it's been monstrous. I want to explain, tell you about... him,' she says. 'But not now, you have to leave.'

Flynn places his arm on my shoulder. I think it means he agrees. Oh god, I feel... heartbroken. Totally heartbroken. The rain is my grief, drenching me, drowning me.

I raise Piper up close to my face. I don't want to ever forget her perfect little face, the way her fur was always Persil-white before I took her to The Farm and put her through all that. The way she would always greet me with total love, how she would follow me *everywhere*. I love her so much.

I loved her so much.

I am shaking so badly I can barely hold her now. And reluctantly, I hand her over to my mother who gives me an anguished look of thanks. Around us the bodies are scattered like pick-up-sticks. Koji rests his heavy, powerful head against me. He was fond of Piper I think, and her of him, despite her barking and bluster.

'Go,' my mother says softly.

'Come,' says Flynn softly.

Now that my mum's taken my gorgeous little Westie, I see that I have her blood on my hands. Literally. And there's something else – dark splashes land on my arm, over and over, before being obliterated each time by the rain.

It's more blood, but this is my own, pouring out. Another nosebleed.

My heart used to walk outside of my body.

And now it is dead.

28: HUNTED

"What a stupid question, yes of course. The world changed that night for both of us. I was fortunate, in a way. As you can see, I'm confined to this damn wheelchair and I sometimes need a ventilator... but I survived the incident. Others didn't.

"For Echo too, the incident had a profound effect. It gave her instant notoriety, for one thing – remember, at that point her snapshot was one of the most powerful acts of aether people had ever seen. And for me, it confirmed that there is a subset of aethereals – 'bleeders' as they are sometimes known – who can get a nosebleed from an act of aether.

"We are just beginning to understand what it means to be a 'bleeder', and Echo became the most famous of them – a special group within a special group.

"But that night changed her as a person too. She felt responsible for an innocent death. Just a dog, you might say, but a soul she loved completely. She hated herself... and she hated me too. She doesn't understand my work and she took it all very personally – as you might expect of an immature, somewhat entitled teenage girl.

"Truly, the birth of aether was like someone inventing the gun and then only giving them to teenagers – and that was never going to end well.

"I just hope that Echo, wherever she is, can forgive me. And forgive herself. Before too many more people get hurt."

— From the TS Interviews with Doctor Magellan-Jones

The cold, sharp rain lashed down, beating them. Punishing them as they fled.

He was struggling, even more than when they had been out on the moors. His ribs had gone from painfully sore to brutally agonising. He could feel hard lumps under the skin, and he was grinding his teeth with pain as he dragged Echo as quickly as he could away from the house, trying to keep them out of sight of the cops closing in.

When he'd fallen from the sky, bloody hell it was close — he'd just managed to do something, to use his PK to break the fall.

He heard voices so he pulled Echo down behind a couple of wheelie bins. 'Try and keep your head back,' he said.

On the run again. They'd fled The Farm, and before that he had fled from here, his home town, thinking he'd killed Keel.

Koji didn't bark, didn't give them away. Echo would be drained by that huge snapshot and she was in shock, so Flynn doubted she had any animus, but the dog had come anyway. Padding along in the rain without complaint, already seemingly loyal to her. Flynn certainly didn't fancy trying to shoo the huge beast away.

He waited for the voices to go, then helped Echo back to her feet, keeping her head back to try and stop the blood pouring from her nose.

She was almost catatonic. In the garden she'd been gagging, choking on her grief like a fatal asthma attack, unable to catch her breath. She had done that incredible snapshot over the top of him and her mum and Koji, but after that she had been distraught, the rain turning her long hair into wet snakes, her face a raging Medusa with blood from her nose all over her mouth and chin, even staining her teeth.

Now the shock had set in and she was limp – as lifeless as a shop dummy and just as hollow. He'd tried talking to her, but he didn't know what to say and she didn't seem capable of replying. He just wanted to hold her, comfort her. He wanted tell her it would be ok.

Even though it probably wouldn't be.

And then there was a whirring hum – and a blinding light appeared in the sky. A helicopter searchlight. Hunting them.

'Piper,' whispered Echo listlessly into the rain.

'Come on,' he said breathlessly, trying to pick up the pace.

The helicopter swung towards them with its throbbing blades – its beam scanning the street just over from them. If they were caught he didn't know whether they'd end up interrogated in a police cell or experimented on in a secret lab. He didn't want to find out which.

He started up an alley between two streets. Police helicopters had infrared or something – thermal imaging. He'd seen it on TV, criminals jumping out of a stolen car and hiding behind bins in the pitch black, snared by the helicopter's thermal images as they guided the police on the ground. Maybe he needed to get them among other people to disguise their tell-tale silhouettes, to hide in plain sight.

He pulled Echo down another alley, Koji following. Bollocks, dead end. Back out, limping, wheezing with pain. Where was everyone? Maybe the rain was keeping them indoors. Or maybe their families were keeping them indoors – maybe they didn't have men like Keel and Virgil in their families.

Around a corner – and there was the high street they'd driven down, the one with the coffee shops and restaurants. Come on he willed himself. The road was a couple of hundred metres away but with every agonising step it seemed to stretch away further. Koji looked like he was walking in slow motion, having to keep pausing to not get ahead of them.

'I'm doing my best,' Flynn muttered.

He hefted Echo around the corner, onto the street – they'd come out by the Italian, the one with flaming torches either side of the door. And then –

– and then someone stepped out in front of them, blocking their path.

It was Noah. The shaven-headed black guy who'd held Flynn in the air with PK. At least now he was soaking wet just like them – not up to his little PK umbrella trick, it seemed.

'That was quite impressive,' he said.

Flynn backed away, holding a lacklustre Echo close. Her head was lolling, her nostrils crusted with dried blood. Koji growled at Noah – thunder in the rain – and revealed teeth like bone knives.

'Keep that freak of a dog away from me,' said Noah, 'or I'll break its neck with PK.'

'Just piss off, leave us alone,' Flynn replied. Bloody hell. They couldn't stay here, the police would be closing in. He tried to focus, stay sharp, but his ribs were screaming and he was distracted by the dancing flames of the restaurant torches.

'That snapshot, though,' Noah continued. 'One of the better ones I've seen.' His speech sounded slurred, as if he was drunk or had just woken up. 'My aethereal mind can shield itself better,' he continued. 'But the others… I'm not so sure, bro. Perhaps the Doctor, he might be ok. He's not aethereal, but he does have a strong mind. But the others… woo. I reckon you might be a cop killer Echo, you hear me girl?'

'Leave us alone,' said Flynn again, his blood starting to boil. 'I don't know what this A9 shit is, but we don't want any part of it.' The damn Italian torch fires, they were so hypnotic, he kept glancing at them.

'That's not your call, bro,' sniffed Noah. 'A9 wants you, and I'm here to bring you in,' he said, pointing at his own puffed out chest. 'You know the square root of fuck all about what's going down here. But it's time for your lessons to begin.' He stepped forward to put a hand on Flynn.

No. He was in too much physical pain, Echo was in too much emotional pain and they had both been through too much to put up with any more bullshit from guys like Noah.

And he could still see the twitching, living flames of the Italian restaurant's torches. Heat. Energy. Flame. Life. It was captivating, it was magical, it was…

…aethereal.

He reached out his free arm, grasping in the direction of the nearest torch and just wanted the flames. And they swirled as if hit by a sudden gust of wind and the fire was sucked from the torch, stretching out in a fiery tongue towards him, spitting and spluttering into a loose, spiralling ball of flame. And then Flynn swiped his arm sideways and the fireball span into Noah, engulfing him.

Noah screamed, putting his hands up to protect himself from the bright, boiling orb. The inferno billowed around him – and Flynn pulled Echo back the other way, while Noah yelled and shrieked behind them.

Flynn went as fast as he could now, his breathing shallow as he turned off down a new side street, Echo stumbling as he pulled her, Koji keeping pace easily. Shit, what had just happened? What was that?

Above, the helicopter beam swung across the ground towards them. In the distance, he heard a siren. He kept going, labouring heavily. Echo stumbled again and he had to stop, had to give her a moment to rest, and they sat down on a brick wall between two dark houses.

Then out of nowhere, a voice appeared in his head.

yo flynn

i understand youve discovered pyrokinesis

Someone was forcing themselves into his head, but he didn't know who or where. Noah again?

psyfire man

and echo holy shit

i heard about her multiple target snapshot

This wasn't communication, this was some kind of mind attack.

lemme ask something

does she ever get nosebleeds when she does aether

He sent out a wispr of his own:

who is this

And the reply came back:

be careful flynn

people who play with psyfire get burned

talk soon man

i am ulysses

The presence in his head faded to nothing. Only then did he realise the whirring of the helicopter was now directly above them – and suddenly the blinding searchlight hit them, making it look like they were standing on a glowing moon.

'Shit,' he said. He sighed heavily.

'Flynn,' Echo murmured. She said it so softly, but it still made him jump. She reached out a hand. 'Please, help me stand.'

He helped her to her feet, this beautiful, blood-stained, fragile, formidable, open, unknowable, straightforwardly complex girl. She put her left hand on Koji's head and her right on Flynn's shoulder, and from beneath her dark fringe she looked into his odd-coloured eyes and he looked back at her.

She wiped her hand across her mouth and looked at her fingers as the rain washed them clean again.

'Piper…' she said weakly.

'No, no… that's… it's your blood. Nosebleed,' he said.

'I don't like blood,' she said. 'I'm a vampire that hates the sight of blood.'

And now the sirens of the cop cars bore down on them from every direction. He sighed again, even that causing a sharp pain across his ribcage.

'I think this is it,' he said, grimacing. 'I'm so sorry. I just… there's nothing we can do.'

She said something, but her voice was so faint and the whirring helicopter blades and approaching cop car sirens so loud, he couldn't hear it.

'Sorry, what was that?' he asked.

She looked up at the harsh beam of light from the helicopter. Then she stepped forward and rested her forehead against his, her eyes closed. And she wisprd.

i have sparks in my skull

you have fire in your fingers

and i think together

we can do

anything

EPILOGUE

Physical pain is nothing. It's just nothing, compared to emotional pain.

I've had agonising migraines, I've had terrible period pains, I fell off a trampoline when I was eight and broke my wrist and it's all just *nothing* compared to the soul-crushing anguish of the worst emotional pain.

And you feel emotional pain in your head and your heart and your body, inside and out, *every* moment you're awake. And there's no bandage you can put on, no ice pack you can apply and no painkillers you can take.

My Piper, oh my Piper…

…OMFG.

I once read this post by a hospital doctor about a case she'd been involved with. There was a girl who was really ill, leukaemia I think. She needed a blood transfusion. They discovered her little brother was a match, and the doctor, she asked the boy if he'd be a blood donor. He said yes immediately.

Before they took him through to be prepped, he hugged his mum and dad and told them he loved them. Then as the doctor was about to start the transfusion, the boy asked her, 'Will I die straight away?'

Because he thought giving his blood to his sister meant he would die.

But he'd said yes anyway, without hesitation, to save her.

I mean, when I read that story the first time it made me cry rivers.

Of course, I didn't get the chance to save Piper. In fact... I killed her. Didn't I? Piper is dead because of me.

I don't know what else to say.

I said life has no plot, but you can't help thinking of your life as a movie at least some of the time. Thriller. Comedy. Romance. Action. Whatever.

For the most part I thought my life was just a low budget Family Drama.

Then for a brief few moments, I thought ok: maybe not. Maybe it's a Superhero Origins movie.

But now I realise: the movie of my life is a Tragedy. A gut-wrenching, heart-breaking, soul-crushing Tragedy.

So now I –

– oh shit, the helicopter beam has caught us, Flynn and I. Like ants under a summer magnifying glass. Except the ants would run, but me... I can't. I really can't. Plus... I've got to make a stand. While I still can stand.

My name is Echo Jones.

I am a fragile vampire.

And *this* is where my story begins.

Note from the Author

Thank you so, so much to everyone who supported and encouraged me – friends, family, my agent and all the people who I never met *IRL*, but whose words made a difference to my own. They say you should believe in yourself, but it really helps if someone else does too.

If you enjoyed The Sparks In My Skull, I'd really appreciate it if you could take a few moments to leave a review.

We all face challenges, we all have tough times. Letting each other know about the stories that mean something to us is a great way to reach out and be kind when the darkness closes in.

Thank you.

I D Atkinson

Printed in Great Britain
by Amazon